The king of Egypt said to the Hebrew midwives, whose names were Shiphrah and Puah, "When you are helping the Hebrew women during childbirth on the delivery stool, if you see that the baby is a boy, kill him; but if it is a girl, let her live." The midwives, however, feared God and did not do what the king of Egypt had told them to do; they let the boys live. Then the king of Egypt summoned the midwives and asked them, "Why have you done this? Why have you let the boys live?"

The midwives answered Pharaoh, "Hebrew women are not like Egyptian women; they are vigorous and give birth before the midwives arrive."

So God was kind to the midwives and the people increased and became even more numerous. And because the midwives feared God, he gave them families of their own.

Then Pharaoh gave this order to all his people: "Every Hebrew boy that is born you must throw into the Nile, but let every girl live."

—Exodus 1:15–22 (NIV)

Then Moses stretched out his hand over the sea, and all that night the LORD drove the sea back with a strong east wind and turned it into dry land. The waters were divided, and the Israelites went through the sea on dry ground, with a wall of water on their right and on their left.

The Egyptians pursued them, and all Pharaoh's horses and chariots and horsemen followed them into the sea. During the last watch of the night the LORD looked down from the pillar of fire and cloud at the Egyptian army and threw it into confusion. He jammed the wheels of their chariots so that they had difficulty driving. And the Egyptians said, "Let's get away from the Israelites! The LORD is fighting for them against Egypt."

Then the LORD said to Moses, "Stretch out your hand over the sea so that the waters may flow back over the Egyptians and their chariots and horsemen." Moses stretched out his hand over the sea, and at daybreak the sea went back to its place. The Egyptians were fleeing toward it, and the LORD swept them into the sea.

—Exodus 14:21–27 (NIV)

## MYSTERIES & WONDERS *of the* BIBLE

Unveiled: Tamar's Story
A Life Renewed: Shoshan's Story
Garden of Secrets: Adah's Story
Among the Giants: Achsah's Story
Seeking Leviathan: Milkah's Story
A Flame of Hope: Abital's Story
Covenant of the Heart: Odelia's Story
Treacherous Waters: Zahla's Story

MYSTERIES & WONDERS of the BIBLE

# TREACHEROUS WATERS
## ZAHLA'S STORY

Melanie Dobson

## *A Gift from Guideposts*

Thank you for your purchase! We want to express our gratitude for your support with a special gift just for you.

Dive into *Spirit Lifters*, a complimentary e-book that will fortify your faith, offering solace during challenging moments. Its 31 carefully selected scripture verses will soothe and uplift your soul.

Please use the QR code or go to **guideposts.org/ spiritlifters** to download.

Mysteries & Wonders of the Bible is a trademark of Guideposts.

Published by Guideposts
100 Reserve Road, Suite E200, Danbury, CT 06810
Guideposts.org

Copyright © 2025 by Guideposts. All rights reserved. This book, or parts thereof, may not be reproduced, stored in a retrieval system, or transmitted in any form or by any means, electronic, mechanical, photocopying, recording, or otherwise, without the written permission of the publisher.

This is a work of fiction. While the characters and settings are drawn from scripture references and historical accounts, apart from the actual people, events, and locales that figure into the fiction narrative, all other names, characters, places, and events are the creation of the author's imagination or are used fictitiously. Every attempt has been made to credit the sources of copyrighted material used in this book. If any such acknowledgment has been inadvertently omitted or miscredited, receipt of such information would be appreciated.

Scripture references are from the following sources: *The Holy Bible, King James Version* (KJV). *The Holy Bible, New International Version* (NIV). Copyright © 1973, 1978, 1984, 2011 by Biblica, Inc. Used by permission of Zondervan. All rights reserved worldwide. www.zondervan.com.

Cover and interior design by Müllerhaus
Cover illustration by Brian Call represented by Illustration Online LLC.
Typeset by Aptara, Inc.

ISBN 978-1-961441-18-7 (hardcover)
ISBN 978-1-961441-19-4 (softcover)
ISBN 978-1-961441-20-0 (epub)

Printed and bound in the United States of America

MYSTERIES & WONDERS *of the* BIBLE

# TREACHEROUS WATERS
## ZAHLA'S STORY

**Dedication**

Innocent Mucunguzi

Thank you for welcoming our family to Africa and inspiring people around the world to share Christ's love and provision with vulnerable kids in Uganda.

progressiveministries.org

# CAST OF CHARACTERS

## Biblical Cast

**Aaron** • brother of Moses

**Amram** • father of Moses, Miriam, and Aaron

**Jochebed** • mother of Moses, Miriam, and Aaron

**Joseph and Asenath** • ancestors of Zahla's family

**Miriam** • sister of Moses

**Moses** • leader of the Hebrew people in the Exodus

**Pharaoh** • ruler of Egypt

**Shiphrah and Puah** • Hebrew midwives

## Fictional Cast

**Ahmed** • Egyptian soldier

**Asher** • Zahla's son

**Eliana** • Zahla's granddaughter

**Haken** • the chief wine steward

**Hosea** • Joseph and Puah's oldest son

**Jakar** • shepherd in Goshen

**Joseph** • Zahla's brother

**Lemuel** • Zahla's cousin

**Lydia** • Hosea's granddaughter

**Maya** • Joseph and Puah's oldest daughter

**Merin** • Egyptian soldier and namesake of Asher's grandson

**Ptahmose** • Merin's father

**Raphael** • father of Zahla and Joseph

**Raquel** • acquaintance in Pithom

**Rebecca** • Zahla's cousin

**Seth** • one of the rescued children

**Sivian** • girl lost near the Red Sea

**Zahla** • spirited daughter of Raphael

# GLOSSARY OF TERMS

**abba** • father

**clerestory** • a high portion of a wall that contains windows above eye level

**dodah** • aunt

**felucca** • a usually wooden sailing vessel with one or two sails

**imma** • mother

**natron** • a naturally occurring cleansing mineral similar to baking soda

**radid** • shawl or veil

**saba** • grandfather

**savah** • grandmother

**shedeh** • a spiced drink made from grapes and honey, prized by Pharaoh

# CHAPTER ONE

Thunder roared through the valley and rippled across the sandy path. Zahla hugged her great-grandson to her chest, curling to protect his tiny body from the oncoming storm.

Merin had been born less than a month ago, during the plagues that Yahweh wrought across Egypt after their ruler refused to release the Israelites from slavery. Even though Zahla was nearing her ninety-sixth year, even though their walk out of Egypt had been long, she wouldn't let a drop of rain or blast of wind harm this little one. Zahla lifted her head like a bird facing its enemy. Like an egret shielding its chicks, she'd do anything to protect her family.

The ground shook again, stirring up dust that choked the refugees. While she'd never felt the earth quake, she'd heard many stories of old. The earth had shaken under Yahweh's hand when He brought their world into existence. Shaken when the God of Abraham destroyed the cities of Sodom and Gomorrah.

But what was Yahweh doing now?

Rain would refill their waterskins and cool their skin, but their tents wouldn't shelter them from lightning or the hailstones that had plagued Egypt.

Fellow Israelites pressed around Zahla as they rushed out of their tents and into a valley as if they could escape the storm. The

Hebrew people, along with the others who'd fled Egypt with them, had set up camp below a ridge. Rumors filtered through the crowd about a body of water blocking their journey at the opposite end of the valley. A sea impossible to cross.

Then again, many rumors accompanied their walk out of Egypt. While her eyesight remained strong, she couldn't see beyond the backs of her people or the bend in the path. If there was indeed a sea before them, how could they escape the storm? The Israelites would never turn back toward Egypt.

Merin began to cry, but the noise was drowned in a different kind of sea. The flocks of goats and cattle bleating. The braying of donkeys. Children calling for their *imma* or *abba*. The shuffling and stamping of feet, crushing the sand as the rumbling grew behind them.

Zahla squinted as she searched for the beacon of cloud that had guided them away from Egypt, but it was hidden by dust. And in the midst of the confusion this evening, the threat of a storm, Zahla had lost sight of her oldest son and his children.

Her extended family numbered in the hundreds with the many cousins and children of her nieces and nephew. Only one of her sons had survived the harsh Egyptian taskmasters, and she'd left Egypt two weeks ago with Asher and his family. Asher's wife had passed on five years past, but Asher had three children and almost twenty grandchildren who had accompanied them on this journey.

Until Moses led the Hebrew people away from Egypt, the spacious vineyard in Goshen had been her home, but now home was a cluster of tents among more than a million refugees and their livestock, a number impossible for her to comprehend. Still, she wasn't worried. Like a pigeon, she always found her way back in the evening hours, content knowing that all her family was together in this wilderness. Far from Pharaoh's enslavement.

While Asher had faltered in his faith over the years, her son still fled with the refugees from Egypt, choosing Yahweh's promise of freedom over the oppression of Pharaoh's dark gods. Her grandchildren would see the miracles of Yahweh and freedom prophesied long ago. The smallest ones like Merin wouldn't even remember the bondage, but she wanted all of them to forget the past now and embrace what Yahweh had ahead for them.

Zahla didn't see her family nearby, but at the edge of a pond, among the reeds, stood a girl about five or six years old. Tears trickled down the girl's thin cheeks, and Zahla felt her fear and loneliness as if it were her own. She crept toward the child, scanning the reeds for crocodiles or snakes. With the thunder, the crowds of people, any reptile would surely be scared back into the water, but Zahla had spent a lifetime searching among reeds for the monsters that waited near the shoreline to snatch a little one. No matter how many years she aged, she'd never stop her vigilance in protecting children.

With Merin and his tears secured in one arm, she reached out her free hand, wrinkled and worn, and placed it gently on the girl's shoulder. She didn't want to shout, but her voice had to rise above the clamor. "Did you lose your parents?"

The girl nodded.

"Merin and I will help you find them," Zahla said, nodding at the baby in her arms. "What is your name?"

"Sivian."

"A lovely name."

Sivian gazed across the crowd as if searching for her family as well. While they couldn't see the hills behind them, the thundering hadn't ceased. "What is that sound?"

Zahla was always honest, even with children. "I do not know."

Even though she wasn't certain about the noise, she'd begun to fear the rumbling brought unwelcome visitors instead of rain. That Pharaoh might have changed his mind once again and was still refusing to let Yahweh's people go.

"I happen to be an expert at finding families," Zahla told the girl.

Sivian nodded at the baby in Zahla's arm. "What is troubling him?"

"He misses his imma, I think."

"I understand," Sivian replied before reaching out for Zahla's free hand, while flocks of people rushed by as they moved toward the bend.

One of Zahla's family members would find them soon, before darkness set upon them, and then Asher would help her search for Sivian's parents.

As the crowd flowed through the valley, the thunder began to quiet, and Merin quieted as well. They would gather for news or direction from Moses tonight and wait for the fire. The pillar, she prayed, would turn again into a magnificent tower as it had every other night since they'd begun their desert journey. A flaming monument to their living God.

The pillar was one of many wonders in the past weeks. Fierce signs they'd seen in Egypt to demonstrate the power of Yahweh after He'd seemed silent for hundreds of years. Yahweh had rarely been silent with her, but now His voice—His power—was unmistakable to every man and woman in Egypt.

Their oppressors had suffered greatly when Pharaoh refused to let the people of Yahweh follow Moses into the wilderness, but Pharaoh, that cruel and stubborn man who believed himself a god, was intent on keeping the Hebrew people enslaved. His pride blinded him and his people.

Pharaoh had refused for weeks to free the Israelites, but after the heart-wrenching loss of his son, he relented. The Israelites, along with a handful of defiant Egyptians and slaves from other lands, had spent the weeks since then wandering between hills and through the Egyptian dry lands.

In the daylight hours, her people followed a white pillar that gleamed in the sun. At night, the cloud cylinder was replaced by a flame shooting into the heavens. When the pillar stopped, they set up camp and waited until the cloud began moving again. Then they would step forward with the promise of a new land ahead.

She didn't know when their caravan would finally settle. Even Moses, it was whispered, didn't know where the cloud would lead them next, but they couldn't continue down this path if a sea lay before them. They would have to go back.

Squinting, Zahla searched again for the pillar. Yahweh, she was certain, wouldn't abandon them. Not after all He'd done to free them from the oppression of Egypt.

Voices rumbled around her. People were worried. Distraught. Afraid for themselves and their families. If only they could stop for a moment—breathe—in what should be a quiet, reverent place.

"He has brought us out here to die," a woman nearby complained, and Zahla wished she could cover Sivian's ears.

"We are not going to die tonight," Zahla said, but the woman paid no heed as she continued her rant against Moses.

Even though more than fifty years had passed, the older members of their community remembered well the day that Moses, a Hebrew boy who'd become an Egyptian prince by adoption, killed one of their taskmasters. At the time, many whispered that they were glad someone had finally confronted the whips, the cruelty, but the death of an Egyptian brought more labor for the men and more deaths among the Israelites. And much hatred for the Hebrew-Egyptian prince.

The Israelites both feared and respected Moses. Mixed emotions impossible to untangle in the events of the past month. Moses and Aaron clearly operated under another power beyond their own, and while Zahla believed they heard the voice of Yahweh, some people thought the brothers were listening to a different god.

As the echoes of thunder calmed, the curtain of dust began to peel back. No rain clouds dotted the expanse, no sign of an impending storm. Instead, a wreath of pink and orange appeared as the sun prepared its descent on the western horizon. The white pillar of cloud slashed like a sword through the color, preparing to blaze a new path.

Sivian tugged on her tunic, and Zahla leaned down.

"I am scared," the girl said, her pale brown eyes heavy with fear.

"We will find your parents."

"I know."

As the color flashed around them, Merin squirmed in her arms. "Then what are you afraid of?"

"Yahweh."

"Him you must fear." Zahla paused to comfort Merin. "But the Lord would not have brought us out here to abandon us."

*Unless*, the nagging voice teased inside her.

Unless Yahweh was so angry with the Israelites that He wanted to be rid of them all. She'd heard the stories of old about Yahweh cleansing and renewing their wicked world with a flood. He had promised, in the many colors of a rainbow, that He would never destroy the earth again, but what about His people?

Sivian dug her sandal into the sand. "He killed the others."

Zahla couldn't lean far, but she caught Sivian's gaze in hers. "Who did He kill?"

"The boys in Egypt," Sivian said.

"Ah…" Zahla's chest twisted at the memory. She wanted no child to die, Hebrew or Egyptian, and she didn't believe that Yahweh, the giver of life, wanted to kill either. But an angel of death had taken the lives of Egypt's firstborn sons when Pharaoh refused once again to free the Israelites.

"I do not understand the ways of Yahweh except He created life," Zahla said, "and He wants to free us from slavery. He wants freedom for everyone who follows Him."

And He seemed to want justice for those who'd persecuted her people for hundreds of years.

Merin returned to sleep as if he no longer had to be afraid, and her arm ached with his weight. If only she could sit in her chair, back in Goshen, and gently rock him as he slept. Or rest on a blanket or under the covering of their tent.

But more than rest, she wanted an end to the oppression for her children and their families. To live in a community separate from the gods of Egypt. A place where they belonged and a peaceful future for her descendants.

How her heart longed for peace.

No matter how tired her feet and her arms were, she couldn't stop walking now.

"Look at that!" Zahla exclaimed as the crowd flowed around her and Sivian. The rumors, she realized, were true. The water ahead glowed red from the sun on their backs. It was too wide for swimming and probably too deep for wading.

They'd reached the end of this path.

"What is it?" the girl asked.

"A sea," Zahla said as a gust of salt-soaked air swept over them. They wouldn't be able to drink from this reservoir.

Sivian arched up on her toes in an attempt to see it, and Zahla wished she could pick her up.

"How will we cross it?" Sivian asked.

"It is not possible to cross," she said. "We will have to turn back into the valley."

Wander again in the wilderness.

Merin stirred in her arms, and Zahla gently bounced him. If only she had the strength of her youth. While her mind was still strong, her body failed her.

"Egyptians!" a man shouted behind her.

Zahla's feet dragged in the sand as she turned, Sivian clinging to her side. And she saw the source of thunder along the hillside. Chariots, hundreds of them, were clustered together on the rocks above them, ready to roll into the valley with their swords and might. Like a crocodile waiting for night so it could feast.

The Egyptians had already lost so much by Yahweh's hand. Why must they continue to torment her people?

Pharaoh must have changed his mind again in his fury, refusing to let another God defeat him.

With no weapons to defend themselves, the Israelites were trapped between Pharaoh's warriors and the Red Sea. Between their enemy of old and a new one blocking them from freedom. They were easy prey for those who had enslaved and now wanted to slaughter them.

Zahla's gaze rose to the billowy wings that sprouted from the pillar overhead, gleaming gold as the sun neared the horizon. Despite her confident words for Sivian, her own heart faltered.

Why had Yahweh led them here?

# CHAPTER TWO

"Do not be afraid!" Moses shouted above the cries on the shore. Zahla couldn't see the man who'd brought them out of Egypt, but his voice traveled across the crowd as if Yahweh was carrying his words on the salty breeze. "Stand firm and you will see the deliverance the Lord will bring you today."

Sivian released her grip on Zahla's tunic, standing strong as Moses commanded, twilight threading through her hair. But Merin stirred in Zahla's arms at the current of fear, crying out like some of the adults.

Yahweh, she prayed, would deliver her people, just as He'd done in the past. It was the Egyptians who should be afraid. Whenever they opposed Him, Yahweh's means of deliverance had proved terrifying.

People stomped their feet like horses about to thunder back on the chariots, but she prayed they wouldn't attempt to fight. If the Lord said to stand firm, they would die if they chose to battle their pursuers.

Moses continued, "The Egyptians you see today, you will never see again."

She glanced back at the glimmer of chariots along the ridge. Her life had been shaped by the customs and culture and people of

Egypt, but she never wanted to see another of Pharaoh's warriors. More than anything, she wanted to be truly free from the past.

"The Lord will fight for you," Moses said. "You need only be still."

The shuffling around her began to diminish, but she wasn't certain how long everyone would wait, not after they'd tasted freedom in these weeks away from their oppressors. Could they wait again for deliverance when everything about their situation urged them to either fight or flee?

Then again, they had no place to run. Retreating would be their death, and without a miracle, the Egyptian army would rush down the hill during the night hours or at first light with their swords and chariots. Pharaoh's army no longer cared about returning the Israelites to their position of slavery. The soldiers wanted to massacre her people.

The feet around her may have stilled, but the voices did not. As she held Sivian's hand, waiting for direction, those around her debated the words of their exiled leader.

Should they wait here as he instructed or prepare for a defense against their enemy? But no slingshot, arrow, or sword would stop Pharaoh's men.

"Return to your tents," Aaron shouted, and the crowd stopped to listen again. The Hebrew people had great respect for the older brother of Moses. Unlike Moses, he'd often worked in the brickyard, enslaved alongside many of the Hebrew men.

"Will we die?" Sivian asked, her gaze on the chariots lording over them.

It was an impossible question for Zahla to answer. "No matter what happens, we do not need to be afraid."

Even if fear surrounded them, embedded in their hearts and minds, Yahweh had a greater plan. He'd promised them deliverance. Tonight, she had only to find their tent so Merin could feed from his imma's breast. Then Asher, her oldest son, could help her locate Sivian's family.

The Lord, she prayed, would help all of them find their way home.

"Yahweh led us here for a reason," Zahla continued, her gaze steady on the golden pillar at the water's edge. The chariots held no power over the sky. "He will do another miracle."

"Imma!"

She scanned the heads around her until she found the one who towered over all. Asher elbowed his way through the crowd until he was at her side.

He kissed her cheeks before giving her a reprimand. "You have to stop wandering off!"

"I am not wandering," she insisted. "No more than anyone else."

"The others are able to find their way home."

"I always find my way." Her eyes narrowed, forgetting for a moment the enemy above. "But that tent is not my home!"

"You know what I mean, Imma. Where our family is sleeping."

"I had to see the cloud." Her eyes wandered back to the pillar at the edge of the sea. To the promise that Yahweh was still leading them. What would the Egyptians think when they saw the night ablaze with fire?

Or had they already seen the pillar? Perhaps it had led their enemy to them.

"Come along." Her oldest son opened his arms to take his grandson. "Let me carry Merin."

Zahla shook her head. "I must carry him."

"You cannot rescue every child, Imma," Asher said. Familiar words between them for the past seventy years.

"I will rescue every child that I can." She nodded at Merin. "Especially this one, born from our—"

"From our hearts." He repeated their common words before looking down at Sivian. "But this one is not part of our family."

As if Zahla might have confused her grandchildren.

"Sivian has been keeping me company so I did not get lost."

The little girl looked as surprised as Asher at her declaration.

Zahla took her hand again. "We are looking for her parents."

Asher sighed. "So you were lost together."

"I suppose we were," Zahla said. "I was hoping you could help find them."

Asher looked at the line of chariots, now cloaked in shadows. The pillar's shimmer was fading with the setting sun. "We will wait out the night inside the tent."

If the Egyptians rushed into their camp before morning, it mattered not where they slept, but they were to rise early, Asher told her, as they moved toward camp. They must be prepared to follow the cloud at daybreak.

Not that she would sleep with the chariots looming over them, but maybe some of them could rest as they prepared to see what Yahweh would do.

"Sivian will stay with us until we find her family," Asher said as if he had considered sending the girl away. But Zahla knew her son wouldn't allow this girl to wander through the night. He was too much like his father. Brisk and regimented at times, with a heart that loved deeply and cared sacrificially. Asher would risk his life, if needed, to help a child.

Zahla's legs didn't move as fast as they once did, when she could run faster than some of Pharaoh's soldiers, leaping into the reeds to hide or swimming across the Nile. Now, most of the crowd swept around them as Asher escorted her back to their shared tent.

She was one of the oldest among their people. Perhaps the oldest. She knew of no one else who'd lived ninety-five years in Egypt.

While they walked slowly, they didn't look at the clusters of chariots. Soon the pillar of white would begin to glow orange. Soon the sky would be aflame with fire.

If they hadn't yet seen the fire, perhaps the Egyptians would retreat in fear then. The Israelites could return up the valley to continue their walk into a new land.

"Oh, *Savah.*" Eliana greeted her as they ducked into the crowded tent.

*Savah.* Grandmother. The sweetest of words. How Zahla loved all of her grandchildren and their children.

"We were worried," her granddaughter said as she reached for her son.

Zahla wondered if she worried more about the chariots or that Merin was lost like Sivian in the crowds. "My new friend and I took good care of him."

"You must eat," Eliana said. "We all must find a way to eat even with…"

Eliana glanced at several of the children eating lentils from a bowl. Even though they all knew about the chariots lording over them from the cliff, she held her tongue. Was it faith or fear that kept her quiet?

Sivian joined the family for a meal, but Zahla wasn't hungry. She rolled her few belongings into a blanket in case they had to leave quickly and then smiled when one of the girls offered to share her blanket with Sivian. As the children fell asleep, Eliana retreated to her mat for the night.

Weariness plagued Asher's voice when he spoke again. "Come to bed, Imma."

"I am not tired."

"Without sleep, you will not be well tomorrow."

How could any of them sleep? Yahweh would be working in the night hours. "I will wait up and pray."

Asher sighed. "You pray and pray, Imma, but your God only taunts us."

"Yahweh is your God too, Asher."

"I worship no god," he said, and she understood the conflict in his heart. Asher thought Yahweh had failed him, but even if he had rebelled against Yahweh, even if he doubted His love, the Lord had still rescued him from Egypt.

Tomorrow, she prayed, Yahweh would again rescue her son.

Zahla stepped outside and looked east. The night air was cold, and the pillar had transformed from a column of white to a brilliant fire that spilled from its funneled top, cascading down each side.

A breeze rustled the reeds nearby, the smell of stale water and jasmine reminding her of days long ago. She may have stopped her feet from wandering for the night, but her mind wandered back more than eighty years ago to the Nile. To the night she joined her dear cousin, a midwife by the name of Puah, to deliver Moses's brother into a family who loved him but an empire that didn't want him to live.

She blinked as she looked back at the fire. Perhaps her old eyes were playing tricks, perhaps she was dreaming, but the pillar of fire seemed to be moving toward the camp.

"Asher," she whispered into the tent. "Are you asleep?"

"Not yet."

"Look at this."

A moment later, he joined her. "What is it?"

"The pillar."

He stood in awe like her as the giant torch circled the valley. Then the fire stopped along the cliff like a shield between the Egyptians and Israelites, raining light and warmth into their camp.

"Are we to follow it?" he asked in wonder.

She smiled. "Yahweh must be protecting us from the chariots."

The Egyptians wouldn't be able to pass through the blaze tonight, and any arrows loosed in their direction would be burned in the flames.

Perhaps tonight Asher would finally believe that Yahweh was good.

He turned to her. "You must sleep, Imma. There will be more children who need you tomorrow."

Her eyebrows climbed. "Are you teasing me?"

"I speak only the truth."

She glanced back at the pillar. "The fire will watch over all of us."

Asher escorted her to her mat, and she prayed in the darkness for a miracle for Merin and Sivian and all the children who traveled with them. For the Lord to rescue them as He'd rescued the children long ago.

When she closed her eyes, she dreamed of days long gone of jasmine and reeds and water. Days when she thought they'd never be freed from Pharaoh's oppression.

Days when she, too, had doubted Yahweh.

But in spite of her doubts, Yahweh had rescued her.

# CHAPTER THREE

*Eighty-Three Years Earlier*

The first time Puah asked her to assist with a birth, Zahla had ended up sprawled across the family's earth-packed floor. All while Puah worked alone to deliver a baby girl. Two children had revived Zahla with a cup of water, giggling when her eyes fluttered open.

Puah was only five years older, but sadly, Zahla had little of her cousin's strength or desire to midwife. She hated blood and an imma's screams. The murky waters of birth spilling onto the ground. The bringing of one from another was a miracle, but the process made Zahla's head spin and her skin flush warm.

Puah had laughed off the first incident. The brutal Egyptian heat, she'd said, caused Zahla to pass out. But the second time Zahla attempted to help her cousin, on a much cooler evening, it hadn't gone any better.

The delivery portion sickened her, her stomach tangled into knots at the anguish and blood, but the glimpse of new life was mesmerizing. The wonder of a baby's first breath. The glow of the imma after she birthed. The moments holding a little one who needed care. That was much different than the horrific smells and sounds of labor.

After her third attempt as an assistant, Puah suggested that Zahla find another occupation and that she discover it soon. If not, one of Pharaoh's soldiers would find work, suitable or not, for a thirteen-year-old.

Two years later, Zahla had fully embraced her role as an apprentice for her abba. She tended grapevines for Pharaoh's wine and prepared meals for the many family members who worked with them. They all lived in a village on their ancestors' vineyard in Goshen, almost an hour's walk south from Rameses, the city that Pharaoh was building on the back of slave labor.

The journey to Rameses was much longer during the season of *Akhet* when the Nile flooded its banks and trickled through the vineyards, creating rivulets and ponds in their fields. In those months of Akhet after the harvest was finished, before they began tending new vines, Zahla helped her abba and brother transfer wine into elegant jars for the palace. Every week her brother oversaw a wine shipment up the Nile on a papyrus boat built for Pharaoh's supplies.

Puah found Zahla again during Akhet. A baby was to be born tonight, Puah said, on the outskirts of Rameses. Shiphrah, another midwife, had married yesterday, and Puah was desperate for a companion to accompany her so she didn't have to travel and work alone.

Not all the Hebrew women used midwives. Many had immas or sisters or an older daughter who helped them through their delivery. But Puah was one of the few midwives the Hebrew women trusted with a difficult birth. Her skills, some whispered, were a gift from Yahweh to grow their nation.

The messenger who'd arrived at Puah's door that afternoon said the birth was imminent.

"Is there no other midwife who can attend with you?" Zahla asked as they climbed onto the raft her cousin used to travel down the flooded marsh. A gust of wind rustled the weeds around them and the moon hovered on the horizon, waiting for the dip of sun so it could light the evening hours.

All sorts of creatures crept through the delta at night.

"The imma fears complications," Puah said.

"Birthing children is always complicated." Zahla reached for a reed pole and pressed against the bog, pushing the raft north out of Goshen, toward a village outside Rameses. Crocodiles and hippopotamuses traveled further inland during the rainy season, and she preferred to avoid both of these creatures who hid among the reeds and the soldiers who ruled over them.

Between the muck and infestation of predators, the Egyptian soldiers rarely visited the wetlands during the floods. It was at the end of *Shemu*—the harvest season—when they ventured south. In their annual sweep, the soldiers would capture as many fieldworkers as possible and force them to dig ditches or lay bricks for one of Pharaoh's many new buildings.

How many bricks, she'd often wondered, did Pharaoh need? How many more temples and homes to fill his city before the mud dried up?

After the floodwaters receded, the fieldworkers who survived would return to Goshen to plant for a new harvest or tend to the vines. Those enslaved in the city would make bricks during the sunny season, and the soldiers wouldn't visit Goshen again until after the fields had been cleared.

Puah held the worn birthing basket in her lap as Zahla guided the raft into the deeper places to avoid the animals that found refuge in the marsh.

## Treacherous Waters: Zahla's Story

"It is complicated," Puah said, "to bring a new life into any world but especially to deliver a baby into a world of slavery."

The bulrushes danced in the breeze, and the smell of decaying crops settled over the raft. Zahla hoped any reptile or hippopotamus had already bedded themselves in the taller reeds since she had no weapon to defend them beyond her shoddy pole and the sharp edge of Puah's obsidian blade in her birthing basket.

"We were all born into slavery," she said.

"It is getting harder for our people." Puah sighed. "Pharaoh is frightened because there are so many of us."

His kingdom feared its slave force would turn on their taskmasters, but in her mind, the Egyptians and Israelites seemed to fear each other.

"I want to take away fear," Puah continued, "but Pharaoh wants our people to be afraid."

"I suppose it is the only way he can control us."

And Pharaoh was doing his job well. As he grew older, everyone in Goshen seemed to fear what he might do to their people and land.

"What is the name of the mother?" Zahla asked as she maneuvered the raft around an outcropping of stones.

"Jochebed. It is her second child."

The steady flow of river brushed through the reeds on their left, and Zahla shivered in the cool air. This poor woman needed two midwives who were competent and strong. Who wouldn't collapse at the sight of blood. Being the cousin of a midwife did not qualify her for this job.

"I am not a good assistant for you, Puah."

"I only need you to clean the baby while I care for Jochebed."

She inhaled the river's breath, wishing it could sustain her. "I will try."

When the marshland gave way to soil, they dragged the raft onto shore, and Puah directed Zahla into a village. Jochebed's small home, like the other huts south of Rameses, was plastered with mud and smelled like straw and tallow-fueled smoke from the lanterns. The men here either worked in the fields of Goshen or as laborers in the city. Most of the women in these villages cared for their animals, gardens, and children.

Jochebed labored on a mat while her husband and young daughter, named Miriam, stood nearby. The woman's face was soaked in sweat, her breathing rapid as if it refused to fill her lungs. Puah shooed away two chickens clucking in the front room, their wings spreading as they bobbed into a back courtyard shared with their neighbors.

Puah scanned the room until her eyes settled on a clay jar filled with water. Puah asked Amram, Jochebed's husband, and his daughter to fill a second vessel at the public well.

Jochebed clenched her teeth for several moments before speaking. "I fear something is wrong."

"We will take care of you and your baby." Puah began unpacking the pieces secured in her clay-coated basket and then organized a stack of clean linen, ceramic jars with sesame oil and herbs, and the sharp piece of obsidian that gleamed black in the lantern light. Another jar contained broth made from animal bones to warm Jochebed after she gave birth.

Two mud bricks awaited inside the dwelling to use for a birthing stool. Zahla carefully moved them beside Jochebed's mat, and she marveled for a moment at the bricks, molded in slavery, that were foundational for a new life.

As long as her own hands kept busy, her skin cool, perhaps her stomach would cooperate. She could help Puah instead of distracting her.

Jochebed's pains were coming quickly, her breath shallow. Soon, Zahla hoped, the baby would arrive.

Puah opened a jar and filled her palm with sesame oil. Then she asked Zahla to add three drops of jasmine. As she mixed the jasmine into the oil, Zahla savored the sweet scent. The aroma would calm her as much as it did Jochebed.

Even though Puah was only twenty years of age, she was well-skilled in midwifery, learning from her savah and then her late imma who passed on her birthing basket and knowledge. Now Puah gently massaged the oil into Jochebed's skin and held out her hands so the woman could breathe deeply of the soothing flower.

As the doorway in her body prepared to open, Jochebed groaned with the pains tearing through her abdomen.

"Baby will arrive soon," Puah said as the woman's cries echoed around the room.

Zahla lifted one of Jochebed's arms and assisted in guiding her to the bricks. Puah had covered the smooth stones with linen, and Jochebed knelt on them like so many women before her. When Jochebed wailed again, Puah positioned herself below Jochebed to catch the child.

Amram and Miriam returned to the doorway with the clay jar, Amram's eyes wide in fright. "She is not well."

Puah didn't answer, her focus solely on Jochebed, so Zahla spoke on her behalf. "The pains will bring your child into this world."

This man wished to take Jochebed's agony away; she could see it in his gaze. He deeply loved his wife and wanted to bear her pain, but he was powerless to relieve the anguish of childbirth.

What might it be like to marry one who cared so deeply? How her abba had loved her imma. *Pearl*, he'd called Zahla's imma, for her beauty. After her death, he said he would never marry another. Zahla loved hearing his stories about her imma's life as they worked to cultivate the soil and harvest the grapes, but neither of them ever spoke about her death. The same day that Zahla was born.

The giving of life took her imma away.

Puah's eyes remained on Jochebed even as she spoke to the man behind her. "The baby is breeched, Amram."

Zahla's chest clenched. A breech could harm both imma and child.

"What should I do?" he pleaded.

"You and Miriam need to wait outside and—" Puah balled up another roll of linen and placed it near the bricks so she could kneel beside Jochebed. "Pray that Yahweh will deliver this one for us."

"I will pray." He left the water vessel beside Zahla and retreated with Miriam.

He wouldn't go far, Zahla knew. Probably listening at a crack between bricks even as he petitioned Yahweh on behalf of his wife and unborn child.

Why did the gift of life have to hurt so much?

The night crawled as slowly as one of the lizards climbing their wall, but Puah didn't seem to notice the passing of time or the lizards. She worked steadily beside Jochebed, talking to her and the baby as if the child needed to be coaxed into the world. Then she nodded for Zahla to stand behind the woman.

As Zahla secured Jochebed's back, her gaze wandered to the slender breadth of starlit sky instead of the ground so she didn't have to watch Puah work to free the baby. No matter what her aunts said about Zahla's future as a wife, she didn't think she could ever bring forth life from her own body.

Jochebed wailed as her chest sank toward the ground, and Zahla braced herself as she repositioned the woman's knees on the linen-covered bricks.

"Your baby is coming," Puah said.

Moments later, the cries of a child matched those of its mother. Soon, the entire village would know a little one had arrived.

"A boy," her cousin announced.

Amram would be pleased.

Puah cut the cord with her obsidian blade before Jochebed collapsed back on her mat. As the baby screamed, Puah calmly scanned his body in the lamplight and seemed to find everything in order.

"Well done, Imma."

Zahla couldn't hear Jochebed's response, but one glance at the blood spreading across Puah's linen, and her stomach reeled. She began heaving in short breaths as if she were the one laboring.

"I need your help, Zahla," her cousin whispered, catching her gaze. "You must clean the baby so I can care for his imma."

Puah draped a piece of linen over Zahla's outstretched arms and cradled the baby inside before slinging a second piece of linen over Zahla's shoulder.

"I do not feel well," Zahla said, afraid to look at what remained on the baby.

Puah leaned over, meeting her gaze. "The baby needs you."

The boy cried out, and she pulled him close. "I—"

"And his imma needs me."

With a short nod, Zahla turned away, praying for the strength of an ox to remain upright. Puah had delivered the child. It was Zahla's job to clean and comfort him until he could be fed. It would help no one if Puah had to stop and tend to her along with the child.

With her back to Puah, Zahla sat beside the clay vessel of water and washed off the layers that had sustained him in Jochebed's womb. Soon enough he would grow into a man to live and die at Pharaoh's mercy, but for now, he needed his imma to sustain his life.

As she wiped cool water, the finest of salt, and then oil on his skin, the boy began to cry again. She swaddled him in a dry linen, lest he grow sick in the evening air, and the tight wrap eased his cries.

Puah was still intent on cleaning Jochebed when Amram rushed back inside.

"A soldier is walking our way," he said, his voice trembling.

Why was he afraid? Egyptian soldiers were everywhere in Rameses and the outlying villages, keeping peace among those who toiled to build Pharaoh's storehouses and dwellings. Ensuring with their spears and clubs that no one escaped from the taskmasters.

Laws were many in Egypt but giving birth wasn't a crime. The soldier must be searching for a runaway slave among them.

Had Amram missed a day of work to be with his wife? Perhaps they thought he was trying to escape.

"You and Miriam should slip into the shadows," Puah told him before turning to Zahla. "And you need to hide the baby in the courtyard."

"But why—"

"Now," Puah ordered before returning to Jochebed. "I am afraid you have to return to the stones."

As Zahla rushed across the room, the baby in her arms, Puah lifted the older woman from the bed and repositioned her knees on the bricks.

"Baby is coming now," Puah repeated loudly as if Jochebed were still laboring.

In that moment, Zahla felt like a child again when no one would tell her the truth about what had happened to her own imma. Why did she have to hide tonight? They'd done nothing wrong.

But if Puah and Amram were afraid, if Jochebed in all her pain was willing to return to the stones, then Zahla would care for her baby.

Several donkeys rested in the circular yard, the charcoal pit still warm from the evening fire. She didn't see the chickens that Puah shooed from the hut. Perhaps they'd tucked themselves into another dwelling. She would follow them, but if the soldiers were looking for a runaway slave, they might search each hut.

As the moon slipped behind a cloud, Zahla sank into the shadows on a bed of straw meant for the livestock, the baby swaddled close to her chest. She was grateful the donkeys ignored her as she pressed between them. She draped her woolen *radid* over her shoulders like a tent and covered the baby, hoping the soldier would think they were an animal in the dim light.

The boy remained quiet as if he knew the danger nearby. The nausea that almost consumed Zahla moments ago had vanished, replaced by a new strength to protect this child. Under the veil, she whispered a prayer to Yahweh, the invisible deity her *saba* spoke of with reverence and unwavering faith when he was alive. The God of Abraham, Joseph, and Manasseh.

How they needed a deliverer. The one promised to all the Hebrew people.

"Where is the baby?" the soldier demanded inside the house, the brusque voice of one annoyed by the very existence of this new life. One who cared not whether a child lived or died.

Most of the Israelites knew the Egyptian language, but few of the Egyptians knew how to speak Hebrew.

Puah switched to the language of their oppressor. "I am trying to deliver it," she said as if this were her only concern.

A slap of sandals and the scratch of another chicken in the darkness. "I heard a cry."

At the soldier's words, Jochebed wailed into the night as though she was about to birth a second child. Zahla imagined the man stepping back, and she hoped he would run in the opposite direction. He had no business here.

"We need more water," Puah said.

Zahla didn't know how her cousin maintained her composure. The soldier could easily use his sword or dagger on the midwife and the imma alike.

He snorted. "I do not fetch water for anyone."

The baby wiggled against her, and when he began to cry again, Zahla pressed her finger into his mouth. He tried to suckle it for a moment, but the distraction wouldn't last long. The poor boy wanted his mother.

Jochebed cried out again, and Zahla wondered if the woman's pleas were real. The pain might still be overwhelming, but her cries probably stemmed more now from fear.

Puah spoke again, her voice louder as she pleaded with the soldier. "I am about to lose both the mother and child!"

He laughed. "I do not care about a Hebrew woman or her baby."

A retort must have been playing on Puah's lips, but her cousin didn't respond.

"Dogs, all of you," the soldier spat. "Dust on this forsaken earth."

Rain began falling, and Zahla curled under the tent to keep the baby dry. When Jochebed wailed a third time, Zahla's stomach turned but not because of the blood or birthing. Because she glimpsed this boy's future.

Soon the one in her arms would be molding bricks with his abba and others from the village, at the mercy of taskmasters with their whips and cruel words. No one in the Egyptian kingdom would care if he lived or died. The soldier may call her people dogs and dirt, but it was the Hebrew slaves who farmed much of Egypt's food, cared for their animals, built storehouses, and pressed fruit into wine.

What would Pharaoh do without her people?

The baby squirmed away from Zahla's finger and expelled a weak cry as if he'd exhausted himself. But if Yahweh rescued him in this hour, perhaps He might use the boy's life beyond the brickyard to rescue others.

Puah stepped into the courtyard. "You can bring in the baby."

"But the soldier…" Zahla said.

"He departed." She glanced at the darkened sky. "And the storm will keep him away."

Zahla stood carefully so the baby wouldn't cry again. Then she carried him to his imma. Jochebed leaned back against the wall, and he latched quickly to her breast, contented at last. Jochebed glanced down at him as if she'd found gold in the Nile.

Amram and Miriam stepped into the room after Zahla. She didn't ask where they'd gone after announcing the soldier's arrival.

Zahla studied the curtain over the entrance as if the soldier might return. "Why would a soldier bother with a baby's cry?"

A glance passed between her cousin and Jochebed, an entire conversation of unspoken words.

"Please tell me," Zahla begged. They'd trusted her with hiding this little one. They had to trust her with the truth.

"Pharaoh fears a rebellion," Puah said slowly. "Some have heard rumors that he wants to kill the Hebrew children."

*The snake.* All slithering and scaly and evil. How she despised the man who ruled over them.

Zahla looked at the baby in Jochebed's arms. "Children will not cause an uprising."

"But they will grow into men, and the Hebrew people are already many," Amram said. "Pharaoh wants to decrease our population."

Puah nodded sadly. "He believes it will make us more compliant to do his work."

"Fool," Jochebed murmured, snuggling the child on her chest. "Killing our children… It will only make our people angrier."

Zahla glanced at Amram, the man who had stood in the shadows while the soldier confronted his wife. And she knew, even in their passion, the Hebrews had no way to defend themselves. The Egyptians, with their gleaming swords and chariots, could kill thousands in an uprising. The sharp end of an obsidian stone may cut through an umbilical cord, but it would never penetrate an armor plate or shield.

They had nothing but shadows for defense.

The break of dawn tiptoed across the earthen floor, no place to hide now. Puah glanced at the spread of light, the glistening puddle at the doorway, and dropped to the floor beside Jochebed.

"Still, Pharaoh has made no decree to kill our children," Amram said.

Puah glanced at the door where the soldier had stood. "His men do not need a decree to kill a dog."

Jochebed clapped her hands together over the baby's head as if they were cymbals. "No more talk of killing."

Puah smiled at her. "What will you name your son?"

"Aaron." Jochebed pulled him close to her again. "He will be safe now."

"Aaron," Amram repeated, and Miriam glanced over his shoulder as he took her brother in his arms. "From the house of Levi."

*Aaron.* The name meant "mountain of strength." The promise of redemption.

Perhaps Aaron would be their redeemer.

# CHAPTER FOUR

"Joseph!" Zahla shouted into the mouth of the grotto.

Their forefathers had dug this limestone chamber for their ancestor, and her brother inherited both the name of this ancient ruler and the oversight of his cellar. The chamber stretched more than a hundred cubits underground and offered a dark, humid space to ferment and store Pharaoh's wine.

Abba had built a small house outside the entrance so one of their family members could guard their wares day and night since every jar must be accounted for. If one was damaged, her abba, Pharaoh's chief vintner, would suffer for the loss.

"I am occupied," her brother called back from the depths of the cellar.

While he was adept at storing the jars, Joseph enjoyed hiding in the coolness underground even more than stewarding their prized wine. During *Peret*, the current season of preparation, Abba had to push him to join the others in pruning and training the vines.

But Joseph never tried to escape work during the next season of Shemu. Every able-bodied man, woman, and child in their large family spent the harvest months picking and pressing grapes. For that matter, even those who weren't as able were required to work in some capacity. Without the grapes, there'd be no wine. And without

Pharaoh's wine, the descendants of Manasseh would lose their land and the men would be sent north like so many others to work in the city of Rameses.

Shemu was a celebration, in part, of the independence they'd been able to maintain in Goshen.

Zahla brushed her head covering away from her eyes and glanced at Lemuel, one of her many cousins and today's chamber guard. Propped beside Lemuel was a twisted reed cane that matched his scrawny frame. As if he could deter thieves with a stick.

To her knowledge, no one had ever tried to raid the wine cellar, but Abba wouldn't risk losing their livelihood to an Egyptian thief or desert marauder. His position as vintner was essential for Pharaoh's supply of wine, he explained to any Egyptian who asked about his work. To any Hebrew who asked, he said that it kept his family out of the brickyard.

Instead of thieves, Lemuel was more likely to encounter a wild animal that wandered in from the desert or the fierce winds of a storm. But no threat occupied his attention this afternoon.

"Are you going to help me?" she asked.

Lemuel laughed. "I am not going to drag him out."

Not that he or Zahla could. Joseph was a cubit taller than Lemuel, and even if he didn't like fieldwork, Joseph was built for labor in the vineyards.

Now that Zahla was almost sixteen, her aunts were convinced that she should marry Lemuel, but how could she marry a man who refused to stand up to her brother?

Then again, even if he did confront Joseph, Zahla didn't know if she'd ever marry. She couldn't think of a single unmarried man in their family or community who met her abba's approval as a husband for his only daughter, nor could she imagine giving up a single freedom to matrimony. Her aunts complained often about Abba's lack of oversight, but he would just shrug at their grievances and say Zahla knew how to watch over herself.

She wouldn't disappoint him.

Cool air stole out of the entrance as Zahla stepped closer. She wanted to linger here in the coolness, chilling her face and hands, but Abba had asked her and Joseph to return home.

"Abba wants you," she called to Joseph. "He said it is an urgent matter."

"More urgent than Pharaoh's wine?" Her brother neared the entrance, the glow of his lantern encircling the dark entry, but he wouldn't leave the chamber unless forced.

At least she no longer had to shout into the darkness. "You will have to ask Abba."

"I will ask him when I come home tonight."

She imagined Joseph shrugging like Lemuel, completely unmoved by her appeal. While she'd like to leave him—her only sibling—in the chamber, even lock him in on those days that he goaded her, she still loved him.

Joseph was seven years older, and he remembered well the happy days with their imma. On his best days, he would share a story or two about Imma. On his worst days, he wouldn't even speak to her.

"I suppose you could wait." She leaned back against the craggy wall, her voice quieter. Hopefully, he would have to strain to hear. "But it is unfortunate."

"Not really," he replied, sounding mere steps from the entrance. "I would much rather be sampling the stores down here than pruning vines."

He was only jesting, but it irritated her. "Abba will disown you if he thinks you are tasting Pharaoh's wine."

Joseph laughed as if he hadn't a care in this world. And compared to most Hebrew men, his load was light. As long as he delivered the appointed jars to the wine steward each week and a container of *shedeh*, the spiced drink that Pharaoh prized above any other, no harm would come to her family.

At least that's what Zahla told herself in the weeks after harvest, when soldiers swept through Goshen's fields and retrieved men to work up north. The soldiers never took workers from the vineyards. While laborers were plenty in the barley and flax fields, Pharaoh needed winemakers to store and transport his wine.

Joseph liked to remind his sister that his namesake once ruled over Egypt, second only to Pharaoh. While the history of Israel's sons used to be prized, only the elders spoke about the tribes now. But their vineyard had been owned by the original Joseph, son of Israel, the land descending through the tribe of Manasseh for generations.

Her brother didn't think anyone could force him away from the vineyard, but this Pharaoh was becoming more brutal as he aged. He'd divided the descendants of Israel into small segments and selected taskmasters among them to oversee those enslaved in the cities.

Three moons had passed since she'd accompanied Puah to help deliver Jochebed's son, and she understood why the immas and abbas of their nation grew more afraid of the soldiers. Rumors abounded across Goshen about Pharaoh's desire to eliminate Hebrew boys, and she feared for all the children in Rameses.

Zahla sighed as if she'd given up on coaxing Joseph out of the cellar. "I will tell Abba and Puah that your work detains you."

She waited against the rocks, a smile playing on her lips, and when she glanced over at Lemuel, she saw his smile too. He knew.

One, two, three…

Joseph's head popped out of the darkness like a desert fox, squinting into the light as he searched his surroundings. "Puah is here?"

She silenced the laughter erupting inside her, and Lemuel turned away, scanning the vineyards as if he were looking for a wolf or a leopard. While he didn't laugh, his shoulders trembled as if he was about to keel over.

Her brother, so aloof at times, was completely predictable when it came to Puah.

Zahla shrugged. "Apparently, she is joining us for the evening meal."

Joseph rubbed his hand over his trimmed beard and glanced back at the chamber as if this decision was difficult. "I suppose I can finish my audit tomorrow."

"Abba will be glad to hear it."

He wiped off his brow as he stepped into the light and then pulled his head covering over dark brown locks. "We should all eat together in the chamber."

"The evening will bring cooler air," she replied before saying goodbye to Lemuel.

Joseph stepped ahead of her on the path. "It is never cool enough this time of year."

While he liked to bask in the chilly wine cellar, she knew her brother preferred to spend his evening with Puah.

He thought his intrigue with their cousin a secret, but the entire family knew he was hopelessly smitten with her. For as long as she could remember, Joseph had trailed after Puah like a puppy. It was embarrassing, really. His endless fascination with everything she did or said while all Puah seemed to think about was delivering babies, not having a family of her own.

Zahla would feel sorry for Joseph if he wasn't such a pest. Her brother was much too self-absorbed for someone like Puah, who'd dedicated her life to caring for others.

As they hurried home, they passed several dwellings that housed aunts and uncles who worked at the vineyard. Once the grapes were full and sweet, at least a hundred family members along with harvest laborers would erect goatskin shelters among the rows. They'd work side by side for weeks, handpicking the ripest grapes. Some of the fruit would be dried into raisins, but most would be pressed into wine. In return, the laborers would each receive a large portion of fruit and wine for their household, and the men would be saved for another season from the grueling work in the brickyard.

"Why is Puah here?" Joseph asked.

"She has news to share."

Joseph shook his head as if disappointed over her reasoning to visit, but a midwife was often the best source of information for what was happening among their fellow Hebrews. And Zahla hadn't seen Puah since that night she'd hidden Aaron between the rumps of two donkeys.

In hindsight, the situation with the donkeys might have been comical if she hadn't been so terrified. While her brother might be too distracted to speak tonight, she had many questions to ask their cousin.

As she and Joseph hurried down another long row, passing packed-mud storehouses that held their food and supplies, Zahla smelled roasted perch and hyssop-spiced oil prepared for their evening meal. Then she smiled when she saw the bounty spread on platters in the rectangular courtyard between nine homes including the one where she, Abba, and Joseph lived.

The meal might be simple for someone from the palace, but Zahla considered it a feast. Platters of fish that she'd roasted earlier with fennel and garlic. Crusty bread shaped from barley flour and baked in clay pots among the smoldering embers. A mound of dates and yellow melons grown in the marshlands after the flooded Nile settled back in its bed. And wine from Abba's personal cellar. Her father considered the drink poorer quality from grapes picked late in the season. Perhaps it wasn't as sweet as Pharaoh's shedeh, but Zahla thought it perfect.

Their younger cousins ran circles in the courtyard, and when one of the boys swiped an olive from a platter, his imma slapped his hand before turning him away from the food.

These evenings on the Nile Delta, it often seemed as if her family were free.

Perhaps that was why Puah had come to visit. She lived in a village on the northern edge of the vineyard, close to the city so she could attend births in both Goshen and Rameses. Perhaps she simply wanted to escape, if only for the evening, the threats up north.

Abba stepped out of their house and spotted Joseph. "My son," he said as if Zahla wasn't beside him.

Her abba meant no offense. While she often assisted him during the day, Joseph rarely returned home until the night hours.

Her brother glanced at the brick-rimmed fire. "Zahla said we were eating perch."

"I said no such—"

"Puah?" Joseph exclaimed as if shocked to see her standing among their aunts and uncles. "Why are you here?"

Puah stepped away from the circle. "I have news to share with the family."

"You may visit anytime, even without news."

Of course, Puah could visit anytime. They always welcomed family.

As if his words weren't awkward enough, Joseph continued to stare, but when Puah glanced up at him, Zahla saw something different in her cousin's gaze. Almost like what Zahla saw in her brother's eyes.

Surely not. What could Puah, a successful midwife, see in Joseph and his stomping around in the cellar? Her brother was more mongoose than man.

Abba cleared his throat. "Please, sit. We will eat."

Some of her family unfurled mats near the platters. Others reclined on dry ground or an animal skin. Puah sat beside Zahla with her birthing basket on the ground behind her. Zahla was glad for the dozens of men, women, and children who surrounded them. Glad they could all pool their food for a feast.

Abba bowed his head, and the others followed.

"Blessed are You, O Lord, the Creator of the heavens and the earth. We thank You for the fish in Your river and for Your trees and vines to provide sustenance for my family. Please bless our food and may You protect us…"

Abba's voice broke, and Zahla glanced up. Was her abba crying?

He quickly recovered his voice to finish the prayer, and then he lifted a platter to begin the passing of food.

Zahla tore off a piece of bread and handed the small loaf to Puah. She'd been told Abba had cried when Imma died, but she'd never seen his tears.

As they ate, her abba turned to Puah. "What news do you bring?"

Puah glanced around the circle before looking at the bread in her hands. "I am afraid to share."

Silence met her statement, for while they were all curious, they also worried about what might be changing for their people.

Zahla recalled their conversation on the raft three months earlier when Puah spoke about her role.

"You once said it was a midwife's responsibility to take away fear."

Puah nodded, remembering the words.

"Pharaoh called me and all the Hebrew midwives to his court," she said slowly, her gaze on the glimmering sky above the Nile. "I am afraid he wants us to…"

Words escaped her again until Joseph spoke, his voice kinder than Zahla had ever heard it. "What did he ask of you?"

Puah looked back at Joseph as if he was giving her the strength to continue. "He commanded us to kill any newborn Hebrew that is a boy."

A gasp rippled through the group, and Zahla's mouth gaped open, her head spinning. They'd suspected that Pharaoh might command his soldiers to search for their babies, but how could he demand their midwives, the deliverers of life, kill the children they brought into the world? These women fought to give and sustain life, not steal it away.

Zahla wrapped her arms around her chest as if she could gather all the sons of Israel together and protect them.

"Why has he done this?" Joseph asked.

"Because he fears an uprising among the Hebrew people," Puah explained. "He wants to reduce the male population."

"Coward!" The word leaped from Zahla's lips, and no one disagreed. Instead of demanding his soldiers kill the babies or even killing them himself, Pharaoh planned to turn the midwives against those they loved. To inject more chaos into their clans.

No one was surprised at Pharaoh's fear of an uprising, but why didn't he war against Hebrew adults who could defend themselves? Instead he was like a wicked reptile in the reeds, preying on the weakest among them.

Puah sighed. "The decree is supposed to be a secret."

"No one could keep such a decree secret," Joseph said.

Now the Hebrew people would have to rally around their children. Fight back…if they had any fight left in them.

Zahla watched her younger cousins flit like sand flies between the buildings. Pharaoh may be foolish, but he certainly wasn't stupid. He knew there weren't enough Hebrew men to wage war without weapons, but if the population continued to grow, the Hebrews would soon have enough able-bodied men to defeat his army.

Zahla focused back on Puah. "You would never kill a child."

Did Pharaoh not understand her people? Perhaps an Egyptian midwife would kill at his command, but a midwife like Puah would die before harming a child. None of the Hebrew midwives would kill a baby. The thought was as absurd, as impossible, as the Nile waters turning into blood.

"I am afraid some of the Hebrew midwives fear Pharaoh more than Yahweh," Puah said sadly. "They will do what he commands."

Zahla's heart collapsed. How could they even consider killing the babies they delivered?

Joseph balled his fists as if he might fight both Pharaoh and his soldiers alone. "But not you."

When Puah smiled, Zahla thought her brother might take her hand right there, embarrassing them all. Most of the traditions of propriety had been discarded under their enslavement, but unless a woman was under duress, no man—married or otherwise—was supposed to touch her.

Hooves pounded through the vineyard, and everyone turned. It was probably just a herd of spooked goats or another farm animal, but Joseph reached for a hoe while others lifted crockery or pruning knives to use as weapons in case a hippopotamus or desert animal lumbered into camp.

Instead of a wild creature, a donkey sped into the clearing with a young man on its back. The rider hopped off and scanned their group. "I am looking for the woman called Puah."

Her cousin moved to rise from the mat, but Joseph hopped to his feet first. "What do you want with Puah?"

Her brother's initiative astounded Zahla. Who was this bold man who usually preferred the quiet, dark cellar over the company of his family?

"A woman in labor..." The messenger paused as if to catch his stolen breath, his hand clutching one of the posts that held up their vines. "Shiphrah is requesting help in Rameses."

Puah reached for the birthing basket. "I will go."

"And I will join you," Zahla said, standing with her.

"There is no need," Puah replied. "Shiphrah will be waiting for me."

Zahla shook her head. "You should not journey into the city alone."

Puah turned back to the messenger. "Will you guide me to Shiphrah?"

"I am sorry," he said. "Soldiers are searching for more men to work in the brickyard."

Zahla studied the mud smeared on the young man's face, his tangled long hair. Had he run away from the Egyptians, or did he hold a job in the fields?

If he was supposed to be molding bricks, his overseer would hunt him down and whip him for certain. Some overseers, she'd heard, killed their missing slaves, and now she wondered if Pharaoh applauded these efforts as a warning but also to weed out those who disobeyed.

"I will go," Zahla insisted.

"No, Sister." Joseph glanced across the fields. "I will accompany her."

Abba reached for his arm. "You cannot do this. The soldiers will find you and—"

Her brother's chin lifted in defiance at the word *cannot*. "I will tell any soldier that I am the steward of Pharaoh's wine. They may hate me, but they fear Pharaoh like a god."

"Because they believe he is a god." Puah pulled the basket to her chest. "And they will do anything he demands. You must stay here, Joseph. The soldiers will not care that you are a steward."

Her brother glanced at the messenger before looking back at Puah. "Do you prefer to walk or ride on a donkey?"

"Joseph—"

"I think it would be safer to walk," he continued. "We can hide in the reeds if we hear a horse."

When she didn't reply, he announced that they would walk. Zahla hoped Puah could deter him, but her brother was determined, listening to the messenger's directions to the laboring mother's house.

"May Yahweh walk with you," Abba said quietly, resigned to the whims of his stubborn son. His only son.

What would her abba do if he lost Joseph?

The sun was angling down in the west when Joseph and Puah left for the city, and at their departure, a cloud descended over the group. Her brother would take the needed precautions to avoid soldiers, but what if he thought Puah was in danger? If he defended her against the soldiers, they would kill him.

In the late hours, she heard Abba praying behind the curtain that separated their beds, begging Yahweh, the God that most of their kinsfolk had forgotten, to save Joseph's life.

# CHAPTER FIVE

Puah returned early the next day, as Zahla prepared the morning meal. The baby was a girl, she said, but tears still fell from her eyes.

Joseph hadn't accompanied her home.

"Two soldiers—" Puah's account was interrupted by the tremble in her words.

Abba's hands shook like Puah's voice when he tried to pour her a drink. Part of the wine sloshed into her cup. The rest splattered across the ground.

Puah took a sip and started again. "Two soldiers arrested Joseph on our way home."

Zahla heard her cousin's words, but she couldn't process them. Not yet.

Closing her eyes, she breathed deeply of the spring-soaked air. Then she returned to her preparations for a morning meal, spooning cold lentils into a serving bowl and seasoning them with chopped onions, rosemary, and coriander seed. As long as she kept her hands busy, her focus on the food, she could still her racing mind.

Or, at least, try to still it.

Puah's puffy eyes were red, her cheeks soaked with tears, as she shared her story. She and Shiphrah had worked together all night, delivering a healthy baby girl. Joseph kept the new abba company through the late hours, and at first light, after caring for both the imma and baby, they began their walk south. The soldiers stopped them before they reached the vineyard.

"Joseph told them he was the son of the chief vintner. That he was needed to steward Pharaoh's wine. The men only laughed at him, and then they..." Puah sipped the wine again as if she needed it to find the words. "They beat him with a club and dragged him away."

Abba didn't waste another moment of daylight. He stuffed a cloth filled with dates and cheese into his leather bag, and the women followed as he rushed to the stable. He selected a donkey from their small herd and tossed two furs over the creature's back to use as a saddle.

"Please be careful," Puah begged as he packed a small vessel of his best wine in a pouch.

"I will be home soon," he promised, but Zahla knew he wouldn't return until he located Joseph and secured his liberty.

"I will care for the vineyard while you are away," Zahla assured him.

Puah stepped to her side, and they watched Abba ride his donkey up the vineyard row. Zahla had no doubt he would find Joseph, but what if the overseers forced Abba to mold bricks as well? They might not allow either man to leave the brickyard.

Instead of tears, a chill traveled over her arms and through her chest, settling deep in her bones, and her lungs seemed to freeze.

She gulped in air, trying to warm her insides, but her lungs didn't want to fill. She fell to the ground between the vines and looked up at the Egyptian sun, wishing it would warm her this morning.

"I am so sorry." Puah sat in the dirt beside her. "I never should have allowed him to go with me."

"You would not have been able to stop him." Zahla folded her legs close to her chest. "Once Joseph makes up his mind, it is almost impossible to convince him to change it."

"I fear the taskmasters will convince him with their clubs."

Zahla shivered again, unable to rid herself of the cold. "Perhaps he will annoy them so much, they will demand his release."

Puah managed a smile. "He only annoys you because you are his sister."

"We bicker plenty, but I still love him."

"I know."

"It makes me…" She glanced at Puah and saw fresh tears falling down her cousin's cheeks. "I do not want anyone to hurt him."

Puah reached for her hand, and they both gazed up the row again as though they could see Rameses in the distance. "Do you think your abba will find him?"

"He will do everything possible to find and bring him home," Zahla said, but she knew well that nothing was for certain. How could she continue in this life if she lost her brother and her abba to the Egyptians?

She despised the men and women who oppressed them. Pharaoh and his royal wives and their spoiled princes and princesses who had never worked in the fields but ate mounds of fruit and platters of roasted lamb and drank jars of abba's honey-sweetened wine. The Egyptians, who had never slaved for a day in the brickyard but lived in houses made of sunbaked bricks. She hated the overseers who whipped the men who couldn't keep up with their daily quota, and she loathed the soldiers who did what Pharaoh bid even when it was wicked.

Turning east, Zahla saw the looming pyramids in the east, where members of the Egyptian royalty were entombed. While the bodies of their ancestors were inside, the Egyptians believed their souls had been ferried across the Nile River into the realm of the dead. An eternal paradise.

Did they have slaves to do their bidding in paradise?

Beyond the pyramids, far to the east, was a vast desert and wilderness. Some days she wished she could continue walking past the edge of their vineyard. Beyond the wheat and barley fields in Goshen and the monstrous pyramids and soldiers guarding Egypt's border. She'd heard stories about the harsh climate beyond the border and the marauders who kidnapped and sold people as slaves, but she still dreamed about roaming in the desert. Outrunning the marauders and hiding in the hills.

Beyond Egypt, she might find freedom. Beyond Egypt, perhaps Puah and Joseph and Abba and all of her family could find freedom too.

"I am glad the baby was a girl," she whispered, searching for something good to embrace on this horrific afternoon.

"Me too."

"A new life in the midst of the devastation."

Puah nodded, but she looked as if she might tumble over from exhaustion.

"Did you sleep at all last night?" Zahla asked.

"I am not tired."

Zahla pointed toward the leather curtain that covered the entrance to the house she shared with Abba and Joseph. "Get some sleep, Puah."

"I could not possibly sleep."

"You need to rest before Joseph returns. He will need you…"

Puah glanced at the horizon, seeming to weigh her words. "Will you wake me when there is news?"

"Of course," she replied. "But I suspect you will wake the moment you hear Joseph's voice."

Zahla escorted her cousin into the house and directed her to the bench where Zahla usually slept, the brick covered with a reed mat. Nearby was a basket with several fur blankets. While it was much too warm for a bedcovering, Puah folded one of the furs and tucked it as a cushion under her head. In moments, she was asleep.

Zahla took several bites of the prepared lentils, but her stomach refused any more food. She desperately needed a distraction away from the house.

Eight field workers, most of them family, were pruning the vineyard rows to the west, but she decided to work closer to home so she could watch for Joseph and Abba. With a bronze knife in hand, Zahla knelt alongside a vine and studied the dead wood.

Abba had taught her how to tend their vines when she was a girl, but before he began her training, she used to follow him as he worked, carrying a basketful of supplies and a waterskin to quench his thirst. While he oversaw their large vineyard, he could prune and harvest as quickly as any of the field workers. Even as a child, she had loved watching him prune. He knew, better than anyone, what needed to be stripped away so a vine could flourish.

Zahla scrutinized the vine now as her abba would do. Then she carefully cut off the dead shoots, leaving the healthy buds to flourish. She tossed the debris behind her on the dusty ground to gather later for use on a cooking fire. In a land with few trees, the dead vines, once full of grapes, were prized as firewood.

Both the new and old, she supposed, had value in their own way.

Zahla cut off another worn limb and threw it behind her before gently shaping the new growth on the ropes strung between posts, positioning the vine so it could climb. Eventually the buds and subsequent grapes would bask in the sunlight.

She scooted down to the next trunk and began the process again. In the next month, they'd prune and shape about five thousand of these vines to produce enough wine for the ruler's storehouse. Pharaoh would have his wine, and, as a reward, she hoped he would allow her brother to return home.

As the sun blazed its way across the sky, Zahla tugged her linen covering close to her cheeks. Her skin would be brown again soon enough. She didn't need it to burn today. With rivulets of sweat trickling down her spine, she worked quickly through the afternoon to expel her worry. Worked until she heard the flap of sandals behind her. Then she turned to see Puah with a basket and waterskin in her hand.

"You have to care for yourself too, Zahla."

As she gulped the well water, Zahla glanced at the sun. It would soon set over the horizon.

"Thank you," she said as she handed back the flask.

"You will get sunstroke if you're not careful."

Zahla clipped off another shoot. "The work calms my mind."

"Let me help you," Puah offered as she set down her basket.

"You are supposed to be resting."

"I could not sleep for long."

"We should prepare dinner soon." Zahla eyed the sun again. "For when they—"

"Let us work a bit longer."

When Puah sliced through a vine with her knife, Zahla realized her cousin needed to keep her hands busy as well. So they worked side by side, trimming the plants so they could thrive. How interesting, Zahla thought, that one must cut before one could heal. Sort of like bringing a new life into the world.

Except with the new law, Puah was supposed to take life.

"What are the midwives going to do now?" Zahla asked as they pruned.

"I do not know, but neither Shiphrah nor I would kill a baby." She sighed. "The laws keep changing."

Puah glanced over at her. "That is not all that is changing."

"I am not sure I can handle anything else!"

"I hope you'll be pleased with this change," Puah said although her voice sounded sad.

Zahla flinched. "Is this about Joseph?"

Puah answered with a nod. "Before the soldiers stopped us, Joseph asked if I would like to marry him."

Zahla lowered the knife and stared at her cousin. "What did you say?"

"That I would consider it." Her breath hitched at the memory. "Since my abba is no longer alive, I thought it would be proper to wait a few days to agree to a betrothal, but looking back, I should have just told him yes."

"Do you really want to marry him?" Zahla tried not to sound appalled at the possibility. Still, she couldn't understand why a competent and much-loved woman like Puah who traveled across the city and fields to use her midwifery skills would want to marry a man who preferred spending most of his time in a wine cellar.

"Very much," Puah replied. "I know the two of you do not always see things the same way, but he cares deeply for your whole family and for…"

"For you," Zahla said. "He has been enamored of you for most of his life."

"For me," Puah whispered as if she could hardly believe it. "I want to be his wife. And I want to be your sister."

Zahla placed her knife on the ground and kissed Puah's cheek. "If you truly love him, then there is no one that I would rather have as my sister."

Puah glanced down the row. "I will tell him *yes*, the moment he arrives home."

# CHAPTER SIX

The shuffle of feet woke Zahla, and she squinted in the dark room. "Abba?"

"Go back to sleep, my daughter."

She scooted up against the plaster wall. "Is Joseph with you?"

Abba ducked behind the curtain that divided their sleeping space. "We will talk in the morning."

Her stomach turned when she realized Joseph wasn't in the room.

What had happened to her brother?

Puah stirred on a mat near the window but didn't wake. Better that her cousin remain asleep if Abba didn't have good news.

Zahla moved to the edge of the curtain. "You said you would not return without him."

"I had no choice." Abba's voice broke. "I did not want to leave him there."

"I know." She leaned against the wall. "What happened?"

"I must sleep before I talk."

She wanted to persist, demand that he tell her more, but she would let him rest. After he answered the question that burned inside her. "Is he alive?'

"He is."

Even with that knowledge, sleep eluded her. At first light, Zahla tied her sandals and splashed water on her face and hair. Then she slipped outside and milked their goats. For the breakfast meal, she unwrapped a loaf of flatbread and split it between three plates, drizzling honey over each piece.

When Abba finally joined her and Puah outside, Zahla gaped at the welts on his face. "What did they do to you?"

"The overseers were not swayed by my demand to retrieve Joseph."

"Let me see your back," she said softly.

"Nor were they swayed by my role as Pharaoh's vintner."

"Your back, Abba."

He waved her away. "It is not necessary for you to see it."

"Abba—"

"Our focus must be on your brother."

"We must tend to you first and then we will talk about Joseph." She disliked speaking so harshly to him, but sometimes it was needed to gain her father's attention.

He shook his head, irritated at her demand, but she didn't care.

"Please," she begged. "I cannot lose you to the Egyptians."

Slowly, he pulled back the collar of his tunic, revealing a webwork of lashes. And Zahla—who had never wished harm upon another—wanted to whip whoever had beaten him. Her abba had spent fifty years serving Egypt. His entire life. How dare they treat him like a common slave...

Then again, who among them was common? In her mind, every Israelite—young and old—was remarkable, but the Egyptians had no use for their baby boys or apparently for an old man like Abba, no matter how good his wine.

"I will get my salve," Puah said.

Zahla helped him sit on a stool, and then she added a handful of dates and almonds beside his portion of flatbread and filled a cup with goat's milk to provide him strength for the day. As he ate, she rubbed the calendula salve with aloe vera on his shoulders and back. Then she smoothed on an ointment of wax and honey to protect it.

Her abba oversaw this vineyard, but she thought he should rule their nation. Instead of building yet another monument to himself or the Egyptian gods, Abba would pay men for their labor and make sure everyone had a place to live. He would stop the beatings and welcome the babies. Her abba would require his people to work, as he did with everyone at the vineyard, but if he were in charge, the Hebrew people would be growing more food, raising more livestock in the fields of Goshen, and making a lot fewer bricks.

When she stepped back, Abba pulled up his tunic and continued to eat.

"Please tell us what happened to Joseph," she said as she sat on the ground between him and Puah. Her cousin had forgotten to wear her head covering this morning, and Zahla saw no need to remind her. Puah, who coaxed new life into the world and cared confidently for their Hebrew mothers, looked disheveled and worn. Her long, brown hair was matted, her eyes still red from tears.

Zahla might not have understood it, but it seemed Puah really did care for Joseph. They had only to bring him home, and then not only would Puah be her cousin, but she would become a wife to Joseph, a sister to Zahla, and another daughter for Abba.

"The Egyptians put him to work in the brickyard," her abba said.

Zahla spat. "Monsters."

The men who had taken her brother were worse than monsters, and so were those who kept him. Not even the reptiles along the Nile tormented a person for sport.

Abba finished drinking his milk before speaking again. "The overseer said that only Pharaoh could release Joseph from the brickyard."

Would Pharaoh welcome his favorite vintner from Goshen or—

She refused to consider the alternative.

Zahla glanced at the morning sun and its gleam off the distant pyramids. "So we will go to Pharaoh."

Abba shook his head, the strain wrinkled across his face. "You will do nothing."

"But nothing could mean the end of Joseph's life!" They couldn't possibly stay here when a taskmaster's whip was poised to claim her brother's life.

Puah didn't speak, but she paced circles around them as if she might turn and sprint toward the city.

"You will work the vineyard today, Zahla." Abba stood slowly. "I am going to visit Pharaoh by myself."

"No one should petition Pharaoh alone," Puah said.

"You went before him," Abba reminded her. "Just days ago."

"With a dozen other midwives. And he called for us. I had no choice."

"I have no choice either."

"He cares not about your life or the lives of our people," Zahla told him.

"But he cares very much about his wine."

"I will accompany you," Puah persisted. "As your niece and a midwife and…"

"My future daughter, I hope." Abba patted her shoulder. "Joseph said that he asked you to be his bride."

"I should have told him yes."

"You will give Joseph your answer soon enough, but you cannot go to the palace today. Pharaoh will recognize you, and you must continue your midwifery without another inquiry."

Abba retrieved a jar of the sweet shedeh, the most valued of all royal wines, from the cellar. It was stored in a teal and red ceramic pot painted with leaves and a cluster of grapes hanging from a golden vine. A single eye had been carved and painted near the top as if the gods were guarding Pharaoh's drink.

Zahla wished they could shatter the pottery on the ground and spill the contents that Pharaoh prized. But the wine was their only hope for Joseph's return. She wouldn't touch the wine today, but if Pharaoh refused to let her brother go, if he refused to return the man who'd spent his lifetime producing the palace wine, she would break every single jar in their cellar. Pharaoh would have to acquire his wine somewhere else.

Abba carefully swathed the hand-painted jar with sycamore leaves and a cloud of linen. Then he placed it in a reed basket strapped on his donkey's back. Zahla strung a waterskin over her shoulder, and Puah carried her basket of medical supplies as they stepped up behind Abba. The other workers would have to tend to the vines today.

He eyed the two of them as if they were strangers. "You cannot accompany me."

"I must visit several women in Rameses," Puah explained. "Then I will wait for you on the path outside the city."

Abba turned to Zahla. "Are you visiting these women with Puah?"

She shook her head. "I am visiting Pharaoh."

"You cannot come, Zahla. I could not bear it if the soldiers took you as they did Joseph."

But the Egyptians were more concerned right now with the Hebrew men than their women. She would not let her abba, wounded and worn, visit Pharaoh on his own.

"You will have to tie me up or lower me down the well to keep me away. Even then, I would find a way to help you."

He reached for the lead of his donkey. "Stubborn girl."

But he no longer tried to deter her.

The women followed him quietly between the vines and then north on the dirt pathway until they reached the outskirts of Rameses. While Abba may be worried about her, she knew he wasn't angry. He'd lost his beloved wife the morning after Zahla was born, and now he fought tirelessly for those who remained in his family.

But it was impossible to fight weaponless against those who had swords and chariots and an endless number of zealous soldiers. She whispered a prayer as they neared the edge of the Rameses that Yahweh would fight for them.

When they had crossed through the gates, Puah kissed Zahla's cheek and disappeared into the rambling streets. While she had visited the village south of Rameses many times, Zahla had never been inside the city.

She knew every row in their vineyard, and sometimes it felt like she knew every reed along the Nile as well, but Rameses was nothing like Goshen's fields. Everything in this city was strange to her. The briny odor of fish in the Egyptian marketplace, the stench of animal dung, the yeasty aroma of wheat bread. With no field to escape through, the smells of the city clung to the warm, humid air.

Her jaw dropped when she and Abba rounded a corner, and she saw dozens of wooden stalls lining the busy street, many of them draped with brightly dyed cloth to block the sunlight. The stalls were filled with textile merchants, jewelry artisans, and potters. Food peddlers sold roasted meats, spices, and legumes. Elegant Egyptian women sauntered from booth to booth, each with an entourage of servants, trailing the aromas of cinnamon and frankincense behind them.

The sights were remarkable, the bustle overwhelming. Merchants shouted to capture the attention of those who had coins to buy their wares, but Zahla could barely hear them over the lowing of cattle and squawking of birds and the bleating of goats who weren't fond of the crowds.

"Make way!" a man shouted.

The sea of people divided itself into two streams, pressing against stalls on each side of the street. Abba stretched out his arms to protect the basket on his donkey's back even as a portly woman crushed Zahla against wooden slats. The woman's strong perfume, meant to mask odor, burned Zahla's eyes.

She elbowed the woman away and then ducked through the crowd to search for Abba.

Four chariots rattled through the market, each one pulled by battle-adorned horses in leather and gold tassels with feathers on their headgear. The first charioteer snapped a whip at the crowd, and they pressed closer together so the parade could pass.

Standing behind the charioteer was an archer wearing a short kilt with a painted bow in hand as if he might begin shooting the reed arrows bundled in the chariot beside him.

Did the Egyptians have a reason for parading through the marketplace? The Israelites may have wanted to war against their oppressors, but they and their donkeys and farming tools were no match for Pharaoh's horses and arrows.

After the chariots passed, vendor cries reawakened the market, and the crowd flooded back onto the sand-packed street. Zahla much preferred the gentle calls of the marsh birds in Goshen, the strumming of wind across vines, the sweet laughter of children.

She stopped walking when she heard someone laughing, the sound mixed in with the bartering of goods.

Turning, she watched three Egyptian boys playing together in an alley, safe from the crowd. Boys who might grow up to drive chariots or oversee slaves, like the men who stole Joseph and whipped Abba. None of their immas had to worry that Pharaoh might order the deaths of their sons.

Abba stepped up beside her. "Are you injured?"

"No." Her gaze broke away from the children. "I have never seen anything like those chariots."

"Pharaoh likes to remind both citizens and slaves of his power. He does not care if anyone gets trampled."

Perhaps the Egyptian mothers did have to worry about their little ones.

"The palace is not far now," Abba said as he maneuvered the donkey and wine through the crowded street.

Near the end of the market was a row of majestic homes painted with ochre, malachite, and charcoal symbols on the plaster walls. Built for the noblemen, she thought, and their wives. Those who honored Pharaoh and the Egyptian gods.

Several women watched them from their windows, but no one spoke to her or Abba as they traveled the street. Even though her people shared the land with the Egyptians, and some even shared ancestors, city life was very different from life in Goshen. The Egyptians and Israelites had little in common beyond the fish they ate from the river and grain from the fields. They shared only what the river and land provided.

At the end of the market street, a pristine pool glistened with blue lotus flowers blooming on the surface. As Abba circled the pool, Zahla glanced east to the dusty land that spread out to the pyramids and wondered if the Mediterranean Sea was nearby. She'd never seen the sea, but she knew it was close. Sometimes she could smell the salty breeze that swept up the Nile with the winds.

Was Pharaoh's brickyard in the city? Perhaps Joseph was near them now. Heavily guarded, she suspected, so the men wouldn't attempt an escape on the river or across the barren desert. If someone tried to run, one of the Pharaoh's archers would surely stop him.

She didn't dare ask about the brickyard. Abba needed to focus on the sole mission of rescuing Joseph, not thinking about his enslavement.

They turned another corner, and the street opened wide. Before them was the largest building that Zahla had ever seen. Even bigger than the pyramids. On the lower level of the palace were several entrances including one guarded by a man with a spear and shield.

A terrible cry rang out from behind the building's barred windows, and Zahla jumped.

"It is the prison," Abba said sadly before turning away.

A mountain of steps led from the prison to the palace's towering gate, and as Abba tied up his donkey, she craned her neck to gape at a statue at least ten times her height. The granite figure leering down had the body of a man and the wings of a falcon.

"That is Ra," Abba explained. "The Egyptian sun god."

She studied the sun disk crown on the statue's head, encircled with a golden cobra. "He has no light or breath in him."

"Pharaoh believes Ra and the other gods breathe through him."

Abba carefully removed the ceramic jar from its cocoon of fabric and leaves and reexamined the ceramic and inscriptions on the dark blue glaze of its rounded body and narrow neck. When he stored the wine, Joseph had plugged the top with a stone stopper and wax seal to ensure that no one except those in the royal court could sample Pharaoh's prized wine. Thankfully, it remained intact.

"Yahweh needs no man to breathe for Him," she said as a gust traveled gently up her arms, cooling her head.

He glanced back at the statue. "I wish Yahweh…"

"What is it, Abba?"

"I wish Yahweh would fight for us today."

Instead of looking back at the granite figure, Zahla glanced up at the sun as it neared the center of the sky. The Egyptians may rattle their chariots across the ground, fling their arrows, and make their bricks, but none of them could travel across the sky. And no man—Egyptian or otherwise—could cast the immensity or brightness of sunlight into stone.

"One day, Yahweh will rescue us," she said.

Instead of carrying the jar by its handles, Abba cradled it as he marched through the front gate and the palace courtyard like an invited guest. She followed him through the gates, but her legs stalled under the glare of Ra and the other granite gods lining the path into the palace. None of these gods represented light or life.

Abba turned back. "Will you wait for me outside?"

She took a deep breath. She would not abandon her brother or her abba because of her own fear. "I will visit Pharaoh with you."

After he nodded, she hurried after him. The columns and statues lorded over them on both sides, but she kept her eyes on the palace doors at the end of the walk.

No matter what happened inside the palace, she would not let Abba or Pharaoh or any of the other men know she was afraid.

# CHAPTER SEVEN

A guard stepped in front of Zahla and Abba, a wall of bare chest blocking them from Pharaoh's court.

"Who are you?" the man demanded.

"Raphael," Abba said calmly. "Pharaoh's vintner from Goshen. I am delivering his prized shedeh."

Abba held up the jar so the guard could see the insignia from his vineyard—the cluster of purple grapes and golden vine and omnipresent eye encircled with rays of sunlight.

"Take it to the kitchen." The man pointed his spear toward the edge of the walkway. "You will find the door below."

Abba didn't move. "I must have an audience with Pharaoh."

The guard dared to laugh in her abba's face. "Or an audience with the prison warden."

Even if they had an accent, at least they could speak some of the Egyptian language. She'd never met an Egyptian who understood or spoke Hebrew.

"I am no thief," Abba said.

"We do not allow thieves or dogs inside the palace."

Zahla clenched her hands, wanting to tell this pawn of a man exactly what she thought about his slur. Didn't he know how Pharaoh valued her abba's wine? Sometimes he even sent his palace steward into Goshen to ensure its production. Pharaoh and his guards may despise the Hebrew people, may think they were all dogs, but he still wanted their weekly transport of wine.

Abba didn't seem daunted by the guard's insult. "I have an important request for Pharaoh alone."

The man shook his head as if he couldn't believe Abba's audacity. "Your wine will be welcome inside, old man. Not you or your request."

Zahla huffed. "You are a—"

Abba silenced her with his gaze. More than her pride, more than her defense of Abba, she wanted Joseph to return home. In order to do that, she would have to cushion the many retorts racing across her tongue.

"Ah." The guard smirked, clearly amused when she wasn't trying to be funny. "I have two dogs at my gate."

She would show him who was the—

"What is this?" The clipped question came from a second guard who had stepped up to the gate. This man was a head taller than all of them and wore chest armor engraved with a papyrus plant. The alleged symbol of unity in their land. Instead of carrying a spear, a dagger hung from the man's belt, and a green-striped headdress with jewels woven into the fabric was draped over his hair and shoulders. Slashed across his cheek was a thin scar that looked like a snake about to strike.

Abba turned toward the warrior guard. "I must speak with Pharaoh about an urgent matter in his vineyard."

"Is it of extreme importance?" the guard asked.

Abba nodded. "If not, I would not risk my life in Pharaoh's court."

His gaze fell to the decorated jar in Abba's arms. "The cupbearer will test any drink you bring."

"And he will find my wine both safe and superior."

The warrior tossed a glance at her. "Who is this child with you?"

*Child!* An insult worse than a dog. She was sixteen years old, and he wasn't that much older. How dare he—

Abba's hand slipped away from his grasp on the jar, his palm stretched out at his side. He knew a flood of words was threatening to crash through her lips. This simple signal she knew well. A silent demand to quiet the flood.

"Zahla is my daughter," he said calmly. "She refuses to allow me an audience with Pharaoh alone."

A smile swept across the warrior's lips and then disappeared. Was he going to mock her as well? "Perhaps your daughter will learn that it is safer to stay in the shadows."

"I will learn no such—"

Another warning from her abba's steady hand, and she silenced her retort.

Why was it so difficult to contain the words that brewed inside her? Sometimes they forced themselves out without permission. But words, she knew quite well, could be dangerous. If nothing else, she must contain them for her family's sake. Her words would endanger both of them.

Zahla focused on her hands, pretending she held a stone stopper to plug her lips, allowing only the beneficial words through. "I will stay outside if necessary."

"Pharaoh is in a benevolent mood," the warrior told them. "A daughter was born to him today."

The other guard spat on the ground. "He needs a son."

Zahla felt the eyes of the warrior guard upon her, waiting perhaps for another retort. She'd refuse him the amusement of her words.

The warrior shifted his focus to his comrade. "Open the door for them."

"Merin—"

"The door," he repeated. "It is a simple task."

This time, he seemed to be mocking his fellow guard.

"The only door we should open is to the prison."

Merin looked down upon Abba. "Are you the father of Joseph the vintner?"

"I am."

"I know your son and his transports." Merin turned to his fellow guard. "Neither of us should speak on behalf of Pharaoh. If he has no use for this man and his wine, he will make it known."

Zahla shivered as the door slowly creaked its opening into the court. A cloud of incense floated into the courtyard, and she prayed that Pharaoh would have use for her father and brother alike.

Music played near the door. A lute and lyre. The rhythm of sistrum and drum.

"Make way for Pharaoh's vintner," Merin announced to the small crowd.

The musicians stopped playing, and people divided as if she and Abba were riding a chariot through the market.

"What is this?" a voice seemed to boom from the sky.

Sunlight poured through the upper windows of the clerestory, blinding their view of the royal court, and Zahla squinted until her eyes adjusted to the strange light. Then her gaze landed on an equally strange creature enthroned on a golden chair like one of the statues in the courtyard, except he wore a black wig and winged crown.

This was the god-man, she assumed, that Egypt worshiped.

"Go," Merin whispered behind them.

Abba took the first steps toward the throne, and Zahla scrambled up beside him to face Pharaoh. Others may worship this man, but she despised him, in his extravagant costume and jewels, for enslaving her people and ordering the death of their babies.

"My lord." Abba knelt before the throne and placed the jar on the ground.

Zahla glanced back at the closed door, at the guards standing on both sides and the dozens of people watching from the shadows around the perimeter. And she had no choice but to kneel beside her abba.

The rearing cobra on Pharaoh's golden headdress dipped toward them. "You are a vintner?"

She could see him better now. He wore an odd metal beard strapped to his aging face. Eyes lined with kohl. Wrinkles spilling out under his wig.

"My name is Raphael." Abba rose slowly and lifted the wine. "I am vintner of your royal vineyard."

As Zahla prepared for an insult from the ruler's lips, she imagined again the plug between her lips, stopping any leak of a retort. But Pharaoh was focused more on the jar of shedeh than the man who knelt before him.

It seemed as if the entire court held their breath until Pharaoh lifted a finger and pointed toward the shadowed wall. "See if he tells the truth."

A man dressed in a long white gown, belted with a blue sash, stepped out of the shadows. Then a second man followed.

Zahla recognized Haken, the chief wine steward who'd visited their fields. He knew her abba was an honest man. And he knew that Abba needed Joseph to assist him in the work.

Haken stopped beside Abba. "Greetings, vintner."

Abba stood with the jar clung to his chest. Its safe delivery was a relief, but this sweet wine was still his only collateral. If the wine steward dropped the vessel or didn't approve of the taste, he had nothing else to prove his worth.

A young boy brought forward a clay lantern, the flame fueled by oil. The wine steward held the mouth of the shedeh over its flame until the wax seal melted. Then the steward reached inside and removed the stone plug.

The man with the blue sash—the cupbearer, Zahla assumed—produced a small goblet, and the steward filled it with the bright red shedeh. The cupbearer smelled it first, and the entire court watched, the musicians silent, as he took a long sip. No one spoke in the moments that followed. Waiting upon death seemed entertainment enough for Pharaoh and his court.

Zahla dared another glance around the throne room. Did anyone wish her abba's drink contained poison? While the collapse of their cupbearer might add a bit of excitement to their mundane lives, even the taste of bad wine could prove fatal to both her and Abba.

The cupbearer didn't drop from a poisoned drink. With life still teeming inside him, he handed the cup to Haken. The wine steward took a long sip and then turned toward the throne.

"It is wine from the royal vineyard," Haken declared, and she could hear the delight in his words. Abba's shedeh was still the best in this land.

Pharaoh leaned forward as if he might sample from the goblet. "What is your request, vintner?"

"Soldiers accidentally took my son to work in the brickyard, and I have come to petition for his release."

Pharaoh's eyes narrowed into two black lines. "Why do you presume this was an accident?"

"Those who took him did not realize that I cannot make the royal wine without him."

Silence followed Abba's words. Would Pharaoh consider this a threat? Or perhaps it would anger the court.

Pharaoh's fingers drummed against the armrest, and she wondered if it was a signal for his guards to detain them, but no one stepped forward. "Do you not have other workers in the vineyard?"

"None as qualified as Joseph," Abba explained, and she wondered if Pharaoh had ever learned the name of their ancestor who'd ruled under another Pharaoh long ago. "He has worked by my side for three and twenty years and carefully stewarded your wine, my lord, in our vault. I trust no one else to manage or transport your wine."

Pharaoh seemed to consider his words before lowering his gaze to Zahla. "Who is this girl?"

She focused on the ground so the man—and he was just a man—wouldn't see the defiance in her eyes.

"My daughter."

"Is she capable of good work?" Pharaoh asked.

"Very capable, my lord."

She smiled at the pride in Abba's voice until Pharaoh's next words. "Then she shall deliver my wine."

"I am aging in years," Abba said slowly as if he hadn't anticipated this possibility. "One day soon she will marry, and without Joseph's skill, I fear for the future of your vineyard."

Zahla blinked. She and Abba had never talked of marriage. Most of their discussion focused on the pressing needs that arose with each season. And while she wouldn't disagree with Abba before Pharaoh, she was well-equipped to run the vineyard, the cellar, and the transport of Pharaoh's wine. Of course, she wanted her brother to return home more than she wanted a change in her position, but she could refine her skills if she must so she could protect the future of their vineyard.

Pharaoh glanced around the room as if he might find someone in his court who was an expert at tending vines or stewarding his wine.

"Do you know where your son is working?" he asked Abba.

*Where he is enslaved,* Zahla wanted to say.

Abba rocked up on his toes. "I do."

"Your son…"

"Joseph," Abba reminded him.

"Find this Joseph," Pharaoh commanded the guards who'd escorted them inside. Then he looked back at Abba. "Your son can return home for the planting and harvest seasons, but I need men to dig ditches during the wet season. He must work in the city once the river floods."

"But the transport—"

"I am confident that your daughter can manage the delivery of wine during Akhet." He turned to the musicians as if he might signal them to resume their playing, but he addressed Abba again. "If Joseph does not report to his overseer at the beginning of the floods, I will assign an Egyptian family to oversee the Goshen vines."

Zahla felt as if she might melt into a puddle on the palace floor.

She'd pushed too hard again in her demands to join Abba. If she hadn't insisted in joining him, Pharaoh wouldn't even know that Abba had a daughter.

Joseph may be free for now, but her insistence meant he would have to return to Rameses during the rainy season.

Pharaoh didn't wait for Abba's response. His decision had been decreed, and when he lifted his hand this time, the musicians resumed playing their percussion and strings.

# CHAPTER EIGHT

Abba didn't speak to Zahla or the two guards as they retraced the path under the palace statues and descended the steps.

"I am sorry, Abba," she whispered as they neared the lotus pool. "I should not have pushed so hard."

He patted her arm. "We will find a reason for Joseph to work in the vineyard during Akhet."

Relief flooded through her. Joseph would return home for the pruning and harvest. Then he and Abba would develop a plan for him to remain there for the remainder of the year.

They retrieved their donkey and followed the guards down a long street to the west. Near the muddy edge of the Nile.

Oh, the stories that could be told about this river and plain, she thought, from almost four hundred years of Israelites living in a foreign land. For many of those years, the Hebrew people had lived as welcomed guests after the ancient Joseph and his dreams saved both the Egyptian and Hebrew people from starvation. Joseph married an Egyptian woman, and she'd borne him two sons of mixed Egyptian and Hebrew blood. But after Joseph died, his memory as redeemer was slowly forgotten among the Egyptian people, and the rulers began enslaving their former guests.

Zahla may have a trickle of Egyptian blood flowing through her from Asenath—Joseph's wife—but she was nothing like the men who escorted them to the brickyard. They reminded her of the rearing cobra on Pharaoh's crown. Poised to kill if someone threatened them or their king.

But if the guards were meant to instill fear, she would mimic the mongoose hiding in the marsh. Small but fierce against any kind of snake.

The brick buildings at the city border faded into a sea of laboring men and mud. Each man stood half naked in a pit, filling wooden molds with a mixture of straw and clay. The sun baked their skin brown and hardened the bricks into a bright yellow.

Long rows divided the pits with each path ending on the bank of the Nile. Abba retied his donkey, and Merin motioned for them to follow him and the second guard down one of the rows.

The overseers and their whips were not exposed to the hot sun. They sat under shaded petitions between the pits, shouting commands at the brick workers and those who loaded the finished bricks into boats waiting on the river, ready to erect another building somewhere in Egypt to demonstrate again that Pharaoh was their god.

What would happen if Yahweh shook this land? Crumbled the palace and all Pharaoh's bricks. Then the Hebrew people could rise up among the ruins and destroy these snakes and their whips.

With every step, Zahla searched the clay pits for Joseph, looping down the second and then up the third row. How had Abba found her brother yesterday? The brickyard seemed to stretch endlessly to the north. It could take them days to find him again.

"Joseph?" Merin called out as they walked.

Several men glanced up from the knee-deep mud, but no one responded.

The warrior guard equaled her brother in age. Was it strange for him to be searching among enslaved men? Or did he, like the other guard, think this work suitable for a Hebrew? Only their lineage kept both guards from making bricks.

Merin turned to one of the overseers and then pointed at Abba. "We are looking for this man's son."

"Everyone here is someone's son."

Merin stepped under the petition. "Pharaoh has commanded we find him."

The overseer studied Merin's chest armor, then the jewels sewn into his head covering. "What does Pharaoh want of a slave?"

The second guard stepped up to the overseer with his spear. "Who are you to question Pharaoh?"

Instead of delaying with another question, the man marched across the narrow path to speak with another overseer. And for the first time today, Zahla was grateful for the guard's belligerence.

Abba's shoulders collapsed as he pointed to the pits on their right. "He was working here yesterday."

"They will find him," she said even though she had no knowledge of Joseph's whereabouts. She just couldn't imagine them not locating her brother.

An overseer shouted near the river, and Zahla cringed when she heard the snap of a whip, followed by pain in the brickmaker's cry. The man's wounds, she feared, would be fierce. The humiliation devastating.

Had one of these men whipped her abba in public?

She cringed at the thought.

"How is your back, Abba?" She'd been so focused on their audience before Pharaoh that she'd forgotten to inquire. The relief in Puah's ointment must have worn off hours ago.

"I will recover."

"You are a good abba." Zahla reached for his hand. "You provide well for our family and everyone in your care."

Tears welled up in his eyes, and she released him. It wouldn't benefit any of them if an overseer or guard saw him cry.

She scanned the pits again. They had to find Joseph alive and well. Then they would return to Goshen as a family. Joseph would continue guarding the cellar and arranging the transport each week into the palace.

If Joseph had to leave after harvest, would Abba really allow her to take his place? Perhaps he'd have no choice with Pharaoh's command.

Like her brother's faithful work, she would ensure that not a single jar of wine was broken on its journey to the palace.

The sun had begun its descent toward the river. Would Puah wait for them on the path home? Her dear cousin would be so relieved that Joseph was allowed to return, until she heard Pharaoh's decree. Then she'd mourn again.

Zahla shook her head. They would sort through the future later.

The overseer and Merin climbed onto a brick ledge about four rows to their left, and Merin helped a man in a loincloth climb up from the clay. Then she blinked back her own tears.

It was her brother.

"They found him, Abba."

At those words, her abba wept.

As Joseph drew near, Abba lifted his arms to greet him, but when he saw the lashes on Joseph's back, so similar to his own, he simply patted his hand. "We are taking you home, Son."

Joseph shook his head. "They will not release me."

Zahla couldn't stop her words this time. "Abba told Pharaoh that you are needed in the vineyard."

"He does not care…"

"He cares about his wine," Abba replied.

When Joseph shaded his eyes, she saw the questions in them. As if he could scarcely believe it might be true. Had he thought that he would have to spend the rest of his life working in the brickyard?

"And he listened to you?"

"He listened to reason." Abba lowered his voice. "He wants you to dig ditches in Rameses during the flood season, but we will find a way to keep you home."

Joseph glanced back at the overseer as if worried the whip might flail him again. What torment her brother must have experienced in the past two days.

He looked at her. "Is Puah safe?"

"Safe but terribly worried. It seems there is a question she is anxious to answer."

A hint of a smile played on her brother's lips. "I hope it is a positive answer."

Zahla returned his grin. "I cannot say."

He scanned the brickyard one last time. "I will dig their ditches if I must do so to marry her."

"I have two stubborn children," Abba proclaimed rather proudly as they walked away from Pharaoh's men.

# CHAPTER NINE

*The Red Sea*

"You must sleep, Savah."

*Grandmother.*

The word startled Zahla from her thoughts. Sometime in the past hour, she'd risen from her mat and lifted a whimpering Merin from his basket so the others could sleep. Then she'd slipped outside and settled near the tent to watch the majestic wall of fire.

As the flames shimmered in the night sky, as voices rippled across the valley from others like her who couldn't sleep, Zahla thought of Puah and Joseph and then their firstborn son, born almost eighty years ago. The great-uncle of this little one.

"Neither Merin nor I could sleep," she told her granddaughter. "I did not want him to wake the rest of the family."

"Morning will find all of us soon enough," Eliana said. She would need to feed Merin before her four other children woke and Moses instructed them all on how Yahweh would fight today.

Zahla scanned the wall of fire again that separated their camp from the Egyptian chariots. Hadn't Pharaoh and his army learned that Yahweh would keep fighting for His people? Even when the

Hebrew people had no weapons to defend themselves, Yahweh had battled for them.

Why did the Egyptian army continue to pursue them relentlessly after all that Yahweh had done to free her people? The only reason that made sense to her was Pharaoh's determination to beat this sovereign God. As if he could prove to himself and his people that he was supreme.

"You will need your strength to walk," Eliana continued as if they would simply travel out of this valley once the sun rose. As if Eliana had no doubt that Yahweh would rescue them.

Zahla adored her granddaughter. Adored her many grandchildren and their spouses. Even when their names escaped her faulty memory, they knew she loved them.

"I can no longer sleep."

Her memories of Puah and Joseph and then Merin had kept her company for the past hour. Even the hardest memories, the most devastating of losses, reminded her that they didn't have to face their enemy alone. While He may not always do what she wanted, Yahweh was with them.

Eliana joined her on the ground and reached for her son. "I was worried when we could not find the two of you."

"I would protect Merin with my life," Zahla said, her arms feeling empty without a baby to hold.

"I know." Eliana began to feed him. "But tomorrow we must all stay together, no matter what happens."

A breeze fluttered across them, and Zahla licked its salt from her lips. "Are you reprimanding me?"

"I would be devastated if anything happened to you or him or anyone else in our family."

"It is impossible to keep all nineteen of us together." And that was just Asher's family. The sons and daughters of her other four children and all of their extended family were spread across the valley.

"You cannot wander off today," Eliana said again as if Zahla might be confused.

"I am not wandering." She was slower than most of the travelers and often distracted. If she found another lost child like Sivian, what was she to do?

If only her grandchildren could see how quickly she used to move. One of the fastest runners in Goshen, she liked to think. She'd certainly become faster at running and hiding after her first nephew was born.

Eliana tilted her head. "This is important, Savah."

She sighed. "I will stay with the family."

Eliana looked down at the babe in her arms. "Thank you for helping with him."

"I would carry all five of your children if I could."

"I know." Eliana smiled. "But it is nice to divide them among us."

Zahla glanced back at the fire. "Are you afraid?"

"Yes," she said sadly. "The Egyptians might kill us in the morning."

Confidence swelled inside Zahla. She'd seen much in her life, and it seemed that this time the God of Israel was going to redeem her family. "Yahweh will protect us."

"I do not doubt Yahweh's might." Eliana brushed her hand over Merin's head. "Not after what He did to free us. But we have already lost many we love to Pharaoh's hand."

A parade of faces marched through Zahla's mind. Those who had gone before them. "They remain here in our hearts, I think. As long as we remember…"

Eliana eyed her. "Are you thinking about Saba?"

"I am." Zahla smiled. "In bits and pieces. Your grandfather was the most courageous man. The most loving…"

"I know." Eliana paused. "We all loved him, and we love you, Savah."

Zahla patted her hand. "I am blessed indeed."

"Saba would be proud of how you have cared for our family." Her gaze dropped to Merin. "How you continue to love us."

The winds stirred again, and then they heard a voice in the darkness, shouting from the east.

"Come!" Moses called to the city of tents. "It is time to leave."

Zahla turned slowly to the east as if a bridge had been built in the last few hours for their escape. She couldn't see beyond the bend, even with the firelight, but the sea salt continued swirling around them in the breeze.

Where was Moses leading them next?

"I will fetch Abba," Eliana said, returning the great gift of her son to Zahla's arms as the murmur of voices turned into a roar.

In their weeks of travel, families had learned how to quickly prepare their goods for travel. Asher and his sons took down their tent, and in the flickering light, the whole family folded and packed their things onto the backs of donkeys.

Sivian stepped up beside her with several other children, staring at the wall of fire.

"Are the Egyptians gone?" she asked.

"I do not think so." With the Hebrews trapped in the valley, their enemy would attack, she suspected, when the fire lifted.

People began following Moses east with their animals and children. Swimming across the sea would be impossible—they couldn't even see the other side—and they had no time or material to build boats. The Egyptians with their chariots and swords intended to massacre all the tribes of Israel on the shore before day's end, their blood reddening the sea like the Nile, but God had promised to bring her family out of the affliction of Egypt and into a new land. A place flowing with milk and honey.

Today, she prayed, they would experience another miracle.

The breeze grew stronger as they neared the water, cooling the heat from the fire. Eliana held the hands of two children while her husband carried their two-year-old in his arms. Asher stepped in to help with their fourth boy and another grandchild born to his youngest daughter.

Zahla clung to Merin. This little one, she thought, represented God's faithfulness to the Hebrew people. Unless Eliana wanted to carry him, Zahla would make sure he was safe.

Pharaoh and his men may be readying themselves for a battle, but Yahweh, she prayed, would rescue them before morning.

# CHAPTER TEN

*Eighty Years Earlier*

"Your imma will return soon," Zahla said as she wiped a tear from her niece's cheek and then lowered Maya to a woven rug.

Maya crunched her toes in the wool before wobbling in a circle, her outstretched arms inviting an invisible ensemble to play harps and drums in her head. Puah and Joseph's only child seemed to hear music wherever she went.

Zahla glanced out the doorway of Joseph and Puah's small house to the fields of Goshen. In the distance, an hour's walk south, was Abba's vineyard.

Her dear cousin had become her sister more than two years past when Joseph and Puah married, before the trimmed vines began bearing fruit. Puah continued delivering Hebrew babies after they married, and she also bore fruit of her own.

Maya was the oldest child, and her second baby was due within the month. Zahla helped Shiphrah deliver her since Puah trusted no one else, fearing what another midwife might do if the little one had been a boy. Abba had been ecstatic about becoming a grandfather, and Zahla loved tending to Maya and spoiling her with silly songs and games.

Joseph and Puah now lived between Rameses and Goshen, in a village that housed field workers. In the dwelling that Puah's parents built long ago.

Because they lived on the northern side of the floodplain, her brother did not need to paddle a raft or canoe to the city border when he worked for Pharaoh, but Zahla wondered if living near Rameses caused him distress. Even though it would still be months before the floods, her brother was often morose during the planting and harvest season. And whether it was because he was a married man or because of his memory of the overseers' whip, he was quieter and much kinder to his only sister.

Then again, the kindness might be Puah's doing.

A baby cried in one of the other homes, and Zahla quietly rejoiced that another child had survived Pharaoh's decree. With Puah as a midwife, new life was teeming in this village and across Goshen even as Abba's vineyard continued to produce Pharaoh's prized wine.

When her brother wasn't working in the field or spending time with Puah and their daughter, he continued to oversee the wine storage. Joseph had been vigilant before Abba petitioned Pharaoh for his freedom, but the matter was crucial now. If something happened to Pharaoh's wine, they would all be ruined. Even though thievery remained rare in Goshen, he and the other cousins continued guarding the entrance day and night so no robber would be tempted to plunder their storehouse.

Like her husband, Puah was often gone from their home. Expectant immas called for her or Shiphrah the moment their pains began, often refusing the assistance of any other midwife since it was rumored that several Hebrew midwives had decided to follow Pharaoh's orders to kill the boys. While Zahla struggled to believe these rumors to be true, the immas of Israel trusted Puah to deliver and protect their babies, and she traveled throughout Rameses and Goshen to assist them. Yahweh was still among their people, Zahla thought, and He'd blessed her dear sister for rescuing His children.

Zahla reached out her hands and began twirling her niece on a rug. When they stopped, Maya repeated the word that had drummed its own rhythm in her mind. "Milk?"

"I have the goat milk," Zahla said, extending the ceramic cup that she'd filled earlier.

Maya shook her head. While she'd eaten fruit and bread already, she wanted her mother to appease her thirst.

"You drink goat milk at my house," Zahla said. "And water."

Tears streamed fresh down Maya's cheeks. "Imma?"

When Maya was younger, Puah had taken her daughter whenever she was called to midwife, stopping to feed her when needed, but now, Maya spent many of her days dancing alongside Joseph or Zahla as they worked. Or with one of their many family members in the village who volunteered to help Puah preserve the heirs of Israel by caring for her daughter.

While Maya drank milk or water when she stayed with Zahla, it was different, she supposed, at home. Her imma was supposed to feed her here.

Zahla glanced at the open doorway. Puah had been gone most of the day now. Surely she would return before dark.

"Let us play outside," Zahla said, hoping to find a breeze on this hot day.

She and Maya bounded out the door together, but Maya stopped near the edge of reeds and scanned both directions along the path—one that led south to her abba in the vineyard and the northern path where her imma had seemingly disappeared.

Zahla was supposed to be preparing the evening meal for their vineyard workers, but this morning, when she'd arrived at Puah and Joseph's home to ask if Maya could spend the day with her, Puah said that Joseph had spent last night at the wine cellar. Puah needed to travel into the city right away, and she'd asked Zahla to remain at her house until she returned. It was an urgent matter, she'd explained, that wouldn't take long. She would return before midday.

It wasn't until this afternoon, when Puah still hadn't come home, that Zahla began wondering if Joseph or someone else knew her whereabouts. She'd gone into the city without her birthing basket, but she still might have been stopped along her journey to deliver a baby. Puah wouldn't hesitate to help if a mother and child needed her.

While she still didn't enjoy midwifery, Zahla had learned how to care for Maya in the past two years. And she'd learned from Joseph how to steward and transport the palace wine during the months he worked in Rameses. She would never tell her brother so, but she enjoyed managing the transportation of Pharaoh's wine up the Nile. Even though she had no fondness for the Egyptians, she recognized several of the palace guards now and the chief wine steward who met her at the quay each week.

When the river flooded, Joseph went to work each day near the palace to build or dig or whatever else the taskmasters required of him. Then he returned home to Puah and Maya each night.

The work was hard, but her brother slaved diligently. His body had grown stronger as a result, but Zahla could see his anger at the injustices, seething underneath his calm. This quiet anger sometimes warred against his devout love for his family. While she never talked about it with him or Puah, she worried that one day he would break under the whips.

She'd forever regret the day she went with Abba to the palace. If she hadn't insisted on joining him in the throne room, perhaps Pharaoh would have allowed Joseph to continue transporting his wine for all three seasons.

Zahla sang a lullaby as Maya danced on the packed dirt.

"Bird!" Maya shouted, and Zahla scanned the empty sky.

Maya's giggle replaced her tears. "Bird song."

"Ah." Zahla smiled and began her niece's favorite song about birds, the one with silly sounds that always made Maya laugh. Then Maya squealed in delight as a kingfisher flew overhead with its brilliant orange breast ablaze and blue wings soaring on the breeze.

Zahla stopped singing to watch the magnificent creature soar west over the field.

"He came," Maya whispered as Zahla knelt down beside her.

"Indeed he did," Zahla said. "He must have needed a friend."

They watched the kingfisher rise above the riverbank before dipping toward the Nile. As Maya scanned the sky for other birds, Zahla began the song again, her mind wandering.

What would it be like to fly above the plains of Goshen and the water? To sail on the Mediterranean and explore the opposite shore? Her eyes turned north as if she could see beyond the city, and she wondered anew. What lay on the other side?

Questions like these haunted her in the night hours. The wondering about the beyond. She may never travel farther north than the brickyard or walk two days south where the fields of Goshen bumped into a city called Pithom. But she still allowed herself to dream about a land where she might be free. A country where all the Hebrew people could live without a Pharaoh and his many taskmasters.

"Zahla!"

She swiveled and watched Puah run awkwardly toward the house, her stomach bouncing with every step. At first, Zahla thought she might be laboring, but with her arms flailing overhead, it looked like Puah was running from something.

Zahla glanced up the pathway, her heart racing, but she saw no one in pursuit.

If an enemy was following, where was she—where were they— to hide? The river, with all its reeds, was too far away, and they had no cellar or secret space in their small home.

Maya began crying again when she heard her imma's voice.

"Take her inside," Puah ordered as she drew near.

Zahla startled at the edge in Puah's voice. "What is wrong?"

"Hurry, Zahla."

She lifted Maya and rushed into the house.

Zahla had once watched Puah deliver a baby boy in the midnight hours, a cord wrapped around his neck, but she hadn't panicked. She'd simply loosened the cord and breathed air into the baby's lungs until he could breathe on his own.

But now, it seemed, all her strength and confidence had been swept away.

Puah yanked the curtain over the front door and collapsed on a floor cushion with her hands on her stomach, scarcely able to breathe.

"What is it?" Zahla begged as she placed Maya into Puah's trembling arms.

Puah glanced at her daughter, cuddled up against her. "Pharaoh called Shiphrah and me to return to his court."

A tremor crept up Zahla's spine as she slipped onto another cushion, the memory of the old man with a cobra crown swelling in her mind. "What did he want?"

"I had hoped his decree about killing the baby boys had been a rash decision. That after two years and all of his travels, he would have forgotten what he demanded."

Zahla closed her eyes for a moment to clear her mind. "But he has not forgotten…"

"Nor will he," Puah replied sadly.

Zahla wished she could deliver a poisoned wine that would kill Pharaoh instead of his steward. "Has he nothing better to do than make bricks and worry about our children?"

Puah's gaze fell to her daughter and then to her rounded stomach. "He asked why we have not been killing the baby boys as he decreed."

"He does not know—" Zahla started. "He cannot possibly know what happens in a Hebrew home."

Puah had traveled across Rameses to deliver babies and through the southern fields of Goshen where Pharaoh's soldiers rarely roamed. No Hebrew imma would brag about the life of her infant son in the face of Pharaoh's orders.

"He asked why his soldiers have seen so many boys in the Hebrew villages since they were to be disposed of long ago."

No breeze stole into the warm room, but Zahla still shivered. Almost three years had passed since Pharaoh's decree, and hundreds of Hebrew children had been born. Their mothers may have hidden them for a season, but no one could hide a growing boy for long. They turned too quickly into young men.

Men who might lead a revolution.

"What did you tell him?" Zahla asked.

"That the Hebrew women are strong. They deliver their babies before Shiphrah and I arrive, and neither of us can wrestle a baby boy from his imma's breast."

If the situation weren't so dire, Puah's lie would be comical. Pharaoh would never believe this story. He would punish both women for defying him. Throw them into prison or worse.

Perhaps that's why Puah was so agitated. She feared the soldiers would find her here soon, and neither Zahla nor Joseph could stop them from taking her away.

"How did you get out of the palace?" Zahla asked.

"We thought he would imprison us for life," Puah said slowly as if the words pained her. "Instead, he chose to punish us with a new decree. A horrific one."

Zahla didn't have the courage to ask what Pharaoh ordered next to torment her people.

"We are no longer required to kill the Hebrew boys," Puah continued.

Zahla studied her, confused. "But that is good news!"

"I am afraid it is not." Puah breathed deep as she cradled her daughter against her breast. "Since Shiphrah and I have not followed his decree, he mandated that the Egyptians must take it upon themselves to murder our sons."

A stack of mud bricks seemed to topple on Zahla's chest, stopping her breath. "Any Egyptian?"

She nodded. "Civilian or soldier."

How could the Hebrews continue living among men and women who were supposed to kill their children?

"He has commanded them to throw every newborn Hebrew boy into the Nile," Puah said, a hand dropping to her stomach as if she could protect her child. "What are we to do?"

"I do not know."

Pharaoh was trying to turn his entire nation against the Hebrews. Perhaps he already had. Some of them would be eager to slaughter the Hebrew babies.

Zahla glanced out the edge of the door covering and saw the spray of pink light from the setting sun. On harvest nights like this, when the moon was bright and temperatures cool, her brother and the other field workers would work long into the evening with the curtain of darkness protecting them from the heat. All of them oblivious to this new command to kill their children.

Now that Maya was calm, soothed by her mother's milk, Zahla could hear other children crying again in the village.

How were parents going to stifle the cries of a baby who was hungry or hot or ill? Babies were supposed to cry when they needed care. To remind others of the life within them that needed to be rescued, not destroyed. But now the cries of these babies would attract cruel soldiers and citizens alike to their parents' door.

"Are there any newborn boys in your village?"

Puah shook her head. "Only two boys have been born this year, and they are each more than six months now."

Zahla blinked in the fading light, and the flight of the kingfisher soared through her head again as if it wanted her to follow. "We should pray to Yahweh who sees all," she said. "Pray that He will guide us."

In that small space, on the outskirts of Rameses, the women begged God to save all the children of Israel.

And Zahla vowed that no matter how difficult, no matter her own weakness, she would do everything in her power to partner with Yahweh to rescue their boys.

## CHAPTER ELEVEN

"You must move home," Zahla told Joseph in the flickering blaze of an oil lamp. "At first light."

Usually, the Egyptians avoided this village, but spurred on by Pharaoh's instruction to find and kill the Hebrew babies, the soldiers might travel outside the city to search. Between the vineyard cellar and storehouses and a forest of reeds along the river, she could find plenty of places to hide a child.

Her brother paced across the dirt floor between her and Puah, who clung to their sleeping daughter as if Maya might sprout wings and fly away. He'd worked late tonight, harvesting grapes with the other workers. Much would change in their community tomorrow when word began to spread about Pharaoh's decree.

Joseph combed grape-stained fingers through his hair. "It is too far to walk during Akhet from Abba's house to my work in the city."

Between the heat of the day, the long hours digging ditches, and the fear for his family—her brother's burden was overwhelming. For any man, but especially for one who'd been wounded body and mind by a taskmaster's whip.

Still, she had to help him understand. He may no longer care about his life, but he must protect his wife and children.

"We have another month until the river floods," Zahla said, eyeing the reed basket in the corner. Puah had woven it for Maya and cushioned it with linen. Now the basket was ready for their new little one.

A baby had enough to overcome in its first days of life. It had no chance against an Egyptian sword.

"If your baby is a boy, the soldiers will find him so close to the city," Zahla said. "But if it is a girl, you can return to this house right away."

"Unless Pharaoh changes his mind again," Puah said. "He might start hunting for the girls too."

None of them could predict what Pharaoh might do next.

Joseph waved his hand toward the door. "Give us a moment, please."

Zahla reached for the reed basket instead of stepping away. "I will help you pack tonight."

"Zahla!"

"It will not take us long," she insisted. "Abba can send one of his men with a handcart to retrieve the rest of your things."

"A moment, Sister."

She glanced between the two of them. They were family. They talked about these things together. "Why must you speak alone?"

Joseph sighed. "One day you will marry, and I will ask this question of you."

She shook her head. "I will never marry."

And her brother, in the midst of this awful moment, had the audacity to laugh at her.

She stomped toward the doorway and stepped outside. Goats and donkeys rustled and brayed nearby, and she heard the whisper of voices as their neighbors settled for the night. No child cried out as if they'd already learned the horrific news from the palace.

She didn't intend to marry, no matter what Abba or Joseph said. Not when she could care for the wine and tend to other women's children on her own. Even if she was willing, who would she marry? Abba said no man in their family would be able to tame her tongue or her spirit. And, remembering her visit to Pharaoh with Abba, she thought he just may be right.

Either way, they had more pressing matters at hand.

What would happen tomorrow to the children of Israel? And to her family. Pharaoh knew where Puah lived. She had already angered him when she refused to kill the Hebrew children, and now he knew she was expecting a baby on her own. In his rage, he might send an Egyptian soldier to their village in the days to come to see if she'd given birth to a boy.

If they moved south, Joseph and Puah couldn't live together during the floods, but it was only for a season. Puah could work in Goshen while Shiphrah and the other midwives delivered the babies in and around Rameses. Just until Pharaoh retracted the decree.

In the morning, Zahla would warn the women in this village about Pharaoh's order, and then she'd leave with her brother's family to travel into the safety of Goshen. He had no other choice.

When the voices behind her quieted, she turned. "Joseph—"

He stopped her. "You must let us think."

"We have little time for thinking. You need to—"

"We will let you know what we need."

She leaned back against the wall, watching as Joseph and Puah whispered in tones too low to wake Maya or for Zahla to understand. Then Joseph reached for his wife's hand. "Puah and I have decided to travel south with you in the morning."

Zahla clapped her hands together. "You can stay with Abba and me for now. Then we will build you a house and—"

"We will decide later," he said. "For now, we must rest."

But Zahla would never be able to rest with this new decree trampling like a pack of jackals through her mind. What would happen to all the children who remained in and near Rameses? She'd assist Joseph and Puah, and then they must find a way to help the others.

Turning, she took a step back out into the night. Stars flickered over the village and beyond. Hundreds of them. Thousands, even. A canopy of light, as far as she could see, in lieu of the solitary moon. The stars needed one another to illuminate the night sky.

Just as the children of Israel needed each other to stand against Pharaoh.

Her brother spoke again. "Come inside, Zahla."

"I cannot rest."

"I fear none of us will rest tonight," Puah said before her groan tore through the shadows.

Zahla rushed to her. "What is it?"

Puah glanced at her husband in the lantern light. "The baby is upon us."

"Tonight?" Joseph asked as if she could convince the baby to return on the morrow.

"How long have you been having pains?" Zahla asked.

"Since the afternoon. I had hoped they were false."

"I will get the bricks," Zahla said as she raced toward the storeroom.

Puah called after her. "And the birthing basket!"

Zahla quickly gathered the supplies before speaking to her brother. "You must find Shiphrah."

Puah shook her head. "There is no time."

"But who will deliver—"

Puah stopped her. "You are ready, Zahla."

But she wasn't ready. She could assist Shiphrah if she must as she had with Maya's birth, but she'd never be ready to deliver a baby alone.

"I cannot."

Puah grasped her hand. "We must do this together."

"Please, Zahla," Joseph begged as he placed blankets around Puah. Then he lifted Maya. "This is what we need."

Her brother had never asked a thing of her except, on occasion, to leave him alone. But to deliver his wife's baby by herself? What if the little one was breeched or Puah couldn't push him out or Zahla couldn't stop the bleeding? So many things could go wrong.

She closed her eyes for a moment, remembering well the night that she'd helped Puah deliver Jochebed's son. And then the night she'd held Puah's hand while Shiphrah brought Maya into the world. If there were no complications, she could deliver this one.

They couldn't have complications tonight.

"Take Maya to the neighbors'." Zahla's voice trembled at first and then a fresh wave of strength washed through her. She might be weak, but Yahweh was strong. He could guide her.

Her hands trembled like her voice as she reached for a clay jar. She should have refilled it earlier today. Would have refilled it if she'd known what the night would hold.

She stopped Joseph before he stepped out the door with Maya. "We need water."

He took the jar from her. "I will fill it at the well."

Judging by Puah's erratic breathing, her body bent in pain, he'd have no time to warm it.

"Please hurry," Zahla told Joseph and then knelt beside the woman who'd become her sister. "I will take good care of you."

Puah nodded. "I know."

"We will get this baby born. Another girl, I think."

Puah groaned again before replying. "It is a boy."

"How do you know?"

Puah pushed out her breath, her hand on her stomach as Zahla reached for the jar of sesame oil and added three drops of jasmine. Two years had passed since Maya was born, but she remembered.

"Sometimes an imma just knows," Puah said sadly.

"Then let us focus tonight on bringing this little one safely into the world."

"Hosea," Puah whispered. "That is what we want to name him."

Zahla leaned toward her stomach. "You will have to help me, Hosea, so I can help you."

"I had such hopes for him…"

"We are not going to give up.

"Hope," she whispered as she helped Puah onto the stones.

Hope for redemption in their world.

# CHAPTER TWELVE

Sound bellowed from Hosea's lungs with his first breath, the deep cry of life echoing between their walls and through the village.

"Quiet him," Puah commanded.

Zahla held the baby close to her chest. As the life flow soaked through her tunic, she cut through the cord with Puah's obsidian knife, and then she tied it with thread.

"Hush," Zahla whispered as his imma rested on her mat, offering her finger to his lips in hopes that it would temporarily satisfy. But his cries only grew louder.

Puah stretched out her arms. "Please let me hold him."

Joseph hadn't returned with the clay vessel, but some water remained in a smaller pot. Zahla dabbed it on a cloth as Hosea ate and cleansed Puah the best she could.

Her sister wouldn't be well enough to travel to Goshen, but Hosea must leave at first light. One of their cousins could wet-nurse him until Puah was ready to walk the distance or ride one of Abba's donkeys to the vineyard. Zahla would take Hosea south in the morning, and then Puah and Joseph could follow later.

She turned quickly at the flap of a sandal outside, ready to take the water from her brother and introduce him to his son.

But Joseph didn't walk into the house. An Egyptian man stomped through the door instead. A dark soldier dressed in a brown kilt and leather cap, holding a sword near his bare chest as though prepared for battle.

Hosea had announced his arrival to Pharaoh's men.

Zahla stepped in front of Puah, her hands trembling again. "This is not time for the company of men."

The soldier eyed the blood on her tunic. "We heard a cry."

Her stomach clenched, and she could scarcely breathe. How many others were outside?

If only Puah could return to the birthing stones, as Jochebed had done years ago, but the baby was already at her breast.

"Move," the soldier barked, shoving Zahla out of his way.

She caught herself on a ledge. "Leave us alone."

He yanked Hosea from Puah's arms and declared to whoever was outside. "It is a boy."

"Let's go," another man said.

"A moment," Puah begged. "Please."

But the soldier refused her, turning on his heels.

Zahla's chest felt as if it might explode. What kind of man killed a child? No matter what Pharaoh said, he didn't have to torment a new imma or a baby.

"Please!" Puah begged again, struggling to her knees. Her body might refuse her the chase, but Zahla could run.

Puah's wail, louder than any from her labor pain, echoed across the village as Zahla raced outside. It was the desperate cry of an imma who'd been wronged.

Neighbors awoke and stepped into their doorways. Zahla would have told them what happened except her focus was on the soldier ahead.

Or two soldiers. A second one stood in the shadows nearby. A tall man dressed in a red tunic with a spear in one of his hands. With the other hand, he swiped Hosea from the soldier who'd stolen him. Then he turned west toward the river.

"Wait!" Zahla shouted, but the soldier didn't turn back.

Something smashed on the ground behind her, and she turned to see Joseph beside a puddle, his clay jar shattered on the ground. And her heart felt as if it shattered with the clay.

"Bring him back!" her brother screamed as the soldier in red rushed away from the village.

When Joseph launched after him, the first soldier grabbed his shoulder. Her brother couldn't harm either man, not when they both carried a weapon, but the soldier might fear an uprising from the hundreds of villagers.

"We are following Pharaoh's orders," the man with the leather cap spat.

Curses flew from Joseph's lips, and the soldier slapped his face.

Zahla's stomach churned as she looked between her brother and the other soldier running to the Nile. She could do nothing to help Joseph, and he wouldn't want her to rescue him. He'd tell her to save Hosea.

With the first soldier focused on her brother, Zahla sprinted toward the riverbank. Starlight illuminated the path through the reeds, and she could see the outline of the soldier who'd stolen her nephew. Hosea no longer cried, and she feared the soldier had hurt him as he ran.

Her nephew was only tired, she prayed. Or scared.

"You are a monster!" she shouted as she swept through the reeds.

The soldier pivoted at her voice, and she gasped when she saw the beads on his collar and the jewels on his headdress reflecting in the starlight.

"Merin?"

The warrior soldier who'd insulted her in the palace courtyard, then allowed her and Abba an audience with Pharaoh. The soldier who'd found her brother.

Even if he was rude then, she'd thought him fair. But not now.

A wicked hatred for this man ran through her veins.

With the spear at his side, Merin cradled Hosea in his other hand as if to throw him into the water. If she had a sword, she'd lop off Merin's head and toss it to the crocodiles.

Zahla stepped closer, her eyes narrowing. "Only a coward would kill a baby."

"A monster and a coward?" He studied her in the starlight. "You're no longer a child, are you?"

"I was not a child when you insulted me at the palace."

He looked down at Hosea. "Is this your son?"

"He is my nephew." A well of anger and despair pooled in her eyes and then raced down her cheeks. She may hate this man, but she was still at his mercy. "Please do not hurt him."

*Wicked. Vile. Monstrous.* The words rolled through her mind like thunder, growing louder in her ears. He was the most rotten of men to steal a baby's life.

If he tossed Hosea into the water, she'd dive straight into the Nile. She would retrieve him before a snake or other creature found him.

His gaze flitted across her face and then fell to the wall of reeds beside her. Instead of the Egyptian language, Merin spoke to her now in Hebrew. "Do not move, Zahla."

How dare he use her name, in the sacred language of her forefathers!

She stepped toward him, her heart raging. "You can tell me nothing."

Merin lifted his spear. "Do. Not. Move."

Was he going to kill her before he took Hosea's life? She had no weapon for defense, but she wouldn't run away. He would have to kill her and Hosea together.

She braced herself when he lifted the spear. Closed her eyes. It was too late for regrets now, but she wished she could have watched Hosea and Maya grow. Even with the pain of slavery, she'd wanted a few more years in this life.

A burst of air brushed past her face. Then a thud when the spear hit—

Not her. Not the ground. Something else.

Merin handed Hosea to her and then rushed past as he followed the trajectory of his weapon.

As she cradled Hosea, she felt her nephew's chest swelling with air, grateful that he still lived. Puah's milk, she hoped, would help him survive this night.

"It is safe now," Merin said as he reached for the shaft of his spear.

Her mouth fell open as he lifted it. At his feet, only a few steps from her, was the enormous carcass of a crocodile. Somehow in the darkness, among the reeds, Merin had struck the ribbing between head and spine. The only soft spot in its armor.

All of her accusations were swept away in a current of awe. The crocodile could have killed her. Would certainly have killed Hosea if Merin had thrown him into the river.

This monster of a man had saved both of their lives.

Words slowly formed on her lips. "How did you know it was there?"

"Its eyes were glowing."

She took a breath, forming words that sounded foreign to her in Egyptian or Hebrew. "You saved my life."

How was she to reconcile that with the man intent on throwing her nephew into the river?

He scanned the slow-moving surface of the Nile. "Now we must decide what to do with the little one."

She pulled Hosea closer to her chest, and he whimpered, needing to eat and sleep in his first hours of life. She brushed her hand over his damp hair. "I will not let you harm him."

A smile played on Merin's lips. "You have made your intentions quite known."

"Are you mocking me?"

"Admiring, I think."

She shook her head even as her stomach tumbled. "You are mocking me."

But much better to be mocked than harmed.

She glanced back at the village, and she could see the lamplight in the windows and doorways. What had become of her brother? Unless Puah intervened, he would fight until the soldier killed him.

Merin straightened his linen head covering before glancing at the village and then turning back at her. "I will check on Joseph."

"How did you remember our names?"

"Pharaoh is extremely particular about his wine," he said. "And it is my job to know everything that is important to Pharaoh."

"And hunt for Hebrew children."

He turned the spear until its head pierced the sky. "I would not have harmed your nephew."

"What would you have done?" she asked in wonder.

Instead of answering her question, he asked another. "Have you ever used a spear?"

She eyed the offered weapon. "I will learn quickly."

"I am certain you will." He poked the shaft in the reeds until he tapped on something hard. "You can borrow my canoe."

She watched in amazement as he removed his jeweled head covering and balled it into a bed. Then he handed her his spear. "It is a weapon and a pole to guide the boat through the reeds."

"You are letting us go?"

"I am sending you away," he said. "You will need to find a place to hide him."

She stepped carefully into the papyrus canoe and placed Hosea on the linen. "I will."

"Be careful, Zahla." He held the vessel steady with his foot. "The river is dangerous tonight."

"I know."

"Stay in the Delta," he warned.

"I know how to paddle through these channels."

He smiled again. "Of course."

"Please take care of my brother." She paused before pushing the canoe away from the bank. "And yourself."

"Ahmed will not care about a baby when he sees the crocodile."

*Thank you.*

The words echoed through her mind, words she should have said as she pressed the spear into the water like a pole, but Merin had already turned back toward the village.

"Ahmed!" he called, his voice booming across the riverbank. "I need your assistance."

Zahla ducked into the reeds and pushed the raft away, toward a channel that would lead her home.

"Where is the rat?" she heard Ahmed bark.

"In the river," Merin replied. "Look what I found."

A low whistle pierced the night before Ahmed asked, "What happened to the canoe?"

Then she lost the sound of their voices as she turned into the channel.

"You're going to be okay," she whispered to Hosea when he began whimpering again. And she prayed that Joseph would be okay too.

A soldier and a crocodile. A night filled with stars. And a spear to aid their rescue.

Yahweh's creativity would never cease to amaze her.

# CHAPTER THIRTEEN

"Here they come!" Zahla whispered to the baby swaddled in her arms.

Abba slowly escorted Joseph and Puah across the vineyard row, both of their bodies still recovering from the night Hosea was born. Maya raced ahead of them, and Zahla picked her niece up alongside Hosea, kissing her cheeks again and again.

Maya giggled at her silliness, and Zahla's heart felt as if it might spill over at this sweet reunion.

Three excruciating days had passed since she'd paddled her nephew home through the channels in Goshen. Abba had been shocked to see her and Hosea and the jeweled headdress that she refused to explain. But he'd acted quickly when she told him about Pharaoh's decree to kill the male babies. Lemuel vacated the dwelling beside the wine cellar, and Zahla and Abba relocated temporarily so they could care for Hosea in the small house.

Hosea was contented for now, his hunger soothed by a wet nurse. Puah had delivered multiple children in their family over the last year, and the mothers were quite willing to help Hosea thrive while his parents were recovering in the north.

No soldiers had arrived to search the vineyard, and why would they? Only she and Merin knew what happened on the Nile, and she hoped he'd returned safely to Rameses and been assigned other duties.

Then again, he had said he would never throw a baby into the river. Perhaps he was the best man to be assigned this horrific task of hunting down the newborn children.

None of them knew how long Pharaoh considered a baby to be new in this world.

One of her aunts wove a basket with a punctured lid so Zahla could swaddle Hosea and tuck him behind the jars in the cool cellar if soldiers arrived. Perhaps it was naive, but she hoped any soldier would avoid the wine cellar for fear of breaking Pharaoh's cache.

Puah's arms stretched wide as she drew near her son, and Zahla placed Hosea in them.

"My baby," Puah said before whispering words for him alone.

Then she kissed Zahla's cheeks and ducked into the house with both Hosea and Maya. In that quiet space, Zahla hoped they could spend hours upon hours as a growing family.

Joseph kissed Zahla's cheek. "Thank you for saving his life."

"I would do anything to protect him and Maya."

"I know." Joseph's left eye was purple, his arm slashed. Ahmed had no whip, but it seemed he'd used his sword that night until Merin called his name. Puah would have used her many ointments on Joseph's skin already. Zahla wouldn't humiliate her brother any further by probing.

"We have much to discuss," he said.

Zahla sat with her abba and brother outside the cellar entrance, their gaze to the north in case Pharaoh, in his desperation, sent his men to Goshen.

"One of the soldiers had my son," Joseph said, "and then he was gone and so were you. Puah and I grieved all night, fearing you and Hosea were both dead."

"The soldier…" She paused. Abba and others in their family had asked about that night, but she couldn't tell anyone what Merin did. It would take only one person repeating the story, even with the best of intentions, for word to spread through Goshen about a soldier who'd defied Pharaoh's order. If the story found its way to the palace, Merin would surely be killed.

Abba had returned the jeweled head covering to her, and she'd tucked it away. One day she would tell her family about Merin's heroic act, but for now, for his sake, she would hold that information close to her heart. Protect him as he had protected her.

"Zahla?" her brother prompted.

She pressed her fingers against her temples to clear her thoughts. "I am sorry. What did you ask?"

"How did you steal Hosea back from the soldier?"

"It was not difficult," she said slowly, her mind reliving the flashes of fear. Then her relief after his spear landed and he transferred Hosea into her arms. "He was distracted by a crocodile."

Joseph scanned her face. "You are too modest, Sister."

"The moment those men saw that crocodile, neither of them cared anymore about a baby." She imagined the celebration in Rameses when they returned with their prize. They probably used the skin to make body armor or multiple sandals, its fat as medicine. And the meat for food or as an offering to their gods.

Then again, she couldn't imagine Merin fearing or worshiping the Egyptian gods. If he did, he never would have helped her rescue Hosea.

"I believe that crocodile might have saved both Hosea and me," she said.

"And me as well." Joseph glanced back at the house as if Hosea might cry out, but all remained quiet. "The messenger said you took a canoe back to Goshen."

She nodded. "I found one hidden in the reeds."

"An Egyptian canoe?" he asked.

"Perhaps. I did not stop to inquire."

"But the soldiers had spears," he continued. "Why did one of them not stop you?"

She thought of the spear that she'd hidden in the reeds, hoping no one in her family would find it. Abba already suspected that someone assisted her in their escape.

"Some things remain best unexplained," Abba said before she spoke again.

"Yahweh alone should be praised for His deliverance."

The three of them sat for a moment in reverence at this miracle. And she wondered again in the silence why Merin had saved their lives.

"The soldiers do not know what happened to Hosea, and we cannot let them wonder." Abba pointed toward the cave entrance. "We must continue our work as if nothing has changed."

That wasn't a problem with the harvest workers. They wouldn't slow their production, but tomorrow was their scheduled transport to the palace. Pharaoh's steward would send the boat early to retrieve Joseph and Pharaoh's weekly shipment of shedeh and red wine.

Joseph shook his head. "How can I deliver wine to the man who wants to kill my son?"

Abba's voice remained calm in the storm of Joseph's words. "Pharaoh does not know Hosea is your son or that you have a newborn baby in your care."

"Send Lemuel or someone else in my stead," Joseph insisted.

"Haken will ask questions if you do not accompany the shipment, and then he will send soldiers to investigate. Our vineyards will be swarming with them."

And Joseph wasn't their only family member with a newborn.

The soldiers would kill the children, and if the shipments stopped, Pharaoh would hurt their extended family and take over the vineyard.

A curse slipped out of Joseph's mouth. "How am I to return to Rameses? I might see the soldier who attacked me."

"You cannot return," Abba said. "At least, not before the floods."

Zahla rubbed her temples again. "I do not understand, Abba."

He turned to her. "Will you deliver it for him?"

She would gladly transport the wine for her brother's sake, but she'd never escorted a shipment to Rameses in any season besides Akhet. "The steward will ask about Joseph."

"Tell him that we have had an abundance of fruit this season. I need him to stay and work the harvest."

"She cannot lie," Joseph said.

Abba's smile was sad but resolute. "It is not a lie."

She took a deep breath. "I will do it."

In the past, Joseph would have escaped into the cellar to think, but he stayed and paced the dirt between them and the vines. His lips and hands alike were pressed together as if he were considering which carried the greater risk—his sister returning to the palace without him before Akhet or the risk of intrusive questions if he delivered the shipment.

Joseph turned back to Abba. "It was too dark for the soldiers to see well. Even if they are in the harbor tomorrow, they will not remember me."

Abba shook his head. "Haken will still ask about your wounds."

"I will tell him..." His voice faded as he struggled for an answer to this inquiry.

"You must stay at home, Joseph. You have two children to care for now."

Like Abba, she thought, in the years after their imma died. When he'd raised her and Joseph alone. Her heart welled with love for both men. They were heroes to fight for her and their family.

"What if the soldiers recognize Zahla?" Joseph asked.

"They never see me when I go into Rameses. Only the wine."

"I suppose I could go—" Abba started, but Zahla and Joseph both shook their heads.

"Then they would surely know something was amiss," Zahla said.

"Lemuel will travel with you," Abba told her, and she didn't argue about the escort. Lemuel had never delivered the wine alone, but he often went with them.

Joseph returned to his seat beside Abba. "I wish we had another choice."

Abba glanced north again as if he could see the palace. "I am sorry, my daughter."

"It is the right decision," she replied. "Haken will suspect nothing except a bountiful harvest."

Early the next morning, workers loaded their cart beside the cellar, carefully storing ten of the decorated amphorae. Abba escorted Zahla and Lemuel toward the river, and as the three of them moved across the path, Zahla checked the reeds for the reptiles and hippopotamuses that found refuge here.

No matter how long she lived, she would never forget the crocodile that had waited for her and Hosea in the dark. Nor would she forget Merin saving their lives.

She should have thanked him before she paddled away, but she hoped he knew how grateful she was. For thanking him now, in front of his peers, would be a death sentence.

One of Pharaoh's papyrus shipping boats waited for them along the riverbank, and six Hebrew men hopped off to load the amphorae, cushioning them with animal skins. Then they adjusted the sail to catch any wind and took their places by the long oars.

Most Egyptians knew how to row a boat—they believed those who'd died must paddle across a river to reach the afterlife—but only a handful of Hebrews were allowed to transport supplies between Goshen and Rameses.

Sometimes she wondered why these men didn't keep rowing south when they left the quay in Rameses. Travel downriver to hide in Goshen or beyond. Then again, they probably had families in the city. The former Pharaoh encouraged family ties among the enslaved. As if he knew the men wouldn't run away if they had a wife and children to return to each night. The men without families were the most likely to escape.

The square sail flapped overhead as Zahla stepped across the gangplank. Lemuel followed and sat beside her on the narrow seat in the back as the rowers paddled north with the current. The river wasn't strong this time of year, but the steady breeze made for a short journey into the city.

Lemuel pointed west at a sheet of black clouds darkening the horizon. "Let us hope that is only rain."

She nodded. "And a respite from the sun."

Light rain showers would be welcome, but a downpour could mold and ultimately ruin the grapes. And hail could break the wine jars before they delivered them as well as damage the many rows of grapes still on the vines.

Abba would be rushing through the vineyard right now, urging everyone to work faster. And the moment they returned home, she and Lemuel would join the others. Without grapes, wine, and shedeh, they had nothing to offer this kingdom.

Lemuel glanced at the oarsmen ahead before lowering his voice. "Your abba said you paddled home with Hosea four nights past."

This was exactly why she must keep Merin's role a secret from those she loved. Word would spread quickly and endanger his life. "No one else must know."

"It was brave of you."

But she hadn't thought her journey brave. She just couldn't consider any other option.

The rowers pulled their paddles through the river, adding power to the current and wind until they slid past the bank where she'd confronted Merin. The reeds where he'd stored the canoe and killed the crocodile. So much had happened in those moments, and she'd hardly been able to process it.

*Thank you*, she whispered to the wind. And she hoped the warrior soldier, wherever he was, would hear it in his heart.

Only Merin knew that the daughter of the chief vintner was the one who took Hosea and that one of Pharaoh's soldiers had wounded the chief vintner's son.

Would he check on their shipment today at the quay? It would do her well to see him safe, if only at a distance.

As the boat drew near to Rameses, just south of the brickyards, the oarsmen paddled up to the busy quay. Other boats were anchored nearby, all different sizes for shipping, passengers, or fishing for tilapia and perch. At the far end of the harbor was a cluster of sailing feluccas and a long boat painted gold and red with a bright falcon figurehead. For Pharaoh and his family, she assumed.

Her boat docked against a brick wall, near Haken who was waiting beside two carts and a drove of donkeys to transport the wine. She arranged her head covering to obscure most of her face as she glanced across the workers and soldiers who accompanied the wine steward. When she didn't recognize any of the men, she lifted her gaze to scan the soldiers along the perimeter, wondering if Merin was among those who guarded the port so an enemy wouldn't infiltrate the city or a slave wouldn't attempt an escape.

She skimmed the faces a second time until she found him looking back at her from the city gate.

"Where is your brother?"

She jumped at the question, forgetting for a moment her purpose here. And she silently scolded herself as she turned back to Haken. Mistakes like that could be fatal.

"Joseph is helping my abba with the harvest."

"I hope he is well." The words were cordial, but suspicion flickered in his gaze instead of concern. Surely he remembered that Pharaoh's soldier had accosted him.

"He is quite well and will return to work in Rameses after the harvest."

As the workers finished loading the last amphorae into the carts, rain splashed across her arms. "We should return home."

The steward motioned for a handler to lead the donkeys toward the palace. "Until next week then."

Before she stepped onto the boat, she stole one more glance across the quay, but Merin was gone.

# CHAPTER FOURTEEN

"Jochebed had another boy," Puah said as Zahla dumped her stained basket of grapes into a cart.

"Oh no..." Zahla lowered the knife from the grape cluster, her mind spinning at the thought of another child gone. In the past month, she'd heard multiple stories of Hebrew babies thrown from the quay in Rameses, and with every loss of a son, her heart broke again. Now Jochebed's newborn was prey to a nation that had turned hunting Hebrew children into a violent sport.

She desperately wanted to help these children but didn't know how.

Puah glanced down at Hosea, strapped in a sling to her chest, and then she leaned in toward Zahla as if she had a secret. "Shiphrah said the baby is well. Miriam helped hide him from the soldiers."

Zahla exhaled. "You should have told me that first!"

Puah sipped from her waterskin and then rearranged the linen cloth that covered Hosea's head so he wouldn't burn in the sun. Soon, during the hottest afternoon hours, Puah would return to their house by the wine cellar to feed him, but until then, the two women harvested grapes together. "I am used to celebrating when a baby is born."

"Of course. We should celebrate his life." Not the possibility of death.

They were all on edge with Pharaoh's decree.

Zahla filled the teeming handcart behind them with one last basket of grapes. "Do you want to walk with me to the winepress?"

Puah nodded. "I would even tread on the grapes if it would cool me off."

Zahla took a sip of water before lifting the cart's handles. While they all wished for the coolness of rain, they wanted to harvest all the grapes before another storm threatened to ruin or steal them away. She began pushing their load of grapes toward the winepress, and along every row, as far as she could see, men and women worked in pairs to remove the ripe fruit. Diligent but tired in the heat of this season.

Zahla smiled. "Abba may insist that we take a turn stomping in the press."

Puah wiped sweat off her forehead. "Perhaps we could just dive into the basin and take a swim."

Zahla laughed at the thought of them buzzing around like tetra swimming in the Nile, chased by a school of tigerfish. They'd be covered in pomace, their skin and garments stained red. Abba would never approve of such a thing.

"How did Jochebed hide her baby?" Zahla asked as they turned onto the dusty, wide path that connected the rows.

The winepress was to their left, and while they couldn't see it in the outcropping of rocks, the wine cellar was several hundred cubits from the press. Lemuel was probably guarding the entrance now with his stick while Joseph transported the newly filled jars and checked on those fermenting in the chamber.

"Jochebed's daughter secured him in a basket on the river's edge."

"That is terrifying." Zahla stopped and lowered the handles to her waist, the memory flashing back again of the crocodile hidden in the reeds more than a month past. "A baby could not survive in the reeds with all the crocodiles and snakes and—"

"He did not have to wait long," Puah explained. "Jochebed said someone took her baby to a safe place."

Zahla lifted the handles again. "I am relieved to hear that."

Had Merin rescued Jochebed's baby as he'd done with Hosea? And if so, where had he taken him? Even though Zahla had continued to take the shipment into Rameses every week, she hadn't seen him again, and she'd wondered if Pharaoh had sent him away for disobeying his order.

"Is Aaron well?" Zahla asked, remembering his birth before Pharaoh's official decree to kill the boys.

"Shiphrah said Aaron is thriving."

"I am glad to hear it. I hope many more of our children will thrive in spite of Pharaoh."

Music from a lyre and several timbrels streamed up the path as they drew closer to the winepress. Abba always insisted on music as the harvest workers treaded on grapes. A dance of celebration, he called it. A season of thankfulness for the miracle of fruit bursting forth each year from the rain and sun. Dirt and vines.

At times like this, when her family danced and sang together in the fields of Goshen, she often forgot they were enslaved.

"How is Joseph?" Zahla asked as they drew near the press. Thankfully, the wine steward had stopped asking about her brother when she accompanied the weekly shipments, but she continued to worry about his return to Rameses.

"He is always anxious."

"You must be anxious too."

"I fear for him," she said slowly. "That the soldier who hurt him might remember his face. The children and I will stay in the cellar house until after Akhet."

"You will be quite busy here." In the past month, Puah had delivered two girls among their family, with more babies to arrive soon.

Zahla slowed her pace before they reached the press. "I want to help you more with Maya and Hosea."

The lines etched across Puah's forehead relaxed. "I am grateful."

But Zahla was even more grateful. She loved her time with her niece and nephew, much more than trimming vines and picking fruit. And maybe Abba would let her and Maya stomp on grapes together. They'd have fun twirling in the mess of grape seeds and skins and the giant puddles of juice.

Ahead, at the intersection of two paths, was a large basin made of sun-bleached brick. A wood column marked the center of the winepress and offered a handhold, if needed, for the grape treaders. Two troughs channeled juice into dozens of waiting clay jars to transport into the cellar. After the juice fermented, Joseph and Lemuel would transfer the wine into the royal amphorae.

Abba, standing on the edge of the press, towered over four men as they stomped fruit with their juice-splashed legs and splattered loincloths, his arms lifted as he directed the whirlwind of work and music. He called out orders like a taskmaster to those treading grapes and those raking out the pomace and filling the jars. Except Abba had no whip and no need of one, because everyone knew if they didn't harvest enough grapes, if Pharaoh didn't approve of the wine, they would be feeling an Egyptian whip on their backs. None of them wanted to leave Abba's vineyard.

Zahla steered to the end of a long line of carts waiting to unload their grapes into the brick pool.

As they waited, Puah stood on her toes. "I do not see Joseph and Maya."

"They must be at the cellar." Maya was probably entertaining Lemuel while Joseph delivered the new jars of wine.

"I need to leave soon to feed Hosea," Puah said.

A flock of geese shaded the sun, their honks drowning out the lyre and timbrels and chatter of those working. Then another muffled noise. A yell in the distance.

When the honking subsided, the voice shouted again.

"Soldiers!" a woman called, and the music stilled as the word echoed between the rows.

The warning struck like an arrow in Zahla's heart, and she turned to Puah, wide-eyed. She could think of only one reason why soldiers would be visiting during harvest, and he was wrapped in a sling against Puah's chest.

Zahla dropped the handles of the cart, clusters spilling over the sides. Her gaze swept up the line until she met Abba's eyes. Then he shooed them away with his hands.

Puah took off like lightning, and Zahla followed her south. The vineyard might be large, but if the soldiers were intent on finding Hosea, they would search every dwelling in the vineyard and perhaps the cellar.

When they reached the house, Zahla flung open the woven basket made to hide him and checked the linen for fleas and other insects. Thankfully, nothing had taken up residence, but Hosea released a loud cry that echoed through the two rooms and traveled outside. Zahla shivered as Puah quickly unbundled him.

"I will feed him in the cellar," Puah said as she rocked the baby in her arms.

Zahla reached for an oil lantern and rushed out the back door. She wasn't hungry now, not with her mind and heart racing, but they might be in the cellar for the rest of the day. She removed two loaves she had baked in a clay pot heated by a pit of embers. Then she lit a lantern wick.

Hosea's wailing grew louder as the two women swept across the short path between the house and chamber entrance. They found Lemuel resting against the stones, his eyes closed. How was he supposed to protect the wine if he spent his afternoon napping?

She'd have to ask him later. Right now she needed to find a safe place for Puah to feed Hosea before his cries traveled across the vineyard.

She nudged Lemuel's leg with her sandal. "Wake up!"

He unfurled like a hedgehog and sprang to his feet.

Puah continued bouncing Hosea, trying to calm his tears. "Is Joseph inside?"

Lemuel shook his head. "I have not seen him for several hours."

"Please go find him," Puah said as she stepped toward the entrance. "Tell him to hide."

"But the wine—"

Zahla slipped around him. "We will watch over it."

Neither Abba nor Joseph would transport wine until after the soldiers left. None of them wanted to draw attention to this storage space.

Lemuel didn't move. "My job is to guard the cellar."

"Egyptian soldiers are searching the vineyard," Puah said.

Lemuel reached for his stick but didn't step away. "Why are the soldiers here?"

Zahla's stomach turned. Had the man no urgency about him? "We did not stop to ask."

The soldiers might be searching for Hosea or for more men to work in the brickyard. They had no time to consider the possibilities.

Puah glanced over her shoulder at the empty row that ended near her home. "You should make yourself scarce, Lemuel."

He didn't argue again about the wine. Instead, he rushed away with the stick clutched at his side.

Dozens of colorful amphorae shimmered in the flickering light as the women hurried down the stone steps and stepped into the dark chamber. Puah fed Hosea until he calmed and swaddled him in the linen. When he finally slept, she kissed his cheeks and covered him in the basket behind a row of fermenting wine.

How many Hebrew boys, Zahla wondered, were tucked away in baskets across Egypt?

Puah stared at his hiding place for a moment and then turned away. "Pharaoh knew I was about to birth a child. If he heard my baby disappeared, he might have sent his men to search for me."

"If the men come into the chamber, I will speak to them," Zahla said. "They will not recognize you in the shadows."

"But if it is the soldier who tried to steal Hosea away, he might recognize you."

"It was dark, and he was too preoccupied with the crocodile to focus on me."

"I am going to begin dinner." Puah climbed a step. "The soldiers can search our home if they must, take me away even, but they will not find a baby in our house."

Zahla knew that one misstep could harm those she loved. It might be better for Puah to wait here. "I can prepare dinner."

"Please stay with Hosea," Puah said. "If the soldiers come to the house, I will do my best to dissuade them."

"If they come this far, they will want to see the chamber."

Puah glanced back into the darkness. "He will sleep for hours, and the soldiers will think you're working here."

Zahla nodded as she fought back a tremble in her voice. "We cannot let them see our fear."

After Puah left, Zahla placed the lantern on a step and wrapped her woolen radid around her shoulders. She didn't open the basket again for fear of startling Hosea, but she hoped Puah was right, that his full belly and the cool air drifting through the perforated lid, along with the warmth of linen, would keep him content for the remainder of this day. She paced the chamber, singing a lullaby as she walked to soothe him in case he awoke. At least, he would know she was there.

An hour or two passed, and she finally collapsed on the bottom step. A thread of light crept through the entrance above, trailing past her. As if Yahweh could see her in this dark place, and wanted her to know.

While she preferred to be outside, shaded under a palm tree on the hottest days, Zahla understood why her brother liked it in the cellar. The air below the earth was a respite from the aching afternoon sun, and among the vibrant jars and earthen walls, the world outside seemed to disappear. Down here, one could pretend to be in charge. Master of the jars. Their ancestor Joseph once ruled over Egypt, and when the world outside seemed to have gone mad, her brother could rule over this place.

The Hebrew God didn't rule like Pharaoh, but all the stories that she'd heard, the memories of Abba and their elders, reminded her that He was good. And while He gave people an opportunity to repent and turn away from their wickedness, He did not tolerate evil for long.

Was He giving Pharaoh and the Egyptian people this opportunity to change? How long would He wait to rescue His people? If they even were the people of Yahweh anymore. She wasn't certain. So many no longer believed in Him.

Leaning back against the dirt-packed wall, she wondered at what was happening above the chamber. Had the soldiers searched from house to house across the vineyard? Had they destroyed her family's work or possessions? And how long she would have to wait in the darkness? The soldiers would surely want to return to Rameses before nightfall.

Another hour passed in the stillness as she ate the bread and sipped from her waterskin. The weariness from the day, the weeks of work and worry, began pressing against her, and she closed her eyes in the dim light.

Hosea was safe for now.

Yahweh, she hoped, would distract the enemy.

## CHAPTER FIFTEEN

Zahla leaped to her feet, and then her gaze swept across the cellar in confusion as voices floated down from the entrance.

Why was she sleeping in the chamber?

Her mind quickly awakened. Soldiers had arrived in the vineyard, hours ago. She didn't know how much time had passed, but she and Puah had hidden Hosea among the jars.

She hoped the stranger's voice wouldn't startle him now. They'd escaped last time, but no river raft would steal them away from this chamber if the soldiers found him here.

"What is inside the cavern?" someone asked near the entrance.

"We store Pharaoh's wine in the cellar," Abba answered. "The only visitor permitted inside is his steward."

Zahla lifted the lantern and climbed a step to listen to the man's response. "You keep only wine in the cellar?"

At the sound of the man's voice, closer now, Zahla's legs felt as if they might collapse. And her chest did a strange dance. As if it had been counting the moments until Merin arrived.

What was wrong with her?

The man had been extraordinarily kind, but he was Egyptian. A soldier and palace guard. While he had protected her and Hosea on the river, while she was grateful to know he was safe, it was still his job to oppress her people. And it was her job to stand firm against him and any soldiers who joined him. No matter his kindnesses, her heart had no business getting tangled up with his.

She didn't hear Abba's answer before Merin spoke again.

"I see a light," he said. "I will only stay inside a moment."

Zahla scanned the chamber half dazed, searching for the light until she realized that she was holding the source, the oil lantern a beacon in this dark place.

With a quick huff, she blew out the flame, but right away, she realized the absurdity of her action. Merin didn't know she was here, and if other soldiers accompanied him, the lack of light wouldn't be a deterrent. They'd plow through this chamber like oxen in the darkness, breaking one or more of the jars that the chief steward so carefully counted and then blame the destruction on her abba.

Hosea would wake up in the chaos and begin crying for his mother. Then the soldiers would smash every jar until they found him.

She couldn't allow herself to think what might happen next.

Merin had said he didn't want to kill the Hebrew boys, but the other soldiers wouldn't ignore them. If neither Abba nor Puah could convince Merin's comrades to stay out of the chamber, she would have to assist them.

She hurried up the stairs and shielded her eyes as she stepped into the blinding sun. Abba stood immediately outside the entrance as if trying to block it, Merin standing beside him. Relief flooded over her when she saw that no other soldiers accompanied him.

Puah must be preparing dinner in the house, oblivious to Merin's arrival, or she would be trying to persuade him in a different direction.

A tentative smile crossed Merin's lips as he looked down at her, his dark hair lit by the sun. "Hello, Zahla."

She glanced at the ground. "Hello."

What else was she to say? She couldn't thank him for what he'd done in front of her abba. His secret—*their* secret—protected them both.

Abba glanced back and forth between them as though he had a great riddle to solve. "You're acquainted?"

"We met at the palace," she reminded him. "When Merin allowed you and me to visit Pharaoh's court."

Abba studied Merin again as if still trying to comprehend his kindness more than two years past. Then he glanced at the chamber entrance. While the soldier standing before them had been helpful at the palace and in the brickyards, Abba would never trust one of Pharaoh's men.

"I remember now," he clipped. "You called Zahla a child."

Merin flinched. "I no longer think of her as a child."

If she had a shovel, this would be an appropriate time to dig a pit beside the cellar and bury herself in it.

Instead, she scanned the house and vineyard behind them. "Where are the other soldiers?"

"I am here alone," he said.

Another breath of relief escaped her lips. Surely Merin wasn't here to harm Hosea after rescuing him.

An awkward silence settled between the three of them until a cry rose from the depths of the chamber, spilling outside. She wanted to run down the steps and comfort her nephew, bring him upstairs into the light, but that would expose Merin's defiance against the edict.

His loyalty, in appearances at least, must be to Pharaoh.

Abba watched Merin closely, waiting for his reaction to the cries. A test. Abba knew well that Merin should kill both him and his grandson.

Instead of stepping toward the cellar, Merin searched the empty sky. "The birds are quite lively this afternoon."

Zahla craned her neck beside him. "Indeed."

"We've had a recent increase of birds in Rameses as well."

She lowered her gaze to search his face. "I hope they have all flown away."

"A few of them have found nests. I am hoping others will fly away soon."

"Why are we talking of birds?" Abba blurted as if they'd both gone mad.

"Your daughter and I have discovered that we have a common interest in winged creatures."

The last time she'd been this close to Merin was in the starlight, beside the Nile, but she'd never even looked him in the eye. Had he been this handsome at the palace? Strong, yes. Demanding the respect of his peers. But she'd been too angry when they first met to care about his features.

Everything was different this afternoon. His dark brown eyes captured her. Equal parts confident and kind. She couldn't seem to look away.

Abba cleared his throat. "I will ask Puah to help with—"

"The bird," Zahla said, her eyes still on Merin. If Puah knew who was visiting, that this soldier saved her son, she'd welcome him to a feast.

"Zahla?"

She turned slowly. "Yes, Abba."

"Would you join me in the house?"

She nodded toward the vineyard. "I was going to ask if I could give Merin a tour of the remaining rows."

"A tour would be wise," Merin agreed. "I will report back to Pharaoh all I have seen, if not heard."

"I will show you the rest of the vineyard," Abba said.

"You do not have to worry." Zahla patted his arm. "I will be safe."

He turned back to Merin. "Only visit the rows that are being harvested."

Zahla stiffened. While Abba was trying to keep her safe, most Egyptian soldiers would balk at a Hebrew's demand.

Thankfully, Merin was unlike any other soldier. "We will only tour the rows where your workers can see us."

"Very good," Abba replied. "I will find Puah."

"And I will fetch our little bird," Zahla said.

Abba shook his head. "Puah will see to it."

Female workers continued harvesting the grapes as Merin followed Zahla to the nearest row, but the men were notably missing from their labor. Perhaps they'd fled to the outskirts of the vineyard and then kept walking south. They would probably spend the night among their shepherd friends in Goshen and send one among them at first light as a scout.

The women pretended not to notice Zahla and her companion, but they all watched with curiosity and suspicion. Some of the younger women had never seen an Egyptian soldier.

Merin stepped beside her, walking in stride. Several hours remained until sunset, and she wondered if anyone was expecting him tonight in Rameses. A mother or even a wife.

It hadn't occurred to her before that he might be married.

She placed one hand over her chest in an attempt to stop the stirring.

Merin glanced down at her hand. "Are you feeling unwell?"

"I am fine," she replied, but a deep breath did nothing to calm her heart. "We were startled when we heard the cry about soldiers."

"I did not mean to startle you or anyone else in the vineyard."

As they drew near another group, she diverted the conversation. "Everyone works during harvest," she explained. "We pick grapes together and take them to the winepress."

He stopped walking and turned to her. "Your nephew is no longer a newborn."

An aunt in the next row was focused on the clusters, but she could probably hear Merin. Zahla didn't want to speak about Hosea here. "The grapes go straight to the press so we can crush them right away. We do not want any of them to spoil."

"Zahla—"

"The wine is our livelihood."

"You do not have to worry anymore about Hosea. He will be safe here."

She glanced down the long row, toward the riverbank, and lowered her voice. "Are you certain?"

"None of the soldiers want to travel this far south in the heat."

"Except you."

He glanced up at a kingfisher before meeting her gaze again. "I have other reasons for visiting."

The whirling resumed inside her. Like locusts, she thought, swarming. She wanted to know his reasons but feared the answer.

No Hebrew should befriend an Egyptian. And an Egyptian would never befriend them.

Yet, it almost felt like she'd found a friend in Merin. How did one explain a kinship with the enemy? He was certainly no longer her opposition. He'd helped her twice now, potentially to his own detriment.

Could she trust a man bound to serve Pharaoh?

"I feared for you after we left on the canoe," she whispered again so none among her family would hear.

"And I feared for you until you brought the wine into Rameses."

That's why he had been watching from the outskirts, on the quay. They had worried about each other. "What did you tell Ahmed about the canoe?"

"I started chiding him for not securing it well enough in the reeds, but he was too distracted by the crocodile and subsequent celebration to care. He drank so much afterward that he forgot about the boat and the baby."

The harvesters had moved closer to them, and she guided Merin farther down the row. "I told no one what happened on the riverbank."

His shoulders blocked the sunlight, cooling her in his shadow. "That was wise of you."

"Pharaoh would imprison you if he found out. Or worse…"

"He would probably choose the worse."

"If Abba knew that you had saved his grandson, he would kiss both your cheeks and feet as well. You would be a hero among all of my people."

He shook his head. "I did not do it for accolades."

She eyed him curiously, her many questions renewed. "Why exactly did you save him?"

A shadow crossed his face. "That is a bit of a story."

"I would like to hear it." Her gaze fell from his eyes to his sculpted arms and linen-clad chest. While he carried a sword, belted at his side, and a plain replacement head covering for the one she'd borrowed, he had no waterskin or satchel with food. "But first, you must be famished."

"I will eat when I return to Rameses."

She motioned him toward the family's hamlet tucked between rows of vines. "If you do not mind a simple meal, I will feed you."

"Simple meals usually offer the best sustenance."

The more they spoke, the more he frightened her. And not because she feared for her life. What was she to do with such a like-minded Egyptian?

"I will fill a plate for you."

Between the houses, her aunts had prepared a banquet with platters of roasted duck and fish, bowls with cucumbers, onions, and radishes, and pitchers full of water and barley beer.

Merin eyed the low tables filled with food. "This is more than a simple meal."

"It is simple but hardy after a day working in the vineyard."

Merin waited at the doorstep while she retrieved two plates and cups from her house and the jeweled head covering that he had provided to cushion Hosea in the canoe.

She handed him the folded covering. "This is for you."

"Please keep it."

"Someone will find it and ask how I obtained such a thing. I cannot lie."

As he balled the covering up to his side, she hurried alone toward the tables. An aunt placed another bowl beside the duck, and her mouth dropped open when she saw Merin. Then she turned to Zahla. "Why are you entertaining a soldier?"

"He is hungry." And Abba would never allow a traveler to pass through his vineyard without sustenance. Even Joseph, their ancestor, fed the brothers who'd betrayed him.

Not that Merin was a brother or a betrayer. Perhaps like Joseph's brothers, he was becoming a friend.

Zahla filled a cup with well water to quench Merin's thirst and motioned him toward the tables. After he drank, she refilled the cup with Abba's reserved wine and prepared two plates with roasted duck, small loaves of bread, fresh goat cheese, and an array of vegetables. Merin carried two wooden stools as they walked together to the opposite side of the hamlet, closer to the river so they could speak in privacy. Her aunts, she had no doubt, would be watching them.

She nodded back toward the tables as they ate. "My entire family is wondering why you are here."

Merin lowered his plate. "You can tell them that I am ensuring a good harvest for Pharaoh."

She leaned forward on the stool, her linen gown draped on both sides. "And what is your true reason?"

"The reasons are complicated," he replied slowly. "But my main intention is to ask for your help."

"My help?" With the exception of a meal, she couldn't think of another way she could possibly assist him.

"There are…" He paused, and she was concerned about what he might say. "Let us say, there are several fledgling birds flying around Rameses. All of them are in need of a nest."

"Ah." She soaked her bread in a sauce made from garlic and leeks. "You are looking for someone to build the nests?"

"Or carry them to a used one."

Her mind took flight when she closed her eyes, exploring the possibilities. Did he know how much she longed to help? That she wanted nothing more than to overcome this edict and rescue every Hebrew baby.

Now that Hosea was safe, perhaps she could assist Merin in finding a place for the hidden ones. Her family would no longer be powerless in the face of this kingdom trying to curb their population. If they worked together, they could save the sons of Israel.

Zahla looked back into eyes as warm as sand and wondered how she'd ever thought him rude. His kindness, at least away from the palace, abounded. "I would like to help you."

He smiled. "I am glad to hear it."

Other family members began gathering around the long tables, and she saw their curious glances. But if either she or Merin disclosed why he was really here, both his life and the lives of the hidden children would be in jeopardy.

"I want to help," she continued, "but I do not know what to do."

"If I bring the babies to you, can you find them a home? Just until it is safe for them to return to Rameses."

Puah would assist her in finding homes and wet nurses for these children and so would many others in Goshen. None of them needed to know about Merin's involvement.

She glanced toward the river. "How many baby birds are in Rameses right now?"

"I know of three, but I am certain there are others hidden away." His voice cracked before he continued. "I want to find as many of them as I can before…"

When his words faded, she filled in the gap. "Thank you for helping us."

"The soldiers and even the nobles have made a sport of their search," he said. "I do not know how any man or woman can throw a baby into the Nile, no matter who birthed him. But many Egyptians live in great fear of your people, and fear sometimes provokes people to unconscionable actions."

"Or provokes them to do good," she replied. "We can choose good in spite of our fears."

He took a deep breath as if her words were a great relief. "Yes, we can."

How strange, she thought, to be talking like this with a man. Even her male relatives didn't spend much time in conversation with her.

But night would be upon them soon, and he would need to return home.

"Merin," she said quietly, not wanting him to leave yet. "Why are you helping the children?"

"My reason does not matter."

"It matters to me. No other Egyptian cares about rescuing our babies." She studied his neatly trimmed hair cut above his shoulders. His strong jawline and shaved face and confident, steady gaze that seemed to earn respect among his fellow soldiers. And she wanted to know more. "What is your story?"

"My story..." He kicked several lumps of soil into a pile.

"I would like to know it." He owed her nothing, but this man intrigued her more with each moment.

"Can you bear the load of another secret?" he asked.

"I can," she said. "I will tell no one what you share."

"I was born into the home of a nobleman in Pithom," he began, and that didn't surprise her. He had the manners and confidence of a privileged childhood.

"It was not a particularly happy home," he continued, "but my mother was a good woman. Kind and gracious even when my father would rage."

Zahla shivered at the thought of a raging father. Abba would get frustrated, angry even at her whims, but he never yelled. In fact, most of her aunts still said he was much too lenient with his only daughter.

"Did he hurt your mother?" she asked.

"I do not know."

"I am sorry, Merin." He must have been deeply wounded by his father. "I hope he cared for her when he was not angry."

"My father had many mistresses through the years." He shoved the dirt again with his sandal, revealing a glimpse of him as a boy. "Everyone knew about these women, but he was above any law in Pithom. For a long time, he felt the affairs were justified, because his wife did not give him an heir."

"Your mother was not his wife..." she said, slowly understanding the root of his pain.

"The woman who raised me was very kind, but she did not give me life. The woman who birthed me had worked in my father's house since she was a girl. When he called for her, she had no choice."

Zahla felt the depth of his wounds but had no words to comfort him.

"The nobleman's wife had no choice either but to pretend that I was her own. She cared for me as a child and protected me from my father's wrath."

Zahla held her breath, afraid to startle him as the story poured out. As though the words had been brewing inside of him, waiting to share, and she didn't want him to stop.

"I was twelve when my adopted mother died, and the next year, I discovered that the woman who had tended many of my needs also bore me. I was angry at first that others knew the truth and never told me. And then, I am sad to say, I was ashamed of her."

"Is it a secret still?"

"Yes," he said. "A necessary one. Both women are gone now, but the truth would ruin my father. We never talk of it."

Zahla felt the weight of his words and then the deep honor of bearing his secret. Why had he chosen to share this with her when he'd told no other? Perhaps he saw his nobleman father in Pharaoh's fury and wanted to rescue any child from him.

"Zahla," he said quietly, and her chest tightened again at the sound of her name, spoken in such earnest.

"I will not talk of it either."

His gaze seemed to encompass her when he spoke again. "My mother was not an Egyptian woman."

"Was she from Kush?"

"No," he said slowly. "She was a Hebrew slave."

His revelation crashed into her like a wave, knocking her over and sweeping her away. No wonder the man before her seemed like kin. Both Hebrew and Egyptian blood ran equally through him, branching out like channels from the Nile. He had to guard both Pharaoh's interests along with his heritage or he would end up like her family, descended from Joseph and his Egyptian wife.

"My mother's faith in Yahweh was strong, even when she could not see Him," Merin said. "She told me stories of how the Hebrew God had rescued people in the past and how He would deliver them again in the future."

"Joseph, the man who brought us into Egypt, promised that Yahweh would one day lead us back out."

"My mother said Yahweh hates evil."

"That is true." At least, that was what she knew to be true in her heart. She didn't understand why it was taking Yahweh so long to rescue them from their enemies and why He allowed the Egyptians to kill the newborn boys.

"If I were born today," Merin said. "Or if someone discovered the truth of my birth…"

If he'd been born today, if his mother had been discovered, a fellow Egyptian would have thrown him into the Nile. And even now, if they discovered his imma's heritage, an enemy might find a way to strip away his status as a soldier and reassign him to the brickyard.

"Do you have a wife and children in Rameses?"

He shook his head. "I have neither."

The blue of the sky, the breeze along the river, everything seemed to disappear as she focused on the man before her. "I will keep your secret," she said. "And I will help you. We will rescue these children together."

Another sound broke through the stillness. The clearing of a throat.

She turned to see Abba looking down at the soldier. "May I speak with you?"

Merin sprang quickly to his feet. "Of course."

Abba turned to her. "Your nieces and nephews are in need of herding."

After a day's work, she usually oversaw a game of leaping frogs or racing donkeys, but she didn't want to step away now. She and Merin had more to discuss.

She stood beside Abba. "I will stay."

"I want to speak with Merin alone," Abba replied.

Abba never raged at her, that much was true, but he was often aggravated when she defied him. Still, she could convince him to change his mind. "Merin is my…"

Her words faded. How would she explain this strange relationship to Abba? An acquaintance. A partner in the days ahead. She couldn't say that he was a fellow Hebrew and certainly not a…

"Friend," Merin told Abba. "Zahla and I are friends. And I am glad to speak with you alone."

She took a step back even though curiosity stormed inside her as she turned toward the hamlet.

Merin left the vineyard after their discussion, and Abba didn't speak about him until hours later. As they settled into their home that night, Abba paused near her bed.

"I never thought I would find a man strong enough for you, Zahla."

She sat against the wall, her heart light. "And where have you found such a man?"

Abba glanced at the lantern. "Merin has helped us in more ways than the palace entry, has he not?"

She would keep the details to herself, but she couldn't lie to him. "Indeed."

"I will thank him, the next time we see him."

"He works in secret," she said. "He does not want anyone to know."

"Except you," Abba replied, and her heart skipped again.

"I know only what I must."

"I pray you are careful, Daughter."

"I am not worried about my safety," she said although she worried what might happen if another soldier discovered Merin's work.

"Do you think we will see him again soon?" she asked.

"Very soon, I believe."

She didn't sleep much that night, wondering what the men had discussed and how exactly Merin was going to transport babies to the vineyard.

# CHAPTER SIXTEEN

*The Red Sea*

Sea water shimmered red as Israelites crowded on the windy shore, the enemy's roar thundering behind them with shouts from charioteers and whips slashed across their horses' backs.

Freedom was so close for her people. Within steps of their reach.

Could Yahweh overcome an entire army, powered by the Egyptian gods?

*Impossible.*

The word traveled through the crowd like a snake poised to strike. Yahweh had led them into the wilderness and straight to this shore. Did He not know their enemy would follow?

Now they were trapped between fire and water. Terrified by what the Egyptians would do.

Moses, one of the boys rescued long ago, had promised them freedom, but she couldn't blame him for the enemy's pursuit. None of them could. Yahweh, in His mighty power, had used Jochebed's sons to bring their people out of Egypt. But now they needed another miracle.

The fire continued to glow behind them, separating her loved ones from the chariots on the hill. A war, Zahla thought, was taking place in the flames between the Egyptians and the God of Abraham. A fierce fight in the spirit world.

If only the Egyptians would return home and leave them alone. They could turn back now and not a single person, Egyptian or Hebrew, would be injured in these midnight hours.

But she'd learned long ago that rage among the Egyptian soldiers rarely relented. They seemed to revel in hatred, bent on revenge. Did they not remember the many years they'd enslaved the Hebrew people?

She didn't worry about herself. She was ready to cross over the waters of this life into a forever one with Yahweh. But she wanted her son and grandchildren and their many cousins to experience freedom in the Promised Land. And she wanted Sivian, who still clung to Zahla's tunic in these late hours, to grow up free as well.

Family surrounded her now with Eliana and Asher on her right, baby Merin safely in Zahla's arms.

Her extended family, numbering in the thousands, were scattered in the crowd. All the loved ones from her childhood days had slipped from this life before her, but most of their children were on this shore. Hosea, she hoped, was somewhere among them.

Puah and Joseph's firstborn son had survived Pharaoh's horrific edict and eventually took over his grandfather's work as chief vintner in Goshen. Yahweh had rescued Hosea long ago, through the most unlikely savior in an Egyptian solder, and now, as wind blew across the water, as the wall of fire raged behind them, she prayed that God would rescue her entire family again. That none of them would ever forget Yahweh's care for His people.

But even if the chariots broke through the blaze, even if their arrows and swords killed her family, her trust in Yahweh would not falter. Someone's strength, she'd learned, did not reflect their love. Even if little Merin weighed heavy in her arms, even if she couldn't save him today, she still loved her great-grandson with her entire being.

Even if Yahweh couldn't overcome their enemy, she didn't doubt His care.

Another wind swept through the canyon, its breath stirring the sea. And her mind traveled back to their family's vineyard. To the men stomping grapes in the press, red juice pooling under their feet and draining into jars. To the afternoon when the elder Merin first visited the vineyard and changed her life. When he'd planted the seeds of love in her heart to flourish in years to come. When they—with the help of her brother—began rescuing the babies.

"Sivian!" a woman shouted through the noise and wind.

Zahla turned as Sivian unfurled her grasp.

"Imma." The girl breathed the word as if it encompassed everything good and right in the midst of their fears.

Sivian's mother picked up her daughter, squeezing her close in the chaos, and Zahla's heart leaped at the sight.

Then the woman smiled at her. "Zahla?"

She moved closer until she recognized one of her many nieces. "You are—"

"Lydia," she said. "Hosea's granddaughter."

Zahla kissed the woman's cheeks, her heart full. The baby who'd inspired the redemption of so many others was a man now who loved his descendants well. Sivian may have gotten lost along the journey, but her imma and great-grandfather would watch over her now.

"Thank you for caring for her," Lydia said.

"She was taking care of me." Zahla tried to scan the faces nearby, but the crowd was swirling around them like the wind. "Is Hosea with you?"

"He is near," Lydia said. "And he is well."

"I am glad." Her nephew, she prayed, would cross into the Promised Land with his family.

Lydia looked down at the baby. "Will you stay with us?"

"I am traveling with Asher and his daughter Eliana," she said before nodding at the baby in her arms. "This is her youngest son, Merin."

Lydia smiled. "My grandfather will be pleased to hear that name."

Zahla bent toward Sivian. "I am glad you have found your family."

"Our family," Lydia reminded her.

Such beautiful words. The Egyptians may have chariots and arrows and swords, but on this shore, waiting for their enemy to strike, her family had the love and care of one another.

And Yahweh was among them.

Zahla walked away from Lydia and Sivian to rejoin Asher's family, but as people and animals shifted in front of her, the brief joy in her heart collapsed. She had promised her granddaughter that she would stay close, but she didn't see Eliana or Asher in the crowd.

While she still had Merin in her arms, she'd lost his mother.

"Eliana!" she called and then she yelled for Asher.

As the roar of men and horses behind the fire grew louder, no one stopped or even seemed to notice her pleas. She kissed Merin on the forehead and silently begged Yahweh again for the salvation of this boy. That he would be reunited tonight with his family. That he and the others would live.

The winds grew stronger across the valley, and she leaned against a cart so she didn't topple. Moses had said Yahweh would fight for them. Was He planning to chase the Egyptians back with the wind?

But then, even if her people managed to walk around the shores of this sea, their enemy would eventually follow. Instead of returning them to Egypt as slaves, they would slaughter every man, woman, and child in their fury.

The only way forward, she feared, was retreat.

Another roar echoed through the darkness, but this time, it wasn't from behind. It was in front of her. Over the sea. And the chaos around her stilled.

Something was happening to the water.

# CHAPTER SEVENTEEN

*Eighty Years Earlier*

A wave tossed the papyrus boat, tied firmly together with ropes, as the oarsmen pushed Zahla and the empty amphorae away from the quay.

Lemuel hadn't accompanied her to Rameses this week since Abba needed every available man and woman to harvest the last of the grapes. The Hebrew oarsmen, he'd said, would watch over her, and he was right. She no longer needed Lemuel's company, even when the harvest was finished. In fact, it was probably better for him to remain at home so no one else wondered why he wasn't working in the brickyards.

Merin hadn't been at the wharf for the past month, and once again, as she scanned the platform, she was disappointed when she didn't see him among the soldiers.

As the harvest days had neared their end, Zahla's gaze kept traveling north across the vineyard rows, hoping she would see his now familiar stride down the middle path. She knew it was strange to watch in earnest for a soldier instead of fearing him. Not only did she want to see Merin, she desperately wanted to help him with the children. But he hadn't brought her a single bird.

She shivered, hoping that no one had harmed him. It would take a miracle for them to rescue these babies, but Yahweh had done miracles before. What she hoped, what she prayed, was that Yahweh would redeem what had been lost for the Hebrew people.

Perhaps she'd imagined the connection between her and Merin, her hopes extended at Abba's insinuation about finding a man, but she hadn't imagined Merin's request for help. With every day, she feared another Hebrew baby had been killed.

What did Merin have planned?

Two more of her cousins had delivered baby boys with Puah's help, and her entire family would help hide them if other soldiers came to visit. More than anything, Zahla wanted to rescue the children in Rameses as well, but an Egyptian guard would surely detain her if she dared to carry a Hebrew baby out of the city.

The winds blew their sail south, past the edge of Rameses and the first village on the outskirts. Reeds swayed along the bank as if they were dancing for their Creator. A glimpse of beauty, she thought, amidst all of the hardship.

Closing her eyes, she welcomed the coolness across her skin. In this moment, she wouldn't dwell on the hardship in their land or the wickedness of slavery. She would focus on the good. The plentiful harvest and river breeze and the health of Hosea as he grew. The fruit on their vines and the wine that pleased Pharaoh and the promises of Yahweh. One day, she prayed, He would set all of them free.

"Stop!" someone cried out from the shore.

She glanced back at the startled oarsmen and then scanned the wall of papyrus until she saw a man crouched among the reeds. On the bank where Merin had slain the crocodile. Then the man sprang from his hiding place when he saw her, waving both hands above his head as if they might overlook his presence.

But no one could miss this Egyptian, even if he'd traded his formal tunic and jeweled headdress for mud-stained attire and a black wig that covered most of his face. Instead of a soldier, Merin looked like one of a thousand taskmasters who oversaw the slaves.

Perhaps the oarsmen saw the glint of his spear or they feared others were waiting behind him, prepared to imprison them during Akhet. They lowered the sail and dipped their oars into the water, redirecting the grip of wind to the opposite bank, as far as possible from Merin and his spear.

Zahla turned swiftly in her seat. "Please stop."

But they ignored her as they worked to fight the wind.

"This man is a friend," she pleaded with the lead oarsman. "I need to speak with him."

"We have no friends among the Egyptians," he replied.

"This man will not harm me or any of you."

Merin was running now through the reeds, following them along the opposite bank. He carried some sort of vessel in his hand. She prayed that, in his earnest pursuit, he wouldn't tread on a snake or crocodile or disturb a hippopotamus at rest.

"Please," she begged the oarsman again. "If he meant to hurt us, he would have done so at the quay."

"Your abba said we must protect you."

"That man is a friend of my abba's." The boat rocked as she glanced down at her tunic and then tied the billowing linen to her side. Though he was running hard, Merin had fallen behind the boat. Even he couldn't keep up with the wind.

"What are you doing?" the oarsman demanded as she scooted toward the edge. Abba had taught her to swim when she was a child. While she only bathed in the Nile as an adult, surrounded by other women, she hadn't forgotten Abba's lessons.

She hoped the reptiles had been frightened away with their chatter, but if not, perhaps by her splash.

Then again, a splash might alert them to a new source of food.

"If you will not stop, I will have to swim to shore."

It wasn't an idle threat. She'd risk the reptiles if she must, to get to Merin and whatever he carried.

She didn't know whether it was because the lead oarsman feared her abba or because he was simply curious, but he finally directed the boat toward the bank. Then he lowered the gangplank so she could meet Merin when he caught up with them.

Wind whistled through the papyrus, bowing the reeds low as Merin scanned the ground around them. Then, with a great heave of breath, he set the box he carried in the grass.

Zahla studied the black hair draping over his shoulders as he caught his breath, keenly aware of their audience. The oarsmen were watching closely, she was certain, but if she kept her voice low, they wouldn't be able to hear.

"What is in your box?" she asked.

"A gift for you."

She smiled. "You should have brought it to the vineyard."

Another deep breath filled his lungs. "Your father asked me to stay away for now."

"I will speak to him—"

Merin shook his head. "Your father is a good man. He wants to protect you."

"You are a good man as well, Merin."

A smile grew on his lips. "One day soon, I will visit the vineyard again."

Another sound broke through the cry of the wind, and her heart leaped at what sounded like the mew of a kitten. Or the worn cry of a baby.

"He needs to be fed soon," Merin said, bending toward the reeds.

He lifted an intricate leather box from the papyrus cushion, a lotus flower chiseled into the top and a tuft of linen propping it open near the middle strap.

"This is exquisite." Both the box and the gift inside.

"It was my mother's," he explained. And tenderness wove like fine linen through his words. While she could never tell him of her feelings, she loved him for it.

"If I transport this box today, the oarsmen will discover our secret." She glanced back at the boat. "And, I fear, they will talk."

Merin's gaze remained steady on her. "You will have to convince them otherwise."

She scanned the dark wig strung over Merin's shoulders, obscuring most of his face. "None of them will recognize you in the city."

"I worry more about you, Zahla. It is a great risk to save a child."

She smiled. "No Egyptian would be surprised if they found I rescued a baby."

"You…" His voice faded as if the words on his lips must remain unspoken. "I know you will take good care of this one."

He held out the box, and she peeked under the lid. The baby looked sickly in the white cloth, his cry weak, but he still moved. Perhaps the oarsmen wouldn't hear his cries with the wind.

She reached for the box and cradled it in her arms. "I will find a wet nurse for him."

"So many have died already," Merin said sadly. "This one's mother thinks I threw him in the river."

"To save him…"

"She was devastated when I took him. She will be grieving for a lifetime, I fear."

What a strange thing to steal a baby away in order to save his life. She thanked Yahweh for Merin's willingness to do the right thing.

Yet no one could know about his work.

"Perhaps you can return him to his imma next year."

He nodded. "One of us will return him home the moment that Pharaoh reverses the edict."

The breeze blew the edge of her radid over her face, and Merin brushed it away. Then he dropped his hand as if he'd burned it. "I am sorry."

Another woman might reprimand him for his impropriety, but he'd meant no harm.

"Zahla?" the lead oarsman called.

"One moment," she said before speaking to Merin again. "Do you think Pharaoh will change his mind soon?"

"If he does not, the Hebrew people will begin to fight back. He does not want a war inside Egypt."

And neither did she. Many of her people would die in an uprising.

"Will you be able to save more children?"

"I hope so." A cloud passed over his face. "When I find them, I will bring them to you."

"I pray you find many."

Merin studied the intricately carved box one last time as if still deciding whether to leave it with her. Then he turned swiftly and disappeared into the papyrus. She climbed the gangplank and held the box in her lap, the lid propped open. While she'd hoped the wind might cover the baby's feeble cries, a wail escaped the confines of the box and traveled right over her shoulders, to the crew behind. The surprised looks on the oarsmen's faces rattled her nerves, but the boy's cry gave her hope for his survival.

The lead oarsman stared at the box. "He brought you a baby?"

"A Hebrew baby," she explained. "And not long in this life without food. We must get him to a wet nurse right away."

"If the Egyptians discover it, they will kill us."

She lifted the baby to her chest. "Do you want to throw him in the river?"

The wind rustled the sail, flapping like the reeds.

"Because if you do," she continued, "you will have the blood of a kinsman on your hands."

The shock in the man's eyes ebbed into admiration. Then he turned to the others.

"Her secret is our secret," he announced. "We will ignore our ears."

"Thank you." The little one reached out and grasped hold of her finger as if he joined them in their partnership.

When they neared the vineyard, she returned the baby to the box. The men could unload the empty vessels without her. She needed to focus on the precious cargo in her arms.

Puah took the baby without question. As with all the babies that she delivered, Puah gave him life.

Joseph, however, had many questions.

"Where did you find him?" he probed as he escorted her back to the village. It wouldn't be long, only days, before he would have to return to the city to once again serve the man that he hated.

"I did not find him. Someone brought him to me."

"Zahla—"

"I cannot tell you anything else."

When Joseph glanced over, she saw new lines etched across his forehead. The demanding labor in Rameses during the rainy season, the worry about his family, had aged her brother. How much longer would he be able to endure the taskmasters who cared not whether he lived or died or he became chief vintner in his abba's place?

"Did this same person help with Hosea?" he asked.

"My silence will protect Hosea and everyone else in our family."

"I am indebted to him."

They stopped on the edge of the hamlet, the aroma of baked fish clinging to the breeze. Several family members lingered around the tables after their evening meal.

Joseph eyed the orange streaks across the sky. "The storms will be coming soon."

"We will watch over Puah and your children while you are gone."

"Puah cannot keep two babies in our house," he said. "Haken will visit one day or send someone to check the vineyard. It will be hard enough to hide Hosea."

"Hosea is no longer a newborn," she said. "And we have other boys in the vineyard now."

"The risk is still too great to have two babies living in one home."

It was difficult enough to have the Egyptians searching for their children. Much worse to have the oarsmen, many of them fathers, wanting to rid themselves of a baby for their own sake. But now her brother? His own son had been rescued from the enemy. She thought he would advocate for the others.

Her fists drove into her hips, her back stiff. "Would you have me throw him in the river like the Egyptians?"

"Of course not," Joseph snapped. "Why would you think so little of me?"

She took a deep breath. Her mind was still spinning from all that she'd encountered on the river. The people who opposed her. "I am sorry for doubting you," she said slowly. "Much is at stake for our people."

"I want to take this baby farther south." Joseph scanned the vineyard as if he could see the fields beyond their rows. "Someone among the shepherds and farmers will feed and care for him."

"You will help..."

"Of course."

She thought of Merin's face on the bank, his smile of relief and delight as he delivered the baby into her hands. Of Hosea and then Jochebed's second son being rescued. "There will be more."

"Very good." He kissed her cheek. "Before I leave for Rameses, I will find a place where you can take this little one and other babies."

She smiled. "Thank you."

While Merin hadn't been able to rescue more children yet, the one life he'd brought to her mattered. Now this boy had an opportunity to grow and flourish and know Yahweh.

"I am proud of you, Sister."

"And I am proud of you too."

"What will you name him?" Joseph asked, and she saw a new light glimmering in his gaze. For so long, he'd suffered under the brutality of Egypt, but maybe now, he could overcome what Pharaoh had meant for evil. Maybe he could even help Merin in the city when he was forced to return.

She thought a moment and then smiled. "What about Asher?"

The man who was a blessing in their stories of old.

"Tomorrow I will find Asher a new home," Joseph promised.

One of many, she hoped, who would escape Pharaoh's decree.

# CHAPTER EIGHTEEN

*Two Years Later*

Zahla shivered as she and Joseph returned home from their walk into Goshen. Beside them, a donkey pulled a cart filled with wool to weave into blankets for the cooler months. If anyone asked, they'd traveled south to trade from their wine reserve.

The baby who'd traveled with them this morning would be cared for among the Hebrew families who raised sheep and flax and barley for Egypt. He was now one of many boys hidden with those who'd been forced to provide for Pharaoh and his populace.

No Egyptians lived among the shepherds and farmers in Goshen. As long as their fields continued to produce, as long as they delivered their wares into the city, Pharaoh had no reason to visit.

While Merin hadn't returned to the vineyard in the past two years, Joseph had convinced Hebrew families in and around Rameses to allow the Egyptian soldier to take their babies. Sometimes the rescue was dramatic, like that night Zahla had chased Merin to the edge of the river. Other times, he simply stole into a home before the wine transport, where, with many tears, the parents gave him their baby boy to hide.

It was only a season, Joseph told the families, but as the months and then years passed, they'd all begun to realize that returning the boys to their original homes would be detrimental to both their families and those who'd cared for them in Goshen. The Egyptians would ask questions about the growing children, and no one would have a good answer as to where the boys had been raised.

The few parents that Joseph had contacted were grateful for the continued safety of their sons, and they agreed—the children couldn't return until Pharaoh changed the edict.

Pharaoh thought he'd succeeded in his plot to eradicate the boys, but the Hebrew population continued to grow. And in their work together, Joseph had become a partner and friend.

"You are the best of brothers," she told him as they neared the vineyard.

"I am just trying to keep up with my sister."

She grinned. "We make a good team."

"When we must," he joked. "Imma would be proud of you, Zahla."

Her chest expanded at the mention of their imma, and then it seemed to shrivel at the reminder of their loss. "I hope so."

Joseph glanced over at her. "She would be pleased to know that you have found a good man to marry."

Zahla laughed. "There is no man for me to marry in all of Goshen."

"I do not think this man lives in Goshen."

Her mind wandered to the soldier who met her often on the banks of the Nile. She was nearing twenty-one now, and Merin was twenty-four. Five years had passed since they'd first met at the palace, and while she wished for more than an acquaintance, there was no path forward for them to ever be more than partners in this peculiar network they'd created. Still, she looked for Merin every week along the river, and her heart leaped whenever she saw him waiting in that ridiculous wig.

The oarsmen no longer argued about stopping on their return trip from Rameses. They rowed to the shore without question to retrieve the baby in Merin's care. But every time they stopped, she longed to stay with Merin along the river. Talk for hours about family and what they hoped for the future. Not *their* future, even though she sometimes lost herself in the wondering, but a future where Egypt allowed Hebrews to keep all of their children.

The donkey waited beside her when she faced her brother. "How can I marry an Egyptian?"

Joseph glanced across the field as if the answer hid among the flowering stalks of flax. "In time, he will find a way."

The breeze rippled through the pale blue flowers and then they stood tall again as if each blossom had captured a piece of the sky. "Are you talking about Yahweh?"

He smiled. "I was thinking of Merin, but perhaps he and Yahweh will find a way together."

As Joseph nudged the donkey forward, she wondered again what it might be like to have Merin as her husband. The love that had taken root in her heart had carved its way to a place so deep inside her that she thought the reservoir would surely run dry. But it never did. A new well sprang fresh every time she saw him.

What would it be like to see Merin every day? Sleep beside him every night?

If she released her heart to him, she'd never be able to stuff it back into her chest.

Even if he felt the same, Merin couldn't tell anyone about his Hebrew mother, or he might be reassigned to the brickyard. And it would take a miracle as extreme as those of old, like a great flood or Lot's wife being turned into a pillar of salt, for Pharaoh to ever allow one of his soldiers to marry a Hebrew woman.

"I do not know about Merin," Zahla told her brother. "But I am happy for you and Puah. You will have many years together and many more children."

"Three seems like plenty of children for now."

She smiled. "I could never have enough nieces and nephews."

He and Puah decided not to return together to their house near Rameses. Puah and their children remained in the house beside the wine cellar while Joseph worked in the city. Many of Zahla's hours were filled with playing and caring for them when Puah was called to deliver another baby. Their family alone had welcomed fourteen babies since Pharaoh's edict, more than half of them boys.

"Zahla?"

She scanned the flax when Joseph stopped again. "What is wrong?"

Her brother was no longer smiling when he spoke. "Will you continue to watch over Puah and my children when I am gone?"

"Of course." She focused back on him. "Abba and I always watch over them when you are working."

"I mean, when I am gone for good."

While her brother's muscles had grown strong with the hard labor, he moved slowly when he harvested their grapes. As if he'd aged decades in the past four years.

Sometimes it even seemed as if Joseph had passed Abba in age.

"Please do not talk as if you are leaving soon," she said softly.

He patted the donkey's side. "The taskmasters are trying to weed out the weak among us, and I fear—"

"You are one of the strongest men that I know, Joseph."

"Thank you."

"Imma would be proud of you too," she said, and she meant it. She'd learned so much about her brother since he and Puah had married, and with understanding came friendship. Even in those moments when he still annoyed her, she remembered all the good that he had done for her and Puah, and most of all for the children he'd fathered and the dozens they'd snuck out of Rameses.

"We will rescue more children," he promised as he continued up the path.

"Yes, we will."

Their abba's vineyard bumped up against the rows of flax. As they drew closer to the village, Maya rushed out of a row filled with family members who were pruning vines, her arms outstretched for her abba.

"The soldier is back!" she exclaimed as Joseph lifted her.

Joseph glanced at Zahla before speaking. "Which soldier?"

"The one Zahla likes."

"I do not—"

"Everyone knows, Zahla." Joseph grinned again. "Including Mer—"

"Do not say his name!"

With his laughter, the comments about his future seemed to have been forgotten. And the familiar flutter returned inside her. Had Merin brought a child, or did he have another reason for visiting?

She brushed her hands over her face to wipe away some of the dirt that she'd accumulated on her journey. Then she groaned when she glanced at the smears on her hands and the remnants of leaves and wool stuck to her linen sleeves. The bottom of her tunic looked as if she'd been stomping around in mud. So different than the bathed and pampered women that Merin guarded in the palace.

"I am going to stop at the well," she told Joseph.

"A wise choice." He removed a clump of wool from her head covering. "You look like you just wrestled a whole flock of lambs."

"Baaa," Maya exclaimed, mimicking a distressed sheep.

Zahla shook her head. "You are quite precocious for a four-year-old."

Joseph pretended to whisper in Maya's ear, but his words were loud enough for Zahla and the field workers nearby to hear. "As precocious as your *dodah* Zahla."

Maya giggled.

Zahla tousled her niece's hair. "We will make a matching crown of leaves for your head."

"Like a princess?"

Zahla smiled. "A Hebrew princess."

Joseph took Maya's hand, and they continued the journey toward one of the storehouses to deposit the wool. Zahla turned in the opposite direction.

A leather bucket, attached to a rope, rested along the brick rim of the well outside her village. She washed her hands and face with the drawn water and then removed most of the debris from her tunic. The mud ring around her feet would have to wait until she laundered her gown.

Merin was waiting in the village courtyard, and she felt strangely shy to be alone with him, so different from the moments when she hopped off the boat on their way back to Goshen. Here, the stillness felt like a threat to her heart and mind.

She glanced over her shoulder, to her family's home. "Where is Abba?"

"He had to return to his work in the vineyard."

She eyed him curiously. "I am surprised that he allowed you to wait here."

"I asked to speak to you before I left, and he approved."

Abba may not have a choice but to do what the other soldiers bid. Merin, however, would respect his wishes. If Abba allowed it, he must know with certainty that Merin was helping her and Joseph with the children.

"Pharaoh is ill," Merin said. "His advisers are preparing his oldest son to take the throne."

Hope flittered again through her. "Will that change the edict?"

"I fear not. His son is not a good man either."

She shook her head. "Are there no good men in Egypt?"

His gaze fell at her question.

"Except you, Merin. You are good."

"Evil wars inside me every day, but I want to help the children."

She scanned the dirt around his sandals for a basket or box. "Did you bring another baby?"

"I tried," he began, but his voice broke. And she felt deeply of the grief reeling inside him.

"Oh, Merin…"

"Someone else took him from his mother before I arrived."

Tears flooded down her cheeks like the Nile after a storm. She no longer cared how she looked or what he might think of her. "Perhaps it is not too late to find this one."

He glanced at the sky as if it might open up and deliver him from this evil. "I am afraid I waited too long."

Merin's face blurred, and the courtyard seemed to whirl around her.

Yahweh had promised to multiply Abraham's descendants until they spread across the sky like stars, but some of the stars were flickering out. How long would He tolerate the killing of the ones among them who were most vulnerable?

Merin slowly came back into focus, and she stared at him as if he were a stranger. "How can you do it?"

He blinked. "I did not harm the child."

"I know." She paused. "But how can you serve Pharaoh and his court when they are killing babies?"

His lips pressed together, and for a moment, she felt bad about wounding him even more after the loss of this child. But she could no longer understand how he could protect such an evil man in his work as a palace guard.

"I have no choice," he finally said.

The words bricked like a wall between them. She knew if he refused Pharaoh, he would end up as a slave or in prison or perhaps dead, but he had a choice.

"You serve them every day, Zahla, with your wine."

"But I do not worship them."

"I saw you kneel in Pharaoh's court," he said, an observation more than accusation.

"It is different," she replied quickly, but she knew it wasn't. And every week she transported wine up to the palace, serving Pharaoh as Merin did.

"I suppose we both have to do our work well," she said, "if we want to help the children."

Merin picked up a handful of stones and tossed them across the courtyard. "It feels like an impossible place."

She searched his face again. His passionate gaze had flooded with frustration, and she wished she could take back her words. Neither his sword nor his spear would free him from his internal traps. He might be able to spear a crocodile, but he couldn't spear the monsters inside.

Stepping closer, she reached up to run her thumb across the thin scar on his cheek. It reminded her of the flax blowing in the wind. Bent but not broken in the opposition. "How did you get the scar?"

He placed his hand on hers and gently lowered it but didn't let go. "My father gave it to me."

A shudder raced down her spine. "Did he lash your face?"

"He ordered one of his men to do it. I did not want to serve in Pharaoh's guard, but my father had other plans."

"You truly did not have a choice," she said quietly.

"Not if I wanted to retain my life."

"I am glad you did," she said quietly. "Without your work, Hosea and Asher and the others would have drowned in the Nile."

He released her hand and walked toward the well in the courtyard's center, sitting on the brick that surrounded it.

"You have rescued many, Merin," she said. "Dozens of children live because of your service to Pharaoh."

"How is your nephew?" he asked.

She smiled. "Healthy and strong. He brings much joy to our family."

"And those in Goshen are safe?"

"They are," she said. "I suspect Asher will be a shepherd when he grows older."

She always visited Asher when she traveled south. He was weaned now, so another baby could take his place with the wet nurse who'd cared for him. Sadly, his imma had died a few months after his abba collapsed in the brickyard, so even if Pharaoh lifted his decree, Asher would remain in Goshen.

"One day I want to invite him to live in the vineyard," she said. "Once it is safe."

"Perhaps he would be a good playmate for Hosea."

She smiled again. "I believe he would."

He studied her so intently that her heart fluttered. "Once it is safe, perhaps I could visit more often."

She nodded at the doorway into her house. "You are always welcome here."

"I wish things were different, Zahla."

Her imagination wandered again to a future where Merin was living with her in one of these homes. Working beside him during the day. Sharing a bed with him at night.

She shivered at the thought.

"Are you okay?" he asked.

She wrapped her arms over her chest. "I wish things were different too."

"If they were, I would be talking to you about a different kind of future."

She met his strong gaze again, confidence building inside her. "Is there nothing we can do?"

He eyed her curiously. "You are agreeable to a discussion?"

"I am agreeable to more than a discussion, Merin."

Light flooded through his dark eyes when he grinned. "I will ponder it more."

"We can ponder it together."

How different things would be if Merin had been born to a Hebrew father. Or she liked to think it would have been different. If Merin was enslaved in Pithom, they never would have met. And they certainly couldn't have worked together to help the children.

Even if they'd somehow been introduced, even if her heart belonged to him, Abba would still be wary of having her marry someone outside the tribe of Manasseh.

Merin stood and reached out his hands, but before she took them, he withdrew like a gazelle who'd sniffed danger. As he moved toward her house, she glanced around to see what had startled him, but the only thing that moved was a brood of chickens foraging for insects and grain.

Unlike Merin's retreat, an anchor had dropped inside her. She stood frozen among baskets of legumes and barley, tears dampening her eyes. How could he leave now, how could she let him go, when it might be a lifetime before they were alone again?

Merin turned back at the doorway, more than ten cubits away, as if he'd needed space between them to speak again. "Both of my mothers would have loved you."

She wanted to run into his arms. Or take him into hers and never let go. She didn't care what Abba or anyone else thought if they found her and Merin in the courtyard. His body may belong to Pharaoh, but she desperately wanted his heart to be hers.

She willed the anchor to ground her so she didn't frighten him away. "I am more interested in the love of their son."

"No one could love you as much as I do, Zahla."

The anchor line snapped, and her heart seemed to fly out of its cage, soaring above the courtyard. To be loved by this man was more than she ever imagined. Even if they could never marry, she would hold his words forever in her heart, knowing he loved her as she did him.

She took a step toward him, her voice barely a whisper. "What should we do?"

He considered her words before speaking. "We ask Yahweh for a clear path."

"I will pray every day," she said. "For the impossible."

# CHAPTER NINETEEN

Zahla discarded her tunic on the bank and slipped into the cool Nile. Puah and their cousin Rebecca stood on the bank where their family washed themselves and their clothing. The shore had been cleared of reeds so they could bathe without the dangers of a reptile surprising them in the grass, but they remained diligent in watching for any creature lurking underneath the water.

Even though crocodiles usually slept during the day, Rebecca rattled her timbrel in hopes of scaring off anything that might wake as they stepped into the river. While Rebecca played, Puah scanned the surface and nearby weeds for any threats.

When nothing bubbled or slithered around the bank, Zahla stretched out her arms and pushed off the muddy bed, swimming several cubits at the surface before plunging underneath. Then she popped her head back out and smiled at her female guardians. On hot mornings like this, she wished she could linger in the river as Joseph used to do in the wine cellar.

While Abba taught her and Joseph to swim when they were younger, she only swam about once a week now, on the days she bathed. And she never dived into the depths of the river or near sunset when the crocodiles emerged for their dinner. Even with the dangers, she loved immersing in the water. Here, she found freedom that she never experienced on land.

Her gaze traveled upstream as if she might see Merin around the bend, waiting for her on the shore. He'd left their village three days past, but her heart continued to soar at his declaration that he loved her as she loved him. She'd stayed up late into the night hours, begging Yahweh for a way. A path, as Merin had said, to a future together.

Perhaps when Pharaoh died, things might change for the better. Perhaps the new Pharaoh might see the Hebrew people as partners in this land instead of his enemy. If Pharaoh didn't hate their people, he might even allow her and Merin to marry.

Her skin flushed warm, and she dived under the water again, the water rinsing away the dirt and sweat. She could play in the river all day, enjoying the respite from the sun, but the other women needed to bathe. And she needed to return to the cellar soon to help prepare the next wine shipment. She and Joseph would leave for Rameses early tomorrow.

When her brother was home, they delivered the wine together, and he helped her place any baby that Merin brought them. Even on his weakest days, Joseph continued to give life to others.

Zahla finally relinquished the river to Puah. She didn't dry her skin before dressing so she could cling to the coolness as long as possible before the afternoon's heat stole it away.

Puah scanned the river again before stepping into the water. While she remained fearless in her work with laboring women, she didn't tread far into the Nile, drawing water near the shore and pouring it over her skin.

Rebecca continued to shake her tambourine as she spoke to Zahla. "I heard rumors about a soldier visiting you."

Zahla tied the cord around her tunic. "The man is quite interested in our vineyard."

Rebecca lowered her instrument. "I suspect he is more interested in you."

Heat flooded Zahla's face, and she scanned the shoreline again so she didn't have to look at her cousin.

Puah glanced over her shoulder. "Your business should remain your business, Rebecca."

"It is hard to keep it to myself when everyone in the family is talking about this man."

"Play your timbrel!" Puah commanded.

Rebecca rattled an arc over Puah's head before she continued speaking to Zahla. "I have also heard rumors that Lemuel spoke to your abba about matrimony."

She flinched. While she and Lemuel were amiable on most days, she couldn't imagine being married to him. "I have heard no such rumor."

"Lemuel would be a good husband to you," Rebecca said. "And the only real prospect since most of the men in our tribe are already married."

"Abba will decide who I should marry."

Rebecca laughed. "Your abba always bends to your desires, Zahla. Ever since your imma—"

"Enough," Puah said as she dried her skin with a coarse linen cloth. "Zahla and her abba will decide at the right time who she should marry."

"But she is past twenty!"

Zahla crossed her arms. "Perhaps I will not marry at all."

Neither woman replied, but Rebecca had the nerve to snicker. They'd both married a Hebrew man from their tribe, and they assumed she would do the same. But Abba still hadn't insisted that she marry. Instead, he allowed her to work like Joseph alongside him and provided well for her needs. If she married, it would be for more than provisions.

"It is my turn to bathe," Rebecca said as Puah finished dressing.

Zahla tied her sandals and then shook the timbrel while Puah brushed her hair, all three women scanning the water as Rebecca prepared for the final bath.

"Wait!" Puah called before their cousin stepped into the water.

A Nile monitor swam by their toes, and while the lizards weren't poisonous, they could bite when startled. Rebecca waited on the bank until the lizard crept up into a grove of reeds. Then she bathed swiftly near the river's edge.

The sun was creeping its way across the eastern sky as the women turned toward the village to continue their day's work.

"I hope you take better care of yourself," Rebecca told Zahla as they walked.

"I am not afraid of the creatures in the Nile."

"It is not the river that I worry about," Rebecca said.

But how could she talk about her future or marriage to a man like Lemuel when her heart belonged to another?

She forced a smile. "You should not worry about me."

"Your soldier may seem friendly enough," Rebecca continued, "but no Egyptian is truly a friend to the Hebrew people."

"That is why we have one another," Puah said quickly, as if she knew Zahla would begin listing off Merin's many virtues. Zahla longed to tell both women of the love that had rooted in her heart, but she'd learned much in the past two years about feigning indifference.

Rebecca kissed her cheek and left for the house that she shared with her husband and two children. Zahla and Puah continued walking toward the wine cellar to help prepare the shipment.

"Do you think you will bring back another baby tomorrow?" Puah asked.

Zahla shook water droplets from her wrists. "I do not know."

"I worry about you and Joseph when you go into Goshen."

"We risk much less than you did when you refused to kill the babies."

Puah glanced at the vast sky and fields that led south. "I fear my children will lose their abba."

"Joseph is taking great care," Zahla assured her.

"I pray so."

She had never told Puah how they obtained the boys, and she suspected that Joseph hadn't told her much about his involvement in Rameses so she wouldn't worry.

Just talking about it seemed dangerous to their work. Puah wouldn't share the information, but if someone overheard, the rumors would pour through the vineyard.

"One day your children will celebrate how you and Joseph worked to rescue so many others," Zahla said.

Puah stopped on the path, and Zahla's gaze followed hers ahead to the grotto. Then she cringed at the sight of a chariot outside.

Merin had said Pharaoh was ill. Had his son or someone else from the palace come to inspect the wine?

Zahla stepped forward. "I am going to the cellar."

Puah reached for her arm, stopping her. "Your abba would want us to wait until he finishes with the visitor."

But what if Abba needed her now? If something had happened to one of their shipments, she could testify to its safe delivery.

"Your abba will tell us the news soon enough," Puah said.

"I cannot leave him down there alone with a royal guest. He might need my help."

"Sometimes you run straight into trouble, Zahla, when you should be running in the opposite direction."

"I am not afraid of trouble."

Puah smiled. "You rescued Hosea and so many others with your courage. I will always be grateful for what you have done, but other times…"

"Other times what?"

"I fear my children will lose their dodah as well."

"I cannot help myself, Puah. I have to fight for those I love."

"Even a warrior must choose his battles. And before he ever fights, he girds himself with armor and a shield and some sort of plan."

"The battles find me," Zahla insisted. "And I have no armor or shield to defend myself."

"Choose your words as carefully as any warrior would his armor. I do not want any harm to come upon you." Puah kissed her cheek as Rebecca had done, and then she disappeared into the house.

Zahla slipped into the cave entrance and listened as voices rose from the cellar. She quietly descended several steps, her wet skin cold, and in the dim light, she saw Abba speaking with two men.

Neither man wore the extravagant head ornament of royalty, but both were dressed in costly garments. Joseph wasn't among them—he would have hidden with Hosea and his other son the moment he saw the Egyptian chariot.

Only Abba noticed Zahla's descent. His gaze slid over the shoulder of a guest, and with the slightest shake of his head, the curl of his hand, he warned her to wait on the stairs.

Her feet still tugged her forward, compelling her to forge ahead to support her abba as she'd done long ago when she'd followed him to the palace to visit Pharaoh. But then—she stopped—when she insisted on going to the palace, Pharaoh had given her Joseph's job and required her brother to work in the city.

Instead of bursting into the lamplight, Zahla forced herself to remain in the shadows. Even though she wanted to help, perhaps Puah was right. Her presence might make things worse again for her abba.

"Pharaoh is ill," one of the men said, and she recognized the voice of Haken, Pharaoh's wine steward, who met her each week at the quay.

"I am sorry to hear about…" Abba's cough interrupted his reply.

Her abba wasn't sorry for Pharaoh's illness. No one in Goshen would be sad to hear when Pharaoh crossed the waters. He'd punished and murdered many during his reign. Even the Egyptians might not mourn when that monster of a man died.

"Pharaoh is requesting more shedeh," Haken continued. "Right away."

Abba turned to the collection of stored jars. He didn't mention their lack, but she knew the shedeh was already in short supply. "We will add two jars to our shipment tomorrow."

"I fear we cannot wait until morning," the steward continued. "Pharaoh finished the last of it two days ago and wants four jars now in addition to his regular supply."

What would Pharaoh do once they ran out of his favorite drink? Zahla didn't know exactly how many jars remained in the cellar, but she hoped it was enough to keep the ruler satisfied until the end of harvest.

Abba shook his head. "It would be dark by the time the boat returned."

"The sunlight is still long into the evening."

"But the dangers on the river—"

Haken waved his hand as if he could dismiss the dangers. "The Hebrew oarsmen are quite skilled."

"Do you have men to help us load?" Abba asked.

Perhaps her abba had asked the question to demonstrate they had nothing to hide, but she was relieved when the steward shook his head. If Haken sent soldiers to load, she feared they would also search the vineyard homes. While all the babies they'd taken from Rameses were hidden further south, eight boys had been born in the past two years among their family and other vineyard workers.

"I must return to Rameses to make preparations for your shipment," Haken replied. "I am quite certain you have enough men to assist you, and Zahla can help as well. It seems that she works as hard as any man."

If Abba or an uncle praised her work, she would be honored, but the flattery from this man's mouth was disconcerting. Why had he singled her out?

"My daughter is steadfast in all of her responsibilities. She is more reliable than some of my men."

"Indeed. Sometimes I wonder if she is trying to garner the attention of an Egyptian man."

The stone steps seemed to quake under her feet. It was bad enough for her family to recognize her interest in Merin, but it would be detrimental to him if a high-ranking official thought he shared her affection.

She wanted to speak out, fight for Merin, but Puah's warning rang in her ears. She had to choose which battles would be beneficial and which could further harm those she loved.

Abba tried again to keep them off the river tonight. "I can send Zahla and Joseph with the shipment at sunrise."

The steward shook his head. "I need them to bring the shedeh before day's end."

A pause followed this demand, and she knew that Abba was trying to decide which battles to fight as well. Unlike Merin, the steward would not be swayed. The timing of the shipment was a losing battle, enforced by any number of soldiers that Haken could send down, and no Hebrew wanted Pharaoh's men in Goshen.

It would take most of the afternoon to ready the jars and then transfer them to the river, but they had no choice but to transport the shipment before sunset.

"We will prepare it right away," Abba said.

Zahla rushed up the stairs before the men turned.

She and Joseph would have to travel into Rameses and return home before dark. Did Merin know they were coming this evening instead of in the morning?

Perhaps she would see him tonight, even if just a few moments, at the quay or waiting for their boat on the bank.

Then again, if the steward suspected her interest, it would be better if she didn't see Merin at all.

# CHAPTER TWENTY

Sunlight flickered on the western horizon as the oarsmen rowed swiftly out of the quay. With Haken's back to her, ushering the jars toward the city gate, Zahla scanned the wharf. The familiar longing swelled inside her to catch a glimpse of Merin. She wouldn't linger on his face. Only a glance to know he was safe.

She didn't see him, but when she looked back at the port, Haken had turned from the gate, his gaze on her. Zahla looked away, too quickly perhaps, with his words from earlier today rattling like Rebecca's timbrel in her head.

How could he possibly know that she'd pledged herself to one of Egypt's soldiers? Even if Abba and her family suspected her interest, she'd told no one except Merin what was in her heart.

The papyrus boat swept south in the final show of light, the oarsmen just as ready as she and Joseph to finish their work so they could return to Rameses before dark.

"He will not be waiting tonight," Joseph said as they glided away from the quay.

"I know," she replied, her gaze on the winding river path. "I just hope he is not planning to meet us tomorrow."

One of the six oarsmen splashed her tunic when he dipped his oar into the water. Her skin and hair had dried long ago in the arid Egyptian climate, her morning bath almost forgotten in the rush of delivering wine. She brushed off the splash of river water before it soaked through her tunic. No sense inviting illness during the cooler evening hours.

A shimmer fell across the current, and she savored the sun's last dance. This hour belonged to neither the Egyptians nor the Hebrews alone. The golden sky was one of the few things they shared.

An oarsman lowered his paddle, his head turning left. As Zahla followed his gaze, her mouth dropped.

Joseph was wrong about Merin not coming tonight. He was standing on the shore, his head covered in plain linen instead of the wild wig, his legs hidden by reeds. In his arms was another case. After the shipment time changed, he must have worked quickly to secure a baby and meet them here.

The oarsmen lifted their paddles, waiting for her or Joseph to direct them to the shore.

Merin waved at them, and she wondered if he'd missed her as much as she'd missed him. They couldn't linger with the failing light, but how she wanted to hear his voice, to feel him next to her again, if only for a moment.

"Please turn—"

Something rustled the reeds near Merin, and she paused her request.

Merin stood on the bank, seemingly oblivious to the writhing. Was he hoping she'd hurry to retrieve the child? Or was he so focused on their boat that he didn't see or hear what was happening beside him?

He needed to put down the case and spear any beast before it harmed him or the baby.

"Merin!" she shouted, pointing toward the motion.

He didn't turn toward the papyrus nor did he call back. Instead, he seemed to be signaling them away.

Perhaps it was a trick. Another man standing on the bank in Merin's stead.

The twilight blurred her vision, and when she focused again, she saw shadows in the reeds, each one as tall as a hippopotamus. It seemed that a small herd had congregated there—a herd that could take down Merin and the child, and then turn on their boat.

Joseph studied the shudder of the reeds alongside her. "What is that?"

"Perhaps the hippopotamuses are out tonight."

"I have never seen them cluster so close together."

The man she loved would be readying himself for a fight, not standing like a sphinx by the water.

"Something is not right," she whispered.

Joseph turned to the oarsmen. "Keep paddling."

When they lifted their oars, a swarm of men surfaced from the forest of reeds, and Zahla's head jogged between Merin and the men in confusion at first. Then shock.

The soldiers surrounded him, knocking his linen head wrap to the ground. Merin's eyes turned wild, frightened, but he didn't drop the case. Instead he clutched it like an amulet to his chest.

If only the goodness of his heart, the kindness of his deeds, would protect him from harm. But he needed a friend right now. Someone to remind him that he wasn't alone.

She turned to Joseph. While he must return to Puah and their children, she belonged with the man on shore. "I have to help him."

Joseph shook his head. "There is nothing either of us can do."

The sadness in her brother's words plunged to the depths inside her as she struggled for her next breath.

How could she continue in life without the man who'd quietly fought off the evil lurking around them? Who had brought good into her world and the lives of those she loved? Merin's imma had no choice but to watch her illegitimate son be taken from her, and then his abba had forced him to become one of Pharaoh's soldiers. How could she live with herself, even surrounded by family, if she simply watched these soldiers drag him away too?

Hope may be fleeting, but she couldn't let Merin think he was alone. If the soldiers were going to arrest him, they would have to take her too.

She tossed her head covering onto the deck and tied the corner of her tunic into a knot so the material wouldn't weigh as heavily on her skin. They were about fifteen cubits from the shore now. With a few kicks, she would be on the bank.

Joseph grabbed her arm, pleading with her. "It will kill Abba if you dive into the river."

"I cannot let them take Merin away alone."

"They will separate you, Zahla. Before morning, you will both be alone."

The crew dug their oars into the water, and when the boat propelled forward, both she and Joseph slipped from their seat to the papyrus floor.

Yanking herself back up, she looked over the boat's side, and Merin's gaze met hers. Then he lifted the case above his attackers and hurled it toward the river.

Zahla sucked in her breath as the case traveled through the air, the tremor of a cry bleeding out before it splashed into the Nile. Then the river was quiet.

The crew dropped their oars, all of them stunned as the case disappeared under the surface.

How could Merin have thrown a little one into the river? If the soldiers had taken the baby, thrown him into the waters, the death would be on them. But Merin...

She shook her head, refusing to equate the man she loved with the soldiers who'd surrounded him. Merin wasn't a monster.

Questions were no longer an option. Nor were her doubts. Zahla hopped onto the seat and lifted the knot to her waist.

"Do not—" Joseph's plea rang in her ears as she plunged into the water.

She couldn't allow this baby to drown.

The shock of cold instantly cleared her mind and filled it with the realities of crocodiles waking to hunt. Rebecca was not there to scare off the creatures with her timbrel nor Puah to warn her of any danger.

But she wouldn't wait around for the night creatures to discover her. Yahweh, she prayed, would reveal the hiding place quickly since her breath wouldn't last long and neither would the baby's. She had to find the case before the baby drowned.

This section of river was shallower than the middle, only two or three cubits deep. A school of perch swam around her, and in the fading light, she could see the rise of a dark cloud from the bottom. Her hands frantically searched among the grass and mud, hoping the box was the catalyst for the disturbance on the river floor. Then her hands swept over something hard. A woven piece, buckled in the front.

She wouldn't dare open it until she was back in the boat. Right now, neither the water nor the bank was safe for her or the baby.

The case at her side, she pushed to the surface for a breath of air. None of the soldiers would swim out to stop her, but if they saw her, they might throw a spear in her direction.

After a quick glimpse of the boat ahead, she dived back under. Her soaked tunic, along with the heavy case, threatened to tug her to the bottom, but she kicked as swiftly as possible around the stern so the soldiers wouldn't see her. Then she slipped back to the top.

The moment Zahla reemerged, she hoisted the case to the surface in hopes that the air might revive the baby.

Two hands reached over the edge and took the case from her. Then she heard Joseph's voice as she clung to the boat's side. "Keep your head low."

Something slithered across her leg when she ducked again, and her breathing quickened. It was just another fish, she told herself, harmless like the perch. No reason to fear.

"Hang on," Joseph commanded.

The row wasn't as urgent this time, more like a gentle tug, but the oarsmen pushed the boat farther from the shore. Their paddles, she hoped, would ward off anything dangerous under the surface.

When the boat swept around a bend, Joseph leaned back over the edge, his hands outstretched. "I am going to pull you into the boat."

She pressed her feet against the rugged papyrus side, and with Joseph's help, she climbed inside.

The lead oarsman tossed her one of the linen cloths that had cushioned Pharaoh's wine. She dried her face while another crew member held the baby by his feet. She could only see the child's back, but his skin was the bluish color of flax in bloom and he hung as still as a cluster on their vines.

She leaned back against the boat, defeated. The cries had left the boy's lungs, and it seemed his breath was gone too.

"Is he dead?" she asked solemnly, her courage fleeting as the oarsman turned the baby's body. She couldn't bring herself to look into his face.

Joseph reached for the boy. "Not yet."

He rested the little body on his lap and rubbed his stomach.

"Breathe," he whispered before turning the baby over. Then Joseph pounded his back.

Zahla shivered. "You have to be gentle."

"Gentle is not going to revive him."

Joseph struck the baby's back again and leaned him over his knee. Water dribbled out of the child's mouth, and then the greatest of miracles—the boy's leg twitched. A twitch of his leg followed by a tremble in his arms. When a cry rippled across the boat, the crew cheered.

Zahla's tunic was soaked, her body frigid, but warmth spread inside her with the baby's cries. The Nile had almost swallowed this little one, but he began to flourish again, growing stronger with each cry.

The lead oarsman tossed Zahla another cloth, and she wrapped it around the child and held him close. They needed to find a warm dwelling and a wet nurse right away.

"We cannot take him to the vineyard," she told Joseph.

He turned to the oarsman. "Can you row us farther south tonight?"

The man eyed the darkening sky. "How much farther?"

"Beyond the flax fields. This one will find friends among the shepherds."

A half-moon replaced the sun as they paddled past the small harbor where they'd loaded Abba's wine, down into the obscure farmlands of Goshen. With the moonlight as their guide, the boat glided alongside flax and then barley fields.

When they heard sheep bleating in the distance, the crew maneuvered to shore.

Zahla thanked the men, not knowing if she would ever see them again. The following hours would determine their future, and she feared that none of them would be spared from Pharaoh's contempt.

Joseph glanced to the left before speaking to the lead oarsman. "Can you continue rowing south?"

While Pharaoh's edict had stretched far, the thousands who worked the fields and farms in southern Goshen, closer to the city of Pithom, remained cushioned from his rule. Once the crew found a landing place, they could release the boat to the current and quietly work these fields too. Only Haken knew their names and faces, and she doubted the steward would spend a moment of his time searching the many hiding places in this land. Pharaoh's soldiers would never recognize the nondescript crew who rowed one of the many supply boats.

"We must return home," the oarsman said sadly with a shake of his head. "We all have families in Rameses."

Zahla understood. Sometimes they had to risk everything to be with the people they loved. Joseph might be able to hide in Goshen as well, but he'd never leave Puah and his children behind.

She carried the baby off the boat, and Joseph dumped the woven case into the deepest part of the river so it wouldn't be discovered. Then he crossed the plank onto the riverbank. Not far from the bank was a small community of shepherds who'd helped them many times. Many of the boys from Rameses lived among the shepherds' offspring.

As they walked east, scanning the moonlit fields of clover and grass, Joseph reprimanded her. "You should not have jumped in the water."

She sneezed. "I could not let him die."

"I would have dived in after him," he insisted, but she wasn't certain of this.

"All that matters now is that we warm and feed him."

"Jakar will help us."

They found the elderly shepherd reclining by a fire outside his home. When he saw the baby, Jakar called for one of his daughters.

"We will help him regain his strength," he promised as his daughter swept the boy from Zahla's arms.

She was grateful for Jakar and his family's assistance, but still she wished she could care for this child instead of giving him away, wished that her body had the sustenance that he needed.

Zahla coughed and then rubbed her soaked sleeves in an attempt to warm her skin. "I will visit him soon."

Jakar motioned her forward. "Come sit by the fire."

"We have a long walk home," Joseph said, but Jakar's gaze remained on Zahla.

"Your sister must drink something for her cough and then rest before your journey."

"We cannot rest for long," Joseph replied, and Zahla understood. Like the crew, they would have to venture home in hopes of protecting their family. They'd feign ignorance about the woven case and Merin's reason for waiting on the bank. Anything to protect Abba and Puah and the children in their care.

But it would take most of the night to trek home in the moonlight. And the soldiers would surely travel to their vineyard at first light.

"Eat!" Jakar commanded as he handed them each a plate of roasted fish. Joseph devoured his rapidly, but Zahla couldn't stomach anything caught in the river.

Another daughter gave her a warm loaf of bread and a bowl filled with figs. Then the woman steeped acacia leaves into a cup of beer and handed it to Zahla.

"Thank you." She sipped on the drink sweetened with honey before scooting closer to the blaze.

"You have brought us many children," Jakar said.

"I am sorry," Joseph said. "We have only a few trusted places to take them."

"An apology is unnecessary," Jakar replied. "These children are a blessing, not a curse. Every baby strengthens our nation."

"We have no nation," Zahla said sadly, for the children of Israel had never had their own land. They'd been scattered in fragments across foreign soil.

"But one day, we will be a great nation," Jakar replied with a confidence that far exceeded hers. "Yahweh promised Abraham."

One day, she hoped, Merin would join them in this nation. She couldn't bear to think that Pharaoh or his men might take his life tonight. Nor could she comprehend her life without him.

Zahla lowered the sweet drink, reliving again the soldiers accosting him on the bank. Then the flash through the sky as he abandoned the evidence of what they would consider a crime.

If only he could tell her why he'd thrown a baby into the river.

"The Egyptians may travel here to search for this child," Joseph said.

Jakar glanced toward the tent where his daughter resided. "Have we a prince among us?"

"No," Joseph continued. "But he defied the Egyptian army by surviving. The soldiers will not be pleased with his audacity to live."

Jakar sighed. "They would kill all of us if they did not need laborers to survive."

"If we left Egypt on our own accord, they would have to figure out how to work the land," Zahla said.

Joseph shook his head. "Pharaoh is never going to let us go."

"In time," Jakar said slowly. "I believe Yahweh is working even now for our release."

Zahla glanced at the moon as if she might catch a glimpse of Him. "I wish He would work faster."

Jakar smiled. "His timing might bewilder us, but He always keeps His promises."

How she wanted to live to see this covenant kept as Abraham's descendants multiplied. *As numerous as the stars.* That's what God had said.

Each new baby was like another star in the night sky.

"You should stay here until morning," Jakar offered.

Zahla turned to her brother. "Abba and Puah will be riddled with worry."

"And the soldiers might arrive in the morning," Joseph continued. "We have to hide the babies in our family."

Jakar prayed a blessing over them, and then she and Joseph stepped onto the moonlit path between fields. Her tunic was only damp now, her skin much warmer.

"Tomorrow, things will change again," Joseph said as they walked north.

"I know."

"We will tell the soldiers that you never found the case."

"Or I found the case and the baby was dead."

"This is no time for pride, Zahla."

She cringed. "There is no pride left in me! I only want them to stop the search."

They moved from the clover fields into those growing barley.

"What do you think happened to Merin?" she asked, afraid of the answer.

"I cannot predict Pharaoh's actions," he replied sadly, and she realized that Merin had become a good friend to her brother as well.

"He threw the baby as if he was afraid."

Joseph sighed. "He threw the case because he knew that nothing would stop you from rescuing a child."

# CHAPTER TWENTY-ONE

"They are here," Abba said, shaking Zahla's shoulder to wake her. Light flooded through the doorway, and she wondered how long she'd slept. Her swim in the Nile had been short, yet her throat still burned and her entire body ached. As the memory of the soldiers flooded back, her heart hurt like her arms and legs.

But the boy was safe with the shepherds. That was most important. It had taken all night for her and Joseph to travel home, and before they slept, they'd warned their family members that the soldiers might arrive. Then Joseph had returned to his home to make sure his family was safe.

Even though the morning sun had already been on the horizon when they returned, Zahla had changed into a dry tunic and collapsed onto her reed mat.

"I will speak to them, but I want the men to see that you are home," her abba said.

She slowly sat on the mat bed, her head throbbing. "Yes, Abba."

"You have done nothing wrong."

But the right choices were often wrong in Egypt.

"Wash up, and we will meet them together."

How was she to face her enemy today?

Some time had passed since sunrise. An hour or two? She didn't know. She was supposed to be strong in the inquiry of these men. Courageous. But every part of her wanted to crumble. The soldiers had taken away Merin, perhaps even killed him during the night, and she had no way to find out what happened. No way to help the man she loved.

While Abba waited, she splashed cool water on her face in an attempt to wash away the tears and heat that burned through her. Then she covered her hair. Even if her body pained her, even if their enemy wanted to destroy her, she must greet them today.

And if the soldiers were planning to imprison her in Rameses, she would kiss her abba and leave with her head held high.

Two soldiers waited outside, both with leather bands tied around their head coverings and swords hanging at their waists. One man she didn't recognize, his eyes red as if sleep had evaded him, his chin peppered with stubble. The second was Ahmed, the cruel guard who'd mocked her and Abba at the palace for being dogs. The soldier who'd stolen Hosea from Puah and beaten Joseph for trying to stop his newborn son from being drowned.

Ahmed appeared to have enjoyed a proper night of sleep, but he was a traitor of a fellow guard, the most despicable of men.

Ahmed was the dog.

She stepped behind Abba, and while she didn't speak, she glared at the soldiers.

Abba knew something was amiss whenever she arrived with a new box or basket after her wine transport, but he knew nothing of how they'd obtained the babies they sheltered here. Nor did he know where she and Joseph were last night.

Neither soldier before them knew for certain who was involved beyond Merin in helping the children, but they must suspect. Haken certainly did. In fact, she was surprised that he wasn't standing among them.

Was the wine steward willing to overlook such a large offense because he didn't want to replace the vintner? Perhaps his appreciation for Abba's wine had kept him in the palace.

If so, who had sent these soldiers?

"My children already delivered Pharaoh's wine," Abba told the men. "Haken asked us to bring it last night."

"We are not here about the wine," Ahmed spat.

A host of words trembled on Zahla's lips, but she refrained from speaking. They would only lead her into deeper trouble, her raspy voice exposing both her illness and her worry.

Then again, these men had probably deemed her guilty already.

"How is Pharaoh's health?" Abba asked.

"The high priest of Osiris is keeping watch at his bedside," Ahmed said without a trace of dismay. "We are told he sleeps most of his hours."

The priest of Osiris would prepare Pharaoh's body for the funerary rites, which meant the royal physician and family thought he would soon depart for the afterlife.

It also meant the delivery of the shedeh last night was unnecessary.

Had Haken forced an early shipment so he could capture Merin and perhaps her and Joseph at nightfall? Did he want someone else to take over the vineyard?

No matter the reason, she needed to find out where they'd taken Merin and if he was still alive.

"My children said one of your men was attacked beside the river last night," Abba said. "I hope he is in better condition than Pharaoh."

Ahmed glanced at his partner before looking back at Abba. "His condition is none of your concern."

"It becomes my concern if an Egyptian is trying to steal my wine."

*Thievery.*

Zahla wanted to cheer Abba for his ingenuity in protecting the rest of their family. Merin would approve.

"Pharaoh's wine," Ahmed corrected.

"It is my responsibility to deliver the wine without incident to Rameses, and Egypt's responsibility to ensure my family's safe return home."

Ahmed turned to scan the path between their homes. "I would like to speak to your son about this shipment."

Zahla cringed at the demand. Not only had this man tried to kill Hosea, he'd flailed her brother. Would he beat Joseph again or would he imprison him this time?

"My son is in the fields," Abba replied.

Her gaze traveled to the sky, and she realized with a jolt that the sun had already crossed the high point and was descending toward the river. More than a half day had passed as she slept. She hoped Joseph had rested for a few hours before he left home. Whether or not he was actually in the fields, she didn't know, but she was certain his work took him far from the cellar today.

The unkempt soldier glanced around the village, seemingly confused as to his role in this inquiry. "Which field?"

"Why are you still standing here?" Ahmed scoffed.

The soldier stared back at him. "Perhaps you should tell me what I am supposed to do."

"Look for babies!"

The soldier scanned the small village and began walking toward the first house after Abba's. Her family knew that the soldiers might arrive. Surely the baby boys were hidden in the fields, their parents watching closely to change locations if the soldiers drew near.

Her people might not be able to fight off the Egyptians in Rameses, but if these soldiers found one of the boys, if they threatened any of their children in the vineyard, her family would band together to stop them. The consequences of saving a baby's life, they all knew, would be swift and strong, but the tribe of Manasseh, the children of Israel, would ultimately be redeemed. Her family wouldn't let the Egyptians kill a baby on this land.

"Before we find Joseph," Ahmed told her abba, "I must speak to your daughter alone."

"What you must say can be said in front of me."

Ahmed fingered his sword. "Not this time, old man."

Abba didn't move, not even when Ahmed removed his sword. Her abba had no weapon, but he stood as a living shield between her and Ahmed. One that would be slaughtered if she didn't comply.

Ahmed had already betrayed the best of men when he'd stood on the bank with Merin. How dare he threaten her abba too?

"It is all right, Abba," she said, stepping up beside him. Her family could risk their lives for the babies, but she wouldn't allow any of them to lose their life on her account.

Abba didn't take his eyes off the man, who was half his age. A man who had none of his character. "I will not permit you to speak with this man alone."

Not like he allowed her time with Merin.

"We will stay in the village," Zahla promised as if she had a say.

The second soldier continued to trudge in and out of the dwellings with his head down as if had no desire to search. Perhaps not all of the Egyptian soldiers found pleasure like Ahmed in fulfilling Pharaoh's edict. They'd been trained as warriors, she guessed, like Merin. Not to kill children.

When she and Ahmed reached the edge of the village, she balled her hands into fists and faced him. "Why are you really here?"

If she could dive into the river at sunset, she could give this man a black eye before he took her down.

But Ahmed didn't attempt to hurt her. Instead his voice dropped to a whisper. "I need your help."

She stared at him, stunned, before uncurling her fingers. Of all the things that she anticipated Ahmed might do or say, asking for her help was not one of them.

She crossed her arms over her chest. "Killing my abba would not have encouraged me to help you."

"I would not have killed him."

How was she to know what he would or would not do? "You ripped my nephew away from his imma."

He didn't respond.

"And you called my abba and me dogs."

"I call all the Hebrew people dogs," he replied, his voice as cold as the river.

Part of her wanted to toss him into the middle of the Nile and see how he fared. Another part was vastly curious about his request. "Were you one of the soldiers on the riverbank last night?"

He nodded as if it pained him.

"Where did you take Merin?" she asked, her voice trembling.

"I did not take him anywhere."

She shook her head. "How could you turn on a fellow soldier like that?"

He blanched but didn't admit any guilt. "I did not take Merin anyplace, but I know where he went."

Her heart leaped. "Is he alive?"

"I am told he lives."

She stared at the man, wondering why he'd given her this gift. She may despise the messenger, but his message was the best of news.

Still, her mind warred between gratitude for this information and fear at what he might require for sharing what must be a secret.

"What do you want from me?" she asked skeptically.

He glanced both ways at the empty path then back at Abba watching them from the doorway. "I need your help freeing Merin from prison."

"Prison…" She flinched. "Why do you need my help when you put him there?"

A vehement headshake knocked Ahmed's head covering in front of his face, and he swatted it away. "Pharaoh put him there."

Without money, a powerful abba, or even the citizenship of Egypt, how could she, a slave in the eyes of those who'd imprisoned him, garner Merin's release?

"You want to borrow my courage," she said slowly, her throat raw. "You are afraid…"

"I told Merin that he would get bitten if he played with dogs."

"We were not playing."

"Whatever it was you were doing."

Her fists curled again. This man before her, armed with a sword, was a coward. She would never help him with anything else except… she'd do anything to free Merin. "Where is he?"

"Two soldiers escorted him to the prison in Pithom."

Pithom. The place of his birth and home to his abba, the nobleman.

"If he is released," Ahmed continued, "he will be sent to work in Pithom's brickyard."

"You can petition Pharaoh. Tell him it was a mistake."

Ahmed looked at her as though she'd left her mind on the bottom of the Nile. "Pharaoh is too sick to know Merin is gone."

"The new Pharaoh will want Merin to return. He is one of the best guards in Egypt."

Ahmed's eyes narrowed. "How do you know he is one of the best?"

She didn't waver under the intensity of his gaze. "I see how the other men look at him when I bring wine to the quay. Even Haken respects him."

"Haken fears him and many of the soldiers. He thinks they are conspiring against the advisers."

"Are any of the soldiers conspiring against them?" she asked.

"I do not care what anyone does to Pharaoh when I am not on guard," Ahmed said. "Right now I am focused on returning Merin to Rameses."

There must be something the nobleman could do to free his son, but she still didn't trust Ahmed's role in assisting Merin. "Why do you want him released?"

Ahmed's thin lips curled together, his forehead pressed into lines as if he didn't quite understand it himself. Perhaps he was feeling guilty for standing on the bank while the other soldiers beat Merin and dragged him away.

"Because he does not deserve prison for what you and your brother did."

*What she and her brother did?*

She wanted to argue. List Merin's many heroic acts. He'd been the first brick in the foundation of their network. The cornerstone, really. Without him, she and Joseph wouldn't have been able to rescue even Hosea.

Then again, Ahmed didn't need to know that Merin had rescued Hosea first and then dozens of others. She wouldn't tell him anything about their work.

"I will visit him in Pithom," she agreed, not knowing how long it would take to walk to the city south of Goshen. "And I will do everything that I can to secure his release."

"Do you have transportation?" he asked.

"I will find my way."

While she was grateful for the knowledge of Merin's life and location, she didn't thank him for the information. If it weren't for Merin, he'd turn on her.

The other soldier stepped up beside Ahmed, and Zahla's confidence cracked when she saw Rebecca's youngest son in his arms.

"How old is this one?" he asked as the child's chatter bounced between them.

"Three," she lied. Older than Pharaoh's edict.

The soldier studied the child, but since neither man spoke Hebrew, they didn't know he spoke nonsense. "He seems younger than three."

Ahmed smacked his comrade's shoulder. "Since when did you become an expert on children?"

The soldier eyed the boy a moment longer before setting him on the ground. When the boy's sister called for him, he ran back into her arms.

Ahmed's eyes narrowed as he turned back to Zahla. "Where are the other babies?"

She tilted her head, confused. Had he regressed into her opposition, or was he grilling her so the other soldier wouldn't suspect his intent? She would continue to do whatever she could, without Merin's help, to keep any newborn boys safe from him and his colleagues.

Her skin ebbed from hot to cold, and she wrapped her arms over her chest. "We have no children here for you."

"Just because Pharaoh is ill does not mean that we have forgotten his edict," Ahmed said.

"I am quite sure you will never forget it."

He scanned the vines to his right. "We will keep looking until we find any children that have gone missing."

Despite his threats, the men left their vineyard without searching for Joseph or other babies.

When Zahla returned to her bed, long before the sun began its descent, she thought of Merin in his prison cell. Did he think he'd been forgotten? Surely he knew that she would never forget him.

At first light, she planned to begin her walk south, but another three days passed before she was able to start the journey. Weakened by illness stemming from her plunge into the Nile, her body initially refused her the ability to walk, and then a messenger arrived with news.

"Haken sent me," the man told her abba. "He needs more wine immediately."

"To concoct another plot against my family?" Abba asked.

The man shook his head. "To quench the thirst of those attending Pharaoh's funeral."

No matter what their captors believed, the evil ruler wasn't a god.

Pharaoh had crossed the river with the many that he'd murdered, and she wondered at that moment—what had he discovered on the other side?

# CHAPTER TWENTY-TWO

Fires burned in small pits across the city of Pithom as women roasted meat and baked bread. Unlike the extravagant décor and lotus ponds of Pharaoh's residence to the north, Pithom was constructed of brick warehouses and granaries to store the harvested crops from Goshen.

Zahla and Joseph moved from building to building, searching for the prison. When Joseph insisted on joining her journey to Pithom, she hadn't argued. Her body hadn't fully recovered from her sickness, and it hurt for her to speak. In the next hour or so, they would have to tuck away between buildings before guards began patrolling the evening streets, and she wanted to find Merin before they rested.

"Are you hungry?" Joseph asked in the Egyptian language so passersby wouldn't wonder at his heritage.

They'd eaten roasted duck for breakfast with Jakar and their shepherd friends, but even though her stomach rumbled after their long walk, she didn't want to stop searching. "We will eat after we find the prison."

"If we find it…"

"We will find it," she insisted.

The prison in Rameses was near the palace, and while they'd seen the city's brickyard as they searched the streets, she and Joseph hadn't located a palace. And they didn't dare ask for directions. Even though they both spoke Egyptian well enough, they feared unwanted attention if someone recognized their accent or if either of them stumbled over their words.

At least their tunics matched the ones worn by most of the men and women they passed in the streets. As long as they remained quiet, their heads held high with the confidence of those well acquainted with their direction, she hoped no one would notice they were lost.

Near the city center was a temple and two elaborately painted homes that looked more like the royal homes in Rameses. Instead of traveling to a palace here, perhaps Pharaoh sent his vizier or another official to check on the food storage. And it made her wonder—how would the new Pharaoh rule this land?

Things were changing again in Egypt, but this time, both the Hebrew people and the Egyptians were unsettled. The new Pharaoh was rumored to be even more brutal than his father, and she feared he would search anew for the babies taken out of Rameses.

But this morning, she had to focus on securing Merin's release, not her family's future.

If there was no palace in Pithom, did that mean they had no prison? And if there was no prison, did that mean Ahmed had tricked her into traveling south? This trip felt like a prolonged plunge into the Nile, and she didn't want to linger in the depths.

Zahla didn't trust Ahmed, but he had seemed to want Merin freed. If Merin was here, she and Joseph would find him tonight, and then she would convince the nobleman to fight for his son's release.

Finding and then freeing Merin would take a miracle, she knew, like the ones of old. If Yahweh was still able to do miracles, she prayed He would find a way to release the man who'd been rescuing His children.

The marketplace was smaller than the one in Rameses and much less dramatic. With stooped shoulders and weary gazes, Pithom's residents seemed to be as worn as their buildings. As though the accumulation and management of food storage had stripped many years from their lives.

She and Joseph searched among the stalls to speak with a fellow Hebrew or a slave taken captive from another land. Someone who might be sympathetic to the imprisonment of a loved one. Many of the slaves had spent their lives laboring for Pharaoh without the care of a physician or proper food to eat. She wished that Yahweh could set all of them free.

"A pleasant evening to you," a young woman said to a vendor in Hebrew before switching to Egyptian. "I will trade this linen for two fists of olives."

Joseph threw out his arm, stopping Zahla before she stepped toward the stall. "You will frighten her."

The younger woman wore no head covering to protect against the afternoon sun, and her dark hair hung like a curtain between her shoulders.

"Ah, Raquel," the seller snorted as he studied the square of linen. "You jest."

"I assure you, this is no jest."

"One fist of olives," he replied. "And a handsbreadth."

"Ha!" Raquel lifted the square. "I will take my business elsewhere."

The vendor glared at her as if he might smash her will into pieces, but the woman didn't crack. She returned his gaze until he threw his hands into the air. "You steal from me, Raquel."

"I am keeping you honest."

Raquel watched the merchant carefully as he measured the olives in a wooden bowl and then transferred them to her ceramic jar.

"Let's follow her," Zahla whispered to Joseph as the younger woman drifted away with her wares.

His gaze remained on the man straightening his goods at the market stall. "Or we could just ask the seller for directions."

She couldn't explain the urgency stirring inside her, but she knew what they needed to do. "We have to talk to that woman."

They trailed Raquel through the busy streets and cooking fires until the woman disappeared in a dust-cloaked maze. As Zahla scanned the crowded intersection, she saw a stark mud-brick building that looked like many of the Pithom storehouses except for the three windows that stretched across the upper floor, each one barred with metal. A man armed with a spear and shield guarded the heavy front door.

Was Merin imprisoned inside this building? If so, he was only a few steps away, somewhere behind the brick. So close to them and yet—

"I think we found it," she whispered.

"What do we do now?" Joseph asked, his gaze on the guard.

The words, it seemed, were for himself, but she still spoke. "I am not certain."

They'd come so far on this journey, but Merin's abba was the only one in Pithom who could secure his release. She'd inquire about directions to the man's residence except she didn't know his name.

They would have to speak to Merin in order to locate his father, but she couldn't think of a valid excuse to obtain access to an unmarried prisoner. If she asked to see him, the jailor would surely think she was mad.

"I will talk to the guard," Joseph said before stepping toward the prison doors, but the jailor turned him away in moments, threatening with his spear.

"Only family members are permitted inside," Joseph said upon his return. "He would not even tell me if Merin was here."

As she eyed the row of dark windows, Zahla asked the question that had bothered her since she'd learned about the prison. "What if Ahmed lied to us?"

"Why would he lie?"

"He and his men might return to the vineyard while we are gone. They might wreck all of Abba's work searching for the babies."

"I think Ahmed is more interested in harming you and me than destroying a prized vineyard, but if he was planning to hurt us, he would have done that when he visited last time."

Shadows crept long over the mustard-colored prison walls, a breeze sweeping over them.

"We have to find shelter for the night…" Joseph's voice trailed off when Raquel stepped out the prison door.

This time, neither Zahla nor Joseph hesitated. They rushed through the narrow streets behind her.

"Please wait." It pained Zahla to call out with her sore throat, but they had to talk with this woman. "We would like to speak with you."

Fear clouded the woman's eyes at being sought after by a stranger. "I have nothing to offer."

Joseph remained behind Zahla, knowing he'd frighten Raquel even more if he approached.

"You were in the prison," Zahla said in Hebrew.

Raquel nodded slowly, her voice marked by both sarcasm and fear. "My abba has been a guest there for almost a year."

"I am sorry," Zahla said. She would be heartbroken if she had to visit her abba in prison.

Raquel studied her. "What is your interest in my visit?"

"We believe a friend of ours has been taken to the same place."

Raquel's gaze lifted as if she could see the brick walls around the bend. "The younger men are usually sent to the brickyard."

"Merin is an Egyptian," Zahla said slowly. "Pharaoh was not pleased about his friendship to the Hebrew people."

"The rulers are not pleased with any Egyptian who dares to be kind to us," Raquel said. "I heard a man was brought here from Rameses four days past."

Zahla's breath caught in her throat, not knowing whether to be glad that Ahmed had spoken the truth or devastated that Pharaoh's men had truly imprisoned him. To die here, she thought. Far from any fellow soldier like Ahmed who might fight for his release.

Raquel stepped closer so Joseph could hear her whisper. "You must stay away from the soldiers. They are looking for more men to work in the brickyard."

"I am already employed by Pharaoh in Rameses," Joseph said.

Raquel eyed him curiously. "The new one or the former one?"

"I speculate that the new one will require my services like his father."

"We are all speculating now," Raquel said. "News is slow to travel to Pithom."

"After I speak to Merin, my sister and I will return home to learn more."

Raquel glanced back toward the direction of the prison. "The guards would never allow a Hebrew man to visit one of their prisoners. They are terrified of a revolution."

Zahla's heart skipped. "Would they allow me inside?"

"Perhaps," Raquel said. "They have never refused me a visit with my abba."

Zahla glanced at her brother, but he didn't try to dissuade her. They were both willing to risk their lives to help Merin. "How do I gain entrance?"

A group of women turned onto the quiet street, and Raquel motioned Zahla and Joseph toward a shadowed alcove between buildings.

"First of all," she began, "the guard must not find out that you are Hebrew."

She sighed. "No matter what I do, it is impossible to cover my accent."

"I hear no accent."

Perhaps her sore throat was a blessing today.

Raquel continued. "When he asks who you are, say you are pledged to marry Merin, the newly arrived prisoner from Rameses."

She had pledged to marry Merin in her heart, and she wondered if Raquel suspected this to be true as well.

"Do you have food to share with him?" the woman asked.

Joseph opened the leather pack at his side and removed a partially filled waterskin. The shepherds had replenished their supplies, but the bread and cheese were the only sustenance that they had for their evening meal. With nothing to exchange for more food, they'd planned to glean from the fields and waterways on their way home.

"Merin can have my portion," Zahla said.

Joseph held out the pack. "Take him both portions."

"Joseph—"

"He needs it more than I do."

"Thank you." His generosity continued to amaze her.

"Tell the guard you've traveled here to bring Merin supplies."

Zahla nodded as she strapped the pack over her shoulder.

"I would give you some olives, but my abba ate all that I brought today." Raquel glanced at the fading sun. "After your visit, will you join my family for a meal and a night of rest?"

Zahla smiled. "We would be grateful for that."

"I will meet you across from the prison before the sun sets."

After Zahla straightened the leather pack across her chest, she and Joseph hurried back toward the prison. A different man guarded the entrance now.

Joseph kissed her on both cheeks. "Please be careful."

"I will."

"I have not had a moment of peace since you were born, Zahla, but the past months have been exceptional. Between the babies and your jump into the river and now this."

"If I did not try to help, I would wither away like a shriveled grape on the vine."

"I suppose you would." He smiled at her. "Merin is blessed to have you."

She kissed his cheek. Then she rolled back her shoulders and eyed the guarded door.

# CHAPTER TWENTY-THREE

Zahla squinted in the dim light until she saw Merin resting on the crowded prison floor. Scores of men surrounded him, many of them playing some sort of game with clay dice.

She shook the metal bars as if she might be able to break them loose. When they didn't budge, she turned back to the jailer, her voice scratchy. "Let me inside."

The man snorted before his eyes moved up and down her tunic as if he could see underneath. "If I let you in, those men will ravish you and whatever you carry in that sack."

She clutched the leather pack in case she had to smash him over the head. "How am I supposed to give him the food?"

He pointed his wooden rod through the bars as he scanned the dark room. "Which clod are you here for?"

"Merin," she said, the case still secure in both hands. "He is near the window."

"Merin!" the jailor shouted into the cell. "This woman says she brought you food."

A prisoner turned away from the game and slipped up beside her, his fingers reaching through the bars. "I go by Merin."

She stepped back, shaking her head. "You're not the one I am seeking."

The laughter grew louder behind him. "I can hardly hear you."

"My throat is hoarse."

The jailer poked him with his rod. "Get away from her."

As the man retreated back to the circle, she watched the soldier she loved crawl toward the bars. His face was bruised and sweaty from the heat, his beautiful hair matted with blood. And her heart grieved for him.

Had Pharaoh's men broken any of his bones? The gracious soldier she adored, the warrior who'd rescued so many, had become one of the wounded.

"You came," he whispered, his fingers encircling the bar.

"Of course." She cradled his fingers in hers, the first time she'd ever held his hand. How she wished they were far from here. Walking together in the vineyard or through fields of blooming flax.

"You need to see a physician," she said.

He leaned against the bars, his torn tunic revealing stripes like Abba's not so long ago. Her abba's wounds had healed, but the scars, she feared, would remain forever for both men she loved.

"They do not have much use for physicians in here." The other prisoners returned their attention to the game, but Merin's gaze remained fixed on her. "How did you get inside?"

She crept closer to whisper in his ear. "I told the guard I was here to bring supplies to the man that I had pledged my heart to marry."

The smile on his lips must pain him, but it warmed her to see this glimpse of hope. One day, they would marry.

Opening the leather pack, she pulled out the waterskin that Raquel helped her refill at the city well. Merin poured a handful to wash his face and then guzzled the rest of it as she unfolded the linen holding a loaf of bread, figs, and a square of cheese.

"Thank you," he said before slowly eating the cheese and then the bread. Each bite seemed to revive him a little more.

Leaning against the bars again, Merin stretched his bruised feet out from the bottom of his tunic. Had Pharaoh meant to kill him for his disobedience, or was his intent to dissuade others from their rebellion by humbling one of his strongest men?

She glanced around the filthy cell again. "Are they feeding you anything?"

"They bring us gruel. Twice a day."

"We have to get you out of here, Merin."

He shook his head. "We cannot talk about that."

"But we have to—"

"The walls have ears."

Like the vineyard, she thought. Nothing remained secret for long. "Have you seen your father?"

"No," he said, the pain in his voice mirroring his wounds. "He probably thinks I deserve what happened for helping a—"

She shuddered, understanding quite well what he didn't say.

*A Hebrew dog.*

Even though his father had had relations with his house servant, even though he'd raised a son who was both Egyptian and Hebrew by blood, he still thought Hebrews were more like street animals than people.

"But you are his son," she insisted. "He must help you."

"Not every father is like yours, Zahla."

She knew that to be true. Her abba and her brother and this man before her were three of the best men in all of Egypt.

Still, she would speak with his father.

"What is your abba's name?"

"Ptahmose. He keeps track of the city accounts."

Shadows danced across the brick walls when the jailer lit an oil lantern. Then a breeze swept through the cell, the coolness welcome but not the stirring of its stench. Feces. Sweat. Rotting flesh. Merin would not survive long in here without care.

"Did the baby survive?" he asked slowly, and she was tremendously grateful for her answer.

"He survived and is thriving now with a wet nurse."

His shoulders dropped a notch with relief as her mind wandered again to those horrible moments on the river. To the soldiers who wanted to kill the baby and the shock of water on her skin. To the creatures that could have torn open the box and eaten him.

For the rest of her life, she would know that Yahweh still performed miracles.

"Why did you throw the baby?" she asked.

"Because I knew you'd dive for him."

Relief swept over her like the breeze. Joseph was right about Merin's reasoning, but she still needed to hear that he hadn't disposed of the baby to save himself. When the enemy surrounded him, he'd trusted her with the child's life.

Despite the opposition, without a single word between them to create a plan, they'd worked together to save another life.

"You rescued him," she said.

"I am no hero," he said. "But we worked well together. The baby is safe."

She wished she could clean his wounds and gently take him into her arms. Wished that she never had to let him go. After all he'd sacrificed, he deserved a celebration in Goshen, not a crude prison cell. "We will work together again soon."

The jailer nudged her shoulder with his rod. "Time to leave."

She carefully reached for Merin's hand again between the bars. While she feared hurting him with her touch, she wanted him to feel her in this miserable place and know how much she cared.

How was she to leave him in this squalor?

Merin gently squeezed her hand and then released it. "You had better hurry, or they will lock you in here for the night."

When the jailer lifted his rod, poised to strike either her or Merin, she stepped away. Merin may doubt his father's willingness to help, but she would visit Ptahmose before they returned to Goshen and beg him to have mercy on his son.

# CHAPTER TWENTY-FOUR

Both Raquel and her widowed sister worked as seamstresses near the prison. They welcomed Zahla and Joseph for the night into the small home they once shared with their father.

Dinner consisted of roasted catfish purchased from the market along with stewed figs and almonds. While Zahla tried to eat sparingly, she was famished.

"I will bring you a vessel of wine when I return," Zahla told Raquel as they washed the platters and plates together in a courtyard between homes. A square candle, made of animal fat, burned beside a clay urn of water, but most of their light shone down from the stars.

Raquel smiled. "I am glad to hear you will return."

Abba now knew all that Merin had done to stop Ahmed from drowning Hosea, along with his efforts to rescue so many other children. Surely he would allow her to visit Merin until he was free again.

"The prison food is not enough. Merin will die without sustenance."

"Indeed," Raquel said sadly as she scraped food off another plate and scrubbed it with a natron paste. "Many do."

"I fear for his wounds as well. Pharaoh's men beat him severely, and he cannot walk…"

Raquel rinsed the plate with water. "That, I may be able to help with."

Zahla lowered the drying towel. "We would be grateful for any assistance."

"My abba is a physician."

A flood of relief swept through her. "Will the jailer let him help Merin?"

"I will ask when I visit him next."

Zahla began drying the wet plate. "Thank you."

"Abba tires of being Pharaoh's guest, but Yahweh has used him to help many." Raquel glanced over at her. "Do you think that you and Merin will marry after he is released?"

"It is only a dream."

"A good one, I think," Raquel said. "Thankfully, he is nothing like his father."

"What is Ptahmose like?"

Raquel scrubbed a cup and then dipped it into the water. "He is a horrible man."

"But a noble one."

"And unhappy, by all accounts. Neither Pharaoh's favor nor his wealth have brought him any joy. I am told that even the Egyptian people avoid his home."

"I still want to see him." He may not care for anyone else, but surely he would assist his son.

"You should not visit him alone."

"Joseph will go with me."

Raquel smiled. "When you return to Pithom, please consider this house as your home."

She thanked the gracious woman again. How strange and wonderful alike to have made a new friend in the midst of their adversity.

The next morning, Raquel escorted her and Joseph to the home of Ptahmose in the city center. It was even grander than Zahla had imagined. A painted compound of buildings instead of one house.

She studied the carved relief of a falcon, its wings spread, above the large door. "It is stunning."

"And another form of prison, I fear," Raquel said. "I hope your meeting with him goes well."

Her gaze remained on the falcon. "If he helps with Merin's release, all will be well."

"Either way, I will speak to my father about tending Merin's wounds."

Zahla kissed her friend's cheek, and Raquel left them for her own work.

Joseph and Zahla stared at the imposing door another moment before he knocked.

After much persuasion, explaining to the head servant that they were friends of Ptahmose's son, Zahla and Joseph were given an audience with the city's treasury official. Unlike his son, with his lean frame, forged of muscle and courage, Ptahmose was a portly man who rested on a mound of colorful cushions, next to a pool sparkling from sunlight that poured through the open roof. His lips were stained yellow from a bowl of melon in his lap and then ringed purple from his goblet of wine.

Ptahmose didn't rise from his cushioned seat. Instead of a greeting, he directed them to sit before him on the tiled floor. Then he scrutinized her and Joseph as he ate another chunk of melon.

Zahla's throat had lost most of its soreness as she pleaded for Merin's freedom. "Your son is in prison."

"You think you tell me something that I do not know?" he scoffed. "I know everything that happens in Pithom."

"But Merin should not be there. He is a hero."

"Merin has shamed me," he said as if this explained his indifference. "He has shamed me and Pharaoh and the commander of his guard. He deserves no release."

Zahla's hands trembled and then her lips. "It seems you are the shameful one."

His face flamed red. "How dare you ridicule me."

"You sleep with your Hebrew servant and then pretend—"

"Zahla!"

Joseph's warning came too late for her to duck. While the melon didn't hurt, it splattered across her head covering and face.

She slowly wiped the juice off her cheek and then picked up a piece before it fell from her tunic. Staring the wicked man in the eye, she ate the fruit. "Thank you for sharing your meal."

"Get out!"

Her gaze fell to the goblet. "Where exactly do you obtain your wine?"

Joseph's hand pressed against her arm. "Let's go, Zahla."

Ptahmose didn't rise, but he continued shouting as Zahla and Joseph rushed out the door.

"You're going to land both of us in prison," Joseph scolded when they stopped along the street.

Zahla leaned against a pillar. "Merin was right about his father."

"Of course he was right," Joseph replied. "The man is going to do nothing except eat melon and sip his wine while his only son rots away."

"Ptahmose is the criminal in my mind."

Joseph turned toward her as he recalled their conversation. "Is Merin partially Hebrew?"

She nodded. "It is supposed to be a secret."

"I will not speak of it," he said. "But Merin may not be able to keep this secret much longer."

Before they traveled north, Zahla took Merin food from Raquel's table and another skin filled with water. It would give him enough sustenance, she hoped, until she returned.

She didn't tell him about their visit to Ptahmose, but she assured him she would continue fighting for his freedom. While he didn't question her desire to help, she could see the doubt in his gaze over anyone's ability to set him free. And, if she was honest, she'd begun to doubt it herself.

How were any of them to rescue a man that the former Pharaoh had condemned?

In that hour with Merin and then in the weeks to follow, Zahla promised herself that she wouldn't stop working until he found freedom again. She traveled to Pithom as often as she could to bring him food and clean water, but most of all so he'd know she hadn't forgotten him. That no matter what happened, he wasn't alone.

# CHAPTER TWENTY-FIVE

Joseph stared at the broken jars strewn across the cellar. Haken and a swarm of men who answered to the newly crowned Pharaoh had swept through the prized collection that morning, crushing the decorative pottery and splattering what remained of this season's wine.

"The new Pharaoh is just as foolish as his father," Zahla said as she surveyed the damage from the top of the stairs.

While Puah stood beside Joseph among the ruined stores, Abba lowered himself to another step as if he might collapse from the shock of finding the destruction of their wine and their collection of molded and intricately painted jars meant for Pharaoh's table.

Puah wrapped her hand around her husband's arm. "I am sorry, Joseph."

He picked up a shard of clay and studied the piece as if it might contain answers. "Why would he do this?"

Abba rose slowly from his seat. "Pharaoh wants nothing of his father's to remain."

Her brother's voice sounded hollow when he spoke again. She knew he was trying to swim, to breathe, in the flood of bitterness that washed through him. "I doubt he will be tearing down the walls of his father's palace anytime soon."

A trail of light snuck in from the entrance and brushed over Zahla's feet. The clouds must have shifted outside.

"He is not closing the vineyard," Abba said. "He is just making sure that we stay in line with future demands."

Joseph threw the shard, and it shattered against the wall. "I am surprised he is leaving Haken in charge."

Abba stepped beside him. "If this Pharaoh appreciates good wine as much as his father did, Haken will ensure that he receives it."

Haken must know her family had helped Merin with the children, but it seemed he didn't want complete destruction of the royal vineyard as recompense for their disobedience. Nor did he want to rid the kingdom of its best vintner.

Still, smashing the jars only hurt the royal supply. Now Pharaoh and his steward would have to settle for lesser quality wine from another vineyard until after harvest. And someone would have to fire and paint hundreds of ceramic jars for the new Pharaoh's drink.

She paused on that thought. Two months had passed since Merin was imprisoned. Perhaps they could commission the jars from a kiln in Pithom. She could travel there more frequently to oversee the work.

While Abba didn't know about Merin's heritage, he still encouraged her to visit Pithom, so she returned each week with food that her aunts had prepared along with Puah's ointment for his back. Not only did the jailer allow Raquel's father to manipulate and set Merin's fractured ankle, he permitted Merin to change cells to join the older man in a quieter place as he recovered from his injuries.

She'd planned to leave again in the morning, stopping to visit Jakar and all the children on the way, but now she would have to stay to help her family clean up after this disaster. She was content, at least, knowing that Merin was recovering. Raquel would bring him clean water and food when she visited her father.

Maya rushed down the steps past Zahla, staring at the destruction below. "Abba?"

Joseph seemed to snap out of his stupor as he rushed forward to pick up his daughter. "It is going to be all right."

"I will help you clean."

He kissed her forehead. "Thank you, sweet girl."

"We will all work together to clean," Puah said. "This very day. Pharaoh may send men to destroy our jars, but he will not destroy this vineyard."

Zahla retrieved a stack of woven baskets from the storehouse beside Joseph and Puah's home. Then she hung her head covering on a crag and carried the baskets into the cellar.

"We will begin again today," she said as she handed a basket to each person.

Pharaoh might enslave their bodies, but each one of them commanded their own mind and heart. He meant to discourage them, but they'd continue working together as a family.

Someone else stepped through the entrance and stood at the top of the stairs. Zahla couldn't see his face, but her heart soared when he spoke.

"I want to help."

"Merin?" she breathed. Had her ears betrayed her?

"Your soldier is back!" Maya exclaimed, and the others laughed.

Merin was here in the cellar, out of that miserable jail, but she couldn't move. Her head swirled, her feet frozen in the pool of juice.

Joseph nudged her. "Go to him."

With her brother's prompt, the shock dissolved, and she rushed toward the steps before hopping up each one like a hare. She didn't care who was watching. She wrapped her arms around the neck of the man she loved, and he pulled her close.

"You have returned," she whispered.

He kissed the top of her head. "By Yahweh's hand."

A tremble raced through her chest. She'd feared he would never be free again, and yet he stood here alone. Was an escort waiting for him at the entrance?

"If your father has no objection," Merin said, "I wondered if I could speak with you outside."

"No objection from me," Abba called from the shadows.

She took Merin's arm when she reached the top. "Did your father have you released?"

"Not my father," he said, and she could hear the pain woven between each word. "Pharaoh."

She thought of all the broken clay below the steps. The puddles of wine. "Why would he release you?"

He turned toward her before they stepped outside. The scars still marred his face—they always would—and he used a walking stick to support his leg, but she saw beneath every scar, into the heart of the courageous man who'd grown even stronger under Pharaoh's sentence.

"He has changed the edict, Zahla."

"What do you—" She paused. "The one about the babies?"

He nodded. "The very one."

She stared at him in awe, the words strange on her lips. "He is saving the children?"

"Not exactly," Merin replied slowly. "He needs to add more men to his workforce."

"So he will send them to the brickyards?"

"He will put all of the men to work in the fields or the city. When he learned that I am Hebrew, he commanded me to work among you as well."

Work among them? Her heart sprang new wings at the thought. "How did he learn you are Hebrew?"

"My father sent word to Pharaoh." He pressed the bottom of his walking stick into the dirt before looking back at her. "And he sent word to the prison that he disowned me."

"I am sorry, Merin."

He shrugged. "It felt like he disowned me the moment he forced me to join Pharaoh's army."

If Pharaoh no longer required the killing of Hebrew boys, the immas in Rameses would raise their children again in the city. Zahla and Merin weren't needed to help rescue the boys.

"His messenger also brought me a donkey," he continued, "and the supplies to travel north. I never thought my father would tell the truth about my heritage, but it seems he wanted everyone to know my reason for helping the Hebrews."

"Does that mean you will live among our people?" she asked slowly.

Among her family but, even more important, with her.

His smile was tentative as they stepped together into the sunshine. "If you will have me…and someone else."

She shaded her eyes to search his face. "Who else would I have?"

He motioned toward the crag where she'd hung her head covering. "Come here, Asher."

The boy they'd rescued almost three years ago toddled out from a cleft, and Zahla squealed. Rushing forward, she lifted him in her arms and twirled him as she used to do with Maya. How full she felt, her arms and her chest alike, with both Merin and Asher here.

Asher returned her hug and then smiled at Merin. "I waited!"

"You waited well." Merin tousled his hair before looking back at Zahla. "Jakar's family asked me to spend the night before I continued my journey north. Jakar said you might enjoy a visit from this young man."

"I would, but…"

His eyes narrowed with concern. "What is it?"

"I want both of you to stay longer than a visit."

Merin kissed her forehead, his voice gentle and strong. "I think we can do that."

And she smiled. More than anything, she wanted to spend the rest of her life with this man and the boy they'd rescued together.

# CHAPTER TWENTY-SIX

A week later, she married Merin under an arch of blue lotus, white poppies, and yellow acacia flowers that Puah and Maya wove together for the ceremony. Though Pharaoh's men had crushed the royal jars of wine, they hadn't touched Abba's personal reserve. Zahla's entire family, the descendants of Manasseh, took a break to celebrate with food and drink at their wedding feast.

Friends from both north and south joined them. Jakar and his tribe of shepherds attended the wedding along with their families and those children who hadn't returned home. Raquel's abba had been released from prison after Merin, and he traveled north with both daughters to join the celebration. Zahla seated him beside her abba at the feast.

Ahmed wasn't invited to the ceremony, but Merin had visited him after his return. While Zahla didn't know all the words that passed between the men, Merin assured her that the soldier wouldn't visit their vineyard again. While she'd always be thankful that Ahmed told her about Pithom, she would be quite pleased if she never saw him or any Egyptian soldier in Goshen.

They'd invited Merin's father to the wedding, but he didn't reply. And Merin was relieved at his absence. In the last conversation with his father, after his release from jail, Merin had told him that he loved a Hebrew woman. Ptahmose commanded that he never return to Pithom, and Merin happily agreed.

In the hour before dusk, as she and Merin pledged their faithfulness to God and each other, Zahla marveled at what Yahweh had done to bring Merin back to her, to live as her husband, and that this new Pharaoh, a man several years younger than her, had changed his mind about slaughtering the babies.

She was under no illusion that the years to come would be easy—she'd been told this Pharaoh would work the Hebrew men even harder than his father—but she and Merin would be together, and they'd decided that Asher would live with them as their son.

Merin reached for her hand as Abba prayed a blessing over them. That they would be faithful to each other and as fruitful as his vineyard. Then Abba anointed their heads with the sweet fragrance of lotus. Zahla grinned at Merin as the oil ran down her cheeks. When he reached over to wipe it away, one of her aunts gasped at the gesture and another laughed. But they wouldn't fault him for it. Her entire family had come to love this man who stood before them with his fading bruises and walking stick, knowing he would care well for Zahla and help rebuild what Pharaoh had tried to destroy.

Abba lifted a goblet, and when he toasted the couple, the crowd cheered. They'd celebrate with their family and friends for the evening, but it was the night hours she longed for most. To finally be alone with this man she loved.

As the sky darkened and lanterns began flickering across the courtyard, the party feasted on tilapia and lamb. Stewed fruit and barley bread. Salted cheese and carob cakes sweetened with honey.

Zahla ate with their guests, but she barely tasted the food. Her gaze kept wandering instead to the vineyard. She couldn't see it from the village, but her uncles had pitched a tent on the far side of the grotto from Joseph and Puah's home. And her aunts had filled it with blankets and cushions and enough supplies to last a week, although Zahla wasn't thinking about food at the moment.

She turned to catch the glance of the handsome groom beside her.

"Soon," he whispered, and she smiled at him.

*Soon.*

When the meal ended, Rebecca lifted her timbrel, and a lute accompanied her rhythm, followed quickly by the lyre. Jakar was the first to dance, and a flood of guests soon joined him in the center of their courtyard. Puah held Hosea in her arms, and Joseph danced with Maya. The guests laughed and sang and pretended that Pharaoh and his lackeys didn't exist in their world. They found freedom, it seemed, in that moment of joy.

Merin took her hand and led her into the crowd. Even as he leaned against his walking stick, she knew he wanted to dance. Fortunately, Zahla could dance for both of them, and she did. Whirling around him, tossing her hands high and then dropping them as she clapped to the rhythm. She danced until Raquel leaned toward her.

"Go," her friend commanded, pointing toward a doorway that led out of the courtyard.

Zahla caught Merin's eye again, and he nodded.

The others chose to ignore them as they snuck through the chaos and into Abba's home.

"We must fetch the donkey," she said, so Merin could ride to the grotto.

"I am walking," he insisted.

She shook her head. "It is too far."

But he didn't agree. "I am walking to our chamber."

No matter how long it took tonight, how could she object to his decision to accompany his bride on foot?

"Wait for me!" a small voice called, and Asher raced into the room with Puah close behind him.

"I am sorry," Puah said.

Merin smiled at the boy. "Zahla and I were just leaving, but we will all be together next week."

"You cannot camp without me!"

"We will camp with you another time," she promised, understanding his frustration. Though Puah and Joseph would provide well for his needs, she would miss him.

Asher hung his head, disappointed, and she almost gave in. Perhaps she and Merin would have to wait for their wedding night.

But Merin stepped forward. "Next week, lad. We will all camp together."

"I will miss you."

Merin tousled his hair. "And we will miss you, but your imma and I need some time before the three of us become a family."

Perhaps it was the word *imma* or *family* or the promise of camping later in the tent, but Asher finally agreed.

Merin smiled as Puah guided him away. "We better leave before we have more company."

"Maybe we should invite Asher," Zahla said although nothing inside her wanted to wait another moment to be with her husband. "He only wants to be with us."

"He will spend the week playing happily with his cousins."

The sight of him laughing with the children filled her mind.

One day soon, she hoped, Asher would have brothers and sisters to play with him, but what a blessing to have so many cousins nearby.

"Tonight is for us," Merin whispered.

They walked slowly through the starlit rows, the walking stick and an oil lantern their only companions. And her heart sang as they drew near the tent. Sang as he opened the flap for her to step inside.

Finally, they were alone.

Her husband was right. Tonight was for the two of them.

And she savored every moment.

# CHAPTER TWENTY-SEVEN

*Six Years Later*

Zahla circled three of the children that she and Merin had adopted. Then she tossed the leather ball to Asher. He held it overhead for a moment before throwing it to his sister, who attempted to pass it to Hosea. When the ball hit the dirt, Hosea scuffled with Seth, the boy who had almost drowned on the night that Merin was taken away.

Her and Merin's family had multiplied rapidly in the past six years, but instead of her birthing children, Yahweh had filled it with boys and girls who needed a home. Some of them had lost a parent to the overseers' whips, others from illness or an imma who died in labor. While she'd welcome any children from her womb, Zahla decided she was perfectly content if she never had to kneel on the birthing stones. Even if none of the children were truly flesh of her flesh, their quiver was quite full. Though she hadn't birthed any of them, each child had been woven tightly into her heart.

The young ones giggled as they raced around Zahla, and she laughed with them until Maya slipped in beside her. Zahla reached out her arm and folded her niece into it.

She wished that the bird song would make her laugh, but Maya was much too old now to be cheered up by the silly lyrics and calls. The loss of her abba had dampened her joy.

"I am missing him too," Zahla whispered for Maya's ears only. So her niece knew that she wasn't alone.

Their family had lost Joseph at the last harvest. His body, made for a more calculated life, finally succumbed to the hardship of slave labor. Thankfully, he'd been at home when he'd crossed over the water. He simply didn't wake up the morning he was supposed to return to Rameses. It was as though he'd overcome Pharaoh's demands at last, deciding on his own to remain home for the flood season and every season to come.

"He would want you to play with the other children," Zahla said.

Maya's curls rustled over her shoulders with the shake of her head. "I am too old to play."

But then Asher noticed his cousin and smiled. With the slightest nod from Zahla, he lifted the leather ball, scanned the host of children that had accumulated around them, and tossed it to her.

Maya caught the ball, as she always did, and then a laugh dislodged from her throat. Asher's smile grew larger as he waved her into the crowd, and she finally joined them.

Zahla moved away then so Maya wouldn't see her tears.

Clouds were building in the western sky, but she wanted a moment on the river before the rain fell upon them. As she neared the Nile, she heard a guttural cry and turned to see the slender neck of an egret rising above the grass. The bird's head bobbed as she guarded the nest of her newly hatched chicks.

"Well done," Zahla said as she stepped back from the egret's piercing bill.

The bird, she knew, would fight fiercely for its hatchlings.

Zahla stood quietly on the cleared portion of the riverbank where the oarsmen, who'd proven themselves quite faithful, retrieved Pharaoh's wine. The supply was stored now in amphorae of dark blue and gold instead of the teal and red ones commissioned by his father, but the royal insignia with the golden vine and the sunlit eye still decorated every jar.

Lemuel and his young wife now accompanied each shipment into Rameses.

Zahla hadn't traveled back to the city since Merin was imprisoned, but she'd never forget that last voyage with Joseph when Merin was dragged away. The moment her brother had brought life back into Seth's lungs. In the eye of her mind, she'd always see Joseph here on the river, helping her with the children. His memory still lived—would always live—inside her.

Though Puah mourned deeply for her husband, she'd whispered to Zahla that she was also relieved that he'd fallen asleep at home. Spending another Akhet in the city, she was certain, would have taken his life. Puah and their son and four daughters had been able to spend one last harvest with the man they adored.

Still, Zahla wished her brother had been able to see his children and hers grow into adults. Egypt had stolen his life, and though Pharaoh had stopped killing the babies, she continued to battle against her hatred at the man's slaying both young and old men through impossibly hard labor. The Egyptians worshiped the new

Pharaoh as a god as they'd done with his father, but the gods who weren't built of stone always died in their kingdom.

As the sun fell behind clouds on the opposite bank, she watched its fading light glisten on the dove-gray surface and she knew—even though she couldn't see Yahweh—that He was alive. But still she wondered why He didn't stop the people who were tormenting them. If He was just, if He was as powerful as Jakar and the other elders proclaimed, why did Yahweh continue to allow Pharaoh to enslave and kill their people?

Merin stepped up beside her, and she rested her head on his shoulder.

"Are you missing Joseph?" he asked.

"I am sad for him and all the lives lost to greed."

Merin wrapped an arm around her as they watched color bloom from the clouds. "One day, Yahweh will take us to Him."

"Why do you think that?" she asked.

"Because He wants to walk with us in His garden, far from this pain."

"Some days I long to be with Him."

"Me too," he said. "Perhaps we can all walk together on the other side."

Merin had burned his walking stick years ago after his wounds healed. He'd learned the vineyard business from Abba, and she loved waking up every day at his side, knowing they'd reconvene at the village house that he and her uncles had built for them and their children. Until Yahweh accompanied them across the river, she would gladly walk beside this man wherever life took them.

The winds along the Nile grew stronger, stirring the water, and she braced herself for another storm. If Yahweh blew the gusts, if He poured the rain, He could also sweep through this land and rescue every Hebrew, young and old. He could protect the children and the adults.

As she leaned into Merin, Zahla prayed, in the face of the winds, for the impossible to happen. She prayed again that Yahweh, in great mercy and strength, would set her people free.

# CHAPTER TWENTY-EIGHT

*The Red Sea*

Moses stood at the edge of the water, his arms stretched out as the wind spun across the shore. And then the impossible began to happen.

Zahla blinked in awe as the Red Sea curled in the firelight and then stretched upward. Two walls rose like columns, and before them, between the walls, was a path at least a thousand cubits wide.

The sea no longer blocked their way

The crowd stared in wonder at the corridor, but no one moved. Darkness covered the eastern shore, and none of them knew if the waters would plummet as quickly as they rose. But Moses had said that Yahweh would fight for them. That they didn't have to be afraid.

Yahweh was indeed greater than Pharaoh and his army.

The people quieted, waiting for Moses to speak again, but as they waited, their backs began to warm. Turning, Zahla watched as the pillar of fire, the shield between them and the Egyptians, traveled out of the valley and over their heads. Then the pillar stalled above the seawalls as it hovered in the sky.

Yahweh wanted them to follow, but without the fire, who was going to protect them from behind?

Instead of calling out another command, Moses stepped onto the path between the seawalls. He'd led them out of Egypt and now it was time, it seemed, for them to join him across the sea.

Zahla longed to take her husband's hand. To experience the faithfulness of God alongside him. Could Merin see this miracle from the eternal realm? How she wanted to share this moment with him.

As the crowd began to follow Moses, she searched for baby Merin's parents one more time, but she didn't recognize anyone around her. If the sea was willing to stand in defiance against the Egyptians, she would carry him safely, no matter the distance, to the other shore.

The enemy wouldn't kill another of their children.

Her arms were tired, her legs worn, but for ninety-five years, Zahla had persisted despite the opposition. She wouldn't give up until the baby in her arms was safe. Her husband's memory would accompany her as she moved forward, his feet shuffling alongside her, as she rescued one last child.

Stepping onto the path, she expected her sandal to sink into the mud, but the sole held firm on the dry seabed. *Impossible.* The word raced again through her mind, this time in awe.

Pharaoh's men and magicians may be powerful, but none of them had ever parted a sea.

What did their enemy think of the Hebrew God now?

With the wind whipping up the passage, Zahla couldn't hear the chariots, but they must be near. The fire pillar moved slowly forward, and while others hurried around her in their pursuit of Moses, not waiting to see what the Egyptians might do, she crept with the fire.

As people and their animals pressed around her, she glanced back over her shoulder. The chariots were stopped on the shore, and she wondered if they were afraid to follow. Or perhaps they were equally in awe. It would take only moments for them to catch her and Merin and the others who lagged behind the crowd, but she wouldn't let her fear stop her.

One foot in front of the other, the wind spinning around her, she pressed forward. Every step bringing her closer to the eastern side.

She had to take her great-grandson to Eliana before the wind stopped parting the waters.

Merin and the others in his generation would be the first to live in freedom for hundreds of years. A new generation to worship Yahweh without memory of the evil in Egypt. She only hoped they would remember how He brought them out.

Time passed quickly. An hour or two. Maybe three. Her gaze on the blazing pillar, she lost all sense of time.

Column after column of people swept by. Talking, perhaps, but she couldn't hear them over the roar of wind. She stepped carefully around the rocks and logs on the seabed and marveled again at the arid floor where hours ago there had been water.

Her family and friends didn't mean to leave her behind. They probably didn't even notice her absence in their sprint to the far shore. But when the final press hurried around her, she and Merin remained the last refugees on the path. And she began fearing again for his life.

The blast of wind tempered into a breeze, and she could hear Merin's cries above it. He must be so hungry now. His stomach as sore as her back and legs. And her arms, how they ached.

But she couldn't stop.

As the winds decreased, the Egyptians decided to venture between the columns. She could hear the horses neighing behind her. The snap of whips and men shouting from their chariots.

The towering walls of the sea began creeping closer to her, and she wanted to run between them. To race as she'd once done when she played with the children. So many decades had passed in a flurry of stories and people and the many memories of thirty glorious years with Merin as they'd worked and raised their children in the vineyard.

A screech not far behind, the blast of a trumpet. She should sprint, but her body only allowed her another slow step when she wanted to fly.

The chariots, however, should be racing between the columns. Why hadn't they overtaken her?

Firelight flickered on the walls. Red and orange climbing and falling in the dark blue, illuminating a school of fish and a garden of coral.

The shore wasn't far now. Fifty cubits away. A few people still trailed ahead of her with their animals, but most were on the shore. And her heart lifted for a moment, knowing that the others were safe from the collapse of water.

But they weren't safe from the Egyptians. The waters may have parted, but the enemy was still in pursuit. The chariots would inundate the opposite shore before dawn, and without Yahweh's intervention, they would slaughter the Hebrew people on land.

Merin cried again as the sea walls edged closer, the breadth of their path no wider than that miserable cell in Pithom, and she wanted to cry with him. It was too far to shore, the chariots too close.

When she glanced back again, the warriors were less than a hundred cubits behind her. A blink of an eye for a chariot.

Why hadn't they killed her with their arrows and spears?

The archer in the front chariot lifted his bow, and when he released the bowstring, she stopped on the path, bracing herself for its wound. But then the wind—the wonderous power of the perfect storm—lifted the arrow and flung it into the sea.

Her eyes met the archer's for a breath of a moment before the entire chariot tilted. She watched in amazement as a wheel fell off and then another chariot rammed into it from the rear. A third chariot tried to pass the first two, but as the seawalls narrowed, its horse stumbled on the wheel and the wreckage blocked the path of the entire Egyptian army.

Zahla refocused on the pillar of fire in the east. On each step before her. About thirty or forty of them left before she stepped onto land.

"You are going to make it," she told Merin.

Though her family may be on the other side of the water, she and Merin weren't alone. Yahweh had accompanied them in the winds on this wondrous night, swirling around them with comfort and strength just as she'd danced around her wounded husband all those years ago at their wedding feast.

Water splashed over her feet, and she knew it wouldn't be long before the walls fell. Someone, she prayed, would rescue Merin before they were swept away. Carry him into the Promised Land.

A seam opened in the eastern sky, and the fire began to dim. Morning was upon them, but she couldn't take another step.

When had she grown so weak? All she wanted was to save one more child. A descendant of the baby she'd rescued long ago.

But her body had failed her.

A face appeared in the mist. A man. She couldn't make out his features, but he was tall like her husband, his stride as confident as Merin's had been when he confronted the crocodile. The moment he'd spared both her and Hosea's life.

She smiled at the memory. And at the possibility that she'd already crossed to the other side of this life as she'd passed between the columns of water.

While she had wanted this baby to live another day, perhaps Yahweh had ordained something else for them. They'd be safe with Him.

"Merin?" she whispered.

The man stepped out of the mist. "I am afraid you will not be seeing him quite yet, Dodah."

Disappointment and joy shared an equal space in her heart at the sight of her nephew, almost eighty years after Merin had saved him from Ahmed.

Hosea stretched out his arms. "Yahweh wants to rescue every Israelite from the enemy."

Merin had rescued Hosea from the Egyptians, and now, Hosea was going to rescue Merin's great-grandson.

As she placed the baby into Hosea's arms, cold water churned around her ankles. She'd crossed the sea with her family, and here she would die, knowing every member who'd left Egypt would be safe. Their enemy might be close behind, but Yahweh would intervene as Merin had done long ago. He wouldn't let the Egyptians kill her family now.

"Thank you," she told Hosea.

"I am not leaving you here."

"Do not worry about me," she commanded, the shouts of charioteers echoing between the walls of water. "Take the baby to safety."

But Hosea didn't hold Merin for long. A girl raced up beside him, and Zahla recognized Sivian in the morning light, grinning as Hosea lowered Merin into her arms.

Then Joseph's son stepped up beside her. "Every Hebrew will reach dry ground."

"Please, Hosea—"

"Sivian has the baby." He swept her off the ground as though she were a child. "And I have you."

The ground started shaking as Sivian raced ahead of them. And the new light of morning swept over their path as Hosea carried Zahla onto the shore.

# CHAPTER TWENTY-NINE

"Get back," Aaron yelled, waving frantically. Thousands pressed away from the sea as if they were making way for Pharaoh's army, but no chariots rumbled onto the sand this morning. Instead, with one final roar, the peaks of water bowed to Pharaoh and his men.

Zahla would have been knocked off her feet, but she clung to Hosea's arm as the walls crashed back into their bed.

A storm poured over the Hebrew people and their animals, but it didn't sweep any of them away. In that thread of a moment, with one strong surge, the Egyptian army was gone. Then the sea groaned again as if mourning the destruction.

Chariots bobbed in the water, but Zahla saw no man or beast. The enemy that had chased her for a lifetime, the enemy that enslaved her people and killed their babies and took her husband and brother much too young, had been swallowed into the depths.

Pharaoh's order took the lives of his own people.

She wished the chariots would have turned back, wished Pharaoh had chosen to let her people go, but her family finally had life ahead of them as they traveled toward the Promised Land.

Sivian handed baby Merin back to her, and Zahla cradled him close, her gaze on the waves that flashed with a rainbow of colors. Then Moses shouted so all the crowd could hear.

"I will sing to the Lord," he declared, "for He has triumphed gloriously! The horse and its rider He has thrown into the sea!"

Miriam, his sister, shook a timbrel, repeating the verse as she danced through the crowd. And other women followed. They danced and sang like the musicians in the palace, worshiping their King.

Zahla wished she could join them, but her heart danced in her chest instead.

They no longer answered to Pharaoh. Yahweh was leading them now.

"Merin!" Eliana shouted nearby. And then she swept her baby out of Zahla's arms and held him to her chest.

"Please forgive me," Zahla said. "I tried to stay close."

Eliana kissed his cheek and then Zahla's. "I know."

"I did not want to harm him."

"No harm has been done," Eliana said. "You rescued him."

"Sivian carried him to shore."

Eliana took Zahla's right hand, and then Asher reached for her left. Others from their family joined, linking hands and arms, weaving along the shore like a vine. Sons and daughters of their ancestor Joseph and his Egyptian bride. They'd born fruit and been tamed by the pruning. They'd endured storms and heat and floods. Then, after the floods, they'd thrived again, and with each new year, they'd grown stronger.

Yahweh had brought the Hebrew people through the treacherous waters and set them free on this land, using a baby rescued from

Pharaoh's edict, hidden on the Nile, to rescue all of them so little ones like Sivian and Merin could continue growing their family.

A breath of salt spilled over her in the breeze as if Yahweh was surrounding them again in His care. And as her gaze wandered over the crowd, she stopped when she saw the face of a boy about Sivian's age, looking bewildered as the women continued their song. It seemed to Zahla that he needed a friend to help him find his way.

"Imma?" Asher said when she dropped his hand.

"I will return."

"What is wrong?"

"He is lost." Zahla nodded toward the boy. "Yahweh would not want us to leave him alone."

Asher kissed her cheek. "Yahweh is good."

She smiled, her heart overflowing with those wondrous words. "He is."

"I will go with you," Asher said.

Together they would help another lost one find his way home.

# FROM THE AUTHOR

Dear Reader,

Thank you for joining me on this journey back to one of the Bible's greatest mysteries and wonders. It's been an absolute joy to revisit the Exodus story even as I wondered about the personal stories of those who crossed the Red Sea.

What had they experienced before God sent the plagues to set them free?

Two particular things sparked my curiosity as I began working on this book. First, I was inspired by Puah and Shiphrah's courage and the glimpse that Scripture offers us into Yahweh's blessings for their faithfulness. When they refused to kill the Hebrew boys, God gave them families of their own. History doesn't record the length of Pharaoh's edict to throw the newborn boys into the Nile, but it seems the Hebrew population continued to grow.

Second, I was fascinated by the portion of Passover instructions that mentions foreigners living among the Israelite people before the Lord brought them out of Egypt. We know that Joseph married an Egyptian woman so his descendants were partially Egyptian by birth. As I learned more about the foreigners who lived faithfully among the Hebrews, this made me wonder about others of Egyptian descent.

Also, as I read the story of Jochebed's desperation to save Moses, it dawned on me that Jochebed couldn't have been the only Hebrew mother trying to hide her son. In fact, as a mom of two children, it occurred to me that numerous mothers must have tried to thwart Pharaoh's henchmen. And I wondered what happened to those children.

Between Jochebed's desire to rescue Moses, the growth of Hebrew families after Pharaoh's edict, and the fact that foreigners left Egypt with the children of Israel, the plot for *Treacherous Waters: Zahla's Story* began to form. I wanted to tell the story of heroic men and women across Rameses and Goshen who formed a network to help Hebrew mothers find a place for their boys to live.

So many people were gracious in their support as I wrote Zahla's story. A huge thank you to the editorial team at Guideposts—Jane Haertel, Ellen Tarver, Sabrina Diaz, and Rose Tussing—for helping me brainstorm a unique and plausible story inspired by one of history's greatest miracles.

Thank you to the women in my writer's group—Julie Zander, Nicole Miller, Tracie Heskett, and Jana Kaye—whose feedback and encouragement shaped this book. To Michele Heath for adding depth to my plot and characters. To Jessica Hughes for her insight and leadership in our weekly Bible reading and discussion group. We were in the Book of Exodus when I began writing Zahla's story and slowly made our way into Numbers as I finished. Most of our group consists of college students, and I've learned so much from their collective wisdom, authenticity, and questions.

To my amazing family including my parents, Jim and Lyn Beroth, and my husband Jon for their many prayers and support of my ponderings.

And a huge thanks to you, dear readers, for joining me on another journey. I am forever grateful that our Lord is the same yesterday, today, and forever.

With joy,<br>
Melanie

# KEEPING THE FAITH

1. Zahla's aunts believed her father allowed her too much freedom. What do you think about Abba's approach toward parenting? How did it impact Zahla as she grew older?
2. Merin insults Zahla when they first meet, by calling her a child. When did their perception of each other begin to change?
3. While the Exodus story is well known today, the Hebrew people didn't know Yahweh's wind would part the Red Sea. If you imagine stepping into their place, standing at the edge of a sea with your enemy's chariots looming behind you, what would you be thinking when the winds started to blow?
4. Merin and Zahla both felt trapped at times in their circumstances. How did they choose to bring good into their regimented worlds?
5. Each major character had a strong desire or passion; for example, Zahla wanted to rescue children and Abba wanted to create the best wine in Egypt to provide for his family. What is your greatest desire or passion?
6. Pruning is a major theme in this story as the characters cut away dead wood so new life can thrive. Where in your life have you seen or would you like to see the benefits of pruning?

7. What do you think the walls of seawater looked like as the Israelites walked between them? What did it feel and sound like as they walked to the other side?
8. Have you ever been in a situation where you thought God wanted you to move ahead despite your fears? If so, what happened when you continued into the unknown?

# WAVES OF FAITH: THE IMPORTANCE OF THE RED SEA

## By Reverend Jane Willan MS, MDiv

The parting of the Red Sea's waters by Moses, which enabled the Israelites' exodus, has become one of the most extraordinary tales of biblical history. But did you know that the Red Sea's significance goes beyond this miraculous event?

The Red Sea, a narrow inlet of the Indian Ocean that covers an area of approximately 169,000 square miles, serves as a connecting waterway between Africa and Asia. It stretches around 1,400 miles in length and is about 221 miles wide at its broadest point. On average, the sea is 1,610 feet deep, with its deepest point in the central Suakin Trough reaching 9,970 feet.

The Red Sea is renowned for its rich marine life and coral reefs, home to over 1,000 species of invertebrates and 200 varieties of soft and hard corals. It is the world's northernmost tropical sea and has been recognized as a Global 200 ecoregion for its ecological significance. The Red Sea has shaped the course of history as a vital link between continents—nurturing trade, cultural exchange, and the flourishing of great civilizations.

In ancient Egypt, the Red Sea held great significance beyond its geographical features. The pharaohs recognized its strategic importance and used it as a starting point for trade expeditions to distant lands like Punt, believed to be located in modern-day Somalia or Yemen. These voyages brought back exotic goods such as incense, gold, and live animals, which enriched Egypt's economy and culture. From military endeavors to religious pilgrimages, the Red Sea was deeply ingrained in ancient Egyptian society.

The parting of the Red Sea is one of the most dramatic and awe-inspiring events in biblical history. The story began with the Israelites' enslavement in ancient Egypt under the rule of the pharaoh. Moses was chosen by God to guide the Hebrews to freedom. After a series of devastating plagues—from thick darkness to rivers turning to blood—Pharaoh finally allowed the Israelites to leave.

As the Israelites approached the shores of the Red Sea, they found themselves trapped between the advancing Egyptian army and the impassable waters. At God's direction, Moses stretched his hand over the sea, and the Lord drove back the waters with a strong wind, turning the seabed into dry land. The Israelites crossed safely, walking between walls of water. The waters crashed back down when the Egyptians pursued, swallowing Pharaoh's entire army.

Today, historians and archaeologists still seek to find solid physical evidence for the parting of the Red Sea and the Exodus. But while solid physical evidence might be elusive, no one can disprove the truth of this miraculous event.

There are several theories that might explain how the parting of the Red Sea could have occurred through natural phenomena. One fascinating hypothesis suggests that a sustained strong wind could have pushed back shallow waters for hours, creating a temporary land bridge. This concept, known as "wind setdown," has been observed in other bodies of water and modeled by scientists using advanced computer simulations. Another theory proposes that seismic activity, such as an earthquake, could have caused a temporary separation of the waters.

Geologists and climatologists have examined the region's historical weather patterns and geological formations. Some studies suggest that the climate was different during the time period traditionally associated with the Exodus, potentially affecting sea levels and coastal geography.

The possibility of a natural explanation does not diminish the significance of the parting. Rather, such explanations demonstrate how God's divine intervention can operate either through—or outside of—the laws of nature.

The story of the Israelites' exodus from Egypt has had a profound impact on traditions and popular culture, extending far beyond ancient civilization. The parting of the Red Sea also inspired numerous artists, writers, and filmmakers. It has been depicted in Michelangelo's frescoes in the Sistine Chapel and in Handel's oratorio "Israel in Egypt." Hollywood has also been fascinated by this incredible story. Cecil B. DeMille's classic movie, *The Ten Commandments,* which featured the iconic scene of Charlton Heston as Moses parting the sea, established the standard for biblical epics. An animated version of the story was titled *Prince of Egypt*. And Ridley Scott's *Exodus: Gods and Kings* utilized state-of-the-art special effects to portray this miracle for modern audiences. These film adaptations have influenced how millions around the world imagine this ancient event, blending biblical accounts with creative storytelling.

Beyond direct adaptations, the idea of overcoming an impossible obstacle has become a significant theme in much—if not most—fiction and even nonfiction. The concept of a path appearing where none seemed possible mirrors the narrative of the parting of the Red Sea. This enduring motif speaks to a universal human hope: in our darkest moments, when all seems lost, a way forward might suddenly open before us.

This biblical passage's impact on our shared imagination influences our everyday language too. The phrase "parting the Red Sea" has become a common expression, meaning accomplishing something that seems impossible or overcoming incredibly difficult challenges.

The event is significant in both Jewish and Christian traditions. For the Israelites, it was undeniable proof of God's power and dedication to their liberation. This miracle became a fundamental aspect of their faith, representing God's ability to rescue His people from seemingly impossible situations. It is a powerful symbol of liberation from physical captivity and spiritual oppression. In the Jewish faith, this extraordinary happening is commemorated annually during Passover, serving as a powerful reminder of God's deliverance of the Israelite nation. In Christian theology, this narrative also holds significant meaning as a forerunner of baptism and spiritual liberation.

Whether interpreted through religious, historical, or artistic perspectives, this ancient biblical account continues to remind us of God's power and faithfulness. The story of Moses and the Exodus transcends the boundaries of time and our understanding of what is possible, continuing to shape our understanding of the world and our place within it.

*Fiction Author*

# MELANIE DOBSON

Writing fiction is Melanie Dobson's excuse to explore abandoned houses, travel to unique places, and immerse herself in old journals and books. The award-winning author of almost thirty novels, Melanie enjoys stitching together both historical and time-slip stories. She has written four biblical fiction stories for Guideposts.

Five of Melanie's novels have won Carol Awards, and two were finalists for a Christy Award. She is the previous corporate publicity manager at Focus on the Family and now enjoys teaching as an adjunct professor in the Pacific Northwest.

*Nonfiction Author*

# REVEREND JANE WILLAN, MS, MDiv

Reverend Jane Willan writes contemporary women's fiction, mystery novels, church newsletters, and a weekly sermon.

Jane loves to set her novels amid church life. She believes that ecclesiology, liturgy, and church lady drama make for twisty plots and quirky characters. When not working at the church or creating new adventures for her characters, Jane relaxes at her favorite local bookstore, enjoying coffee and a variety of carbohydrates with frosting. Otherwise, you might catch her binge-watching a streaming series or hiking through the Connecticut woods with her husband and rescue dog, Ollie.

Jane earned a Bachelor of Arts degree from Hiram College, majoring in Religion and History, a Master of Science degree from Boston University, and a Master of Divinity from Vanderbilt University.

*Read on for a sneak peek of another exciting story in the Mysteries & Wonders of the Bible series!*

# STAR OF WONDER:
## Dobah's Story
### by Robin Lee Hatcher

*In the month of Tevet, 5 BC*

Dobah held Levi's hand as he took two steps toward his favorite toy, his happy babble bouncing off the walls of the small room attached to her abba's house, the room she shared with her eleven-month-old son as well as her *savta*. Her savta instead of her husband.

Tears welled, but she blinked them away. It did not serve to wish for what could never be. Dover, her husband, had been dead for more than a year. She could not bring him back, no matter how much she wished she could. She could not change what had happened to him, the accident that had taken his life and left her a young, pregnant widow, forced to return home to live with her parents once again.

The sound of *Imma*'s singing in the small courtyard drifted to her, and she lifted Levi into her arms before leaving the room and walking to the front door.

The census commanded by Rome had swelled Bethlehem's population to at least twice its normal size. But now, at last, people had started to return to their own homes. The guest room of Boaz ben David's house had been filled to capacity with male family members who had traveled to the village in obedience to the decree. A few had even slept in the stable. But today, the last of their relations had departed.

"Yosef!"

Dobah heard her imma's cry of delight and saw her arms reach out in a gesture of welcome. Yosef, Dobah's favorite cousin! She darted out into the small courtyard.

There he was, beyond the stone fence, her impossibly handsome cousin. Yosef ben Yakov. And with him was his wife, Miryam, their baby—a few days old now—in her arms.

"Are you ready for us, Machla?" Yosef asked Dobah's imma.

"The *kataluma* is empty at last," Imma answered. "Come in. You can wash your feet and have something to eat and drink."

Balancing Levi on her hip, Dobah moved to open the gate for them.

"Hello, Cousin," Yosef said to her, smiling. His gaze shifted to her son. "Is this Levi? Look how he has grown."

"Yes." She rose on tiptoe and kissed Yosef's cheek. "It is good to see you again."

"And you? How are you?" He gave his head the slightest shake. "I am sorry about Dover. I know it is still hard."

A lump rose in her throat, and she nodded in answer.

Yosef reached back and drew Miryam to his side. "Dobah, this is my wife, Miryam. Miryam, this is my cousin Dobah and her son, Levi."

Miryam's smile was shy. "Yosef has told me much of his family in Bethlehem."

"All good, I hope."

Yosef laughed. "All true, at least."

Imma stepped closer. "We are so sorry there was no room for you until now." Her gaze flicked to the baby. "It is not what we would have wanted. You should not have had to be alone at such a time."

"Adonai provided," Yosef responded softly.

"Come in. You are with family at last." Imma led the way into the house, Yosef and Miryam right behind her. Dobah waited a few moments by the gate, allowing memories to wash over her. Sweet memories of family gatherings—for weddings, births, festivals, and more. So much love. She was blessed to be part of such a family. None of them were wealthy, but money could not buy what was most important.

Levi pumped his arms and squealed his demand for action. Smiling again, she hurried toward the doorway of their home.

The main floor of the Boaz ben David home had one large room for living, eating, and cooking, plus a sleeping area beneath the kataluma. The doorway to Dobah's and Savta's room was also at the back, while a narrow staircase against the wall led to the kataluma. To the left of the main entrance and down three steps was the small stable where the family's livestock—two goats and a donkey—stayed during the night.

"It is such a long way from Nazareth," Imma was saying when Dobah entered the house. "And then to be forced to stay with strangers without a room to yourself. To give birth without loved ones around you."

"Do not concern yourself, Machla." Yosef put a hand on Miryam's shoulder. "We are well."

"Such a difficult time." Imma tsked softly. "It is cruel, what the Romans have done. Your wife should not have had to travel so far at such a time."

"My place was with my husband." The look Miryam gave Yosef was shy and a little uncertain.

Dobah remembered feeling that way with Dover when they were first betrothed. Even after their marriage had been consummated, she'd been unsure what to say or do so much of the time. But at least, when it had come time for her to give birth, she'd been with Imma and her two married sisters. Miryam, on the other hand, had been far from family and friends.

"Your uncle Boaz will return from the vineyard soon," Imma said, pulling Dobah from her thoughts. "He will be glad to see you."

Dobah set Levi on the floor and went to check the stew that simmered above the cook fire. Fresh bread waited on a nearby table, along with cheese, olive oil, and wine. While Bethlehem burst at the seams because of the census, it had been difficult to find items to buy in the market. Her *abba* was more prosperous than many of their neighbors, but even he could not purchase what was not available. Dobah hoped the situation would improve as life returned to normal, especially now that Yosef and Miryam would be with them until baby Yeshua's dedication.

Male laughter from the street announced the return of Boaz from the vineyard. Yosef stood mere seconds before the door opened. But it wasn't her abba who came through the opening first. It was her savta, a tiny woman with deeply wrinkled skin and a near-toothless smile.

"Savta!" Yosef moved to embrace the grandmother he shared with Dobah, lifting her feet off the floor and knocking the scarf from her gray head.

"Put me down," the old woman demanded with a laugh.

He obeyed.

Boaz entered then, and the two men exchanged hugs and slaps on the back.

Dobah smiled as she watched them. It was good they could all be together. Abba would enjoy having Yosef with him during the day at the vineyard, and Imma would love having another infant to fuss over. And young Miryam would have nearly six weeks to rest until the Temple dedication. Then she would be ready for Yosef to take her and the baby on the long journey north to Nazareth.

---

Camels complained, as usual, as the caravan set off on its nightly journey. The sounds were familiar to Menes. As familiar to him as the sound of his own voice, for he had heard the animals' grunts and hums for most of his twenty-five years.

Menes could scarcely remember when he hadn't traveled great distances with caravans, both large and small. Caravans that had taken him from Egypt to Arabia to Syria to Asia. Again and again and then again. He had been a boy of no more than seven when he'd set out on his first journey, apprenticed to a *khabir*, a man of great knowledge and experience. Now a khabir himself and the owner of many camels, Menes hoped this would be his final trip for a while.

His gaze went to the bright light in the sky, and a shiver of anticipation went through him. In all his years, he had never seen anything like it, nor had he been on a journey quite like this one. The magi who had hired him in a city near the Tigris River had told him the light would guide them to their destination. If they were such wise men, as others purported, how could they set off without knowing where they wanted to end up? It seemed a fool's errand. However, they had paid him well. Who was he to say they should know better?

His body rolling with the gait of the camel, he looked behind him. The prosperity of the magi was not in question. Their robes were of the finest quality, and the camels that followed them were laden with precious oils and gold. He had seen their wealth for himself, which was why he also had seen to the hiring of numerous guards to protect them.

He looked ahead, his gaze lifting a second time to the star. It was a wonder. Nearly as bright as a full moon and different from other stars. It didn't remain in the same place night after night. It moved ahead of them. The magi said it would lead them to meet a new king. Menes had doubted the truth of it at first, but the star did seem to be leading them.

Perhaps they were wise men after all.

# A NOTE FROM THE EDITORS

We hope you enjoyed another exciting volume in the Mysteries & Wonders of the Bible series, published by Guideposts. For over seventy-five years, Guideposts, a nonprofit organization, has been driven by a vision of a world filled with hope. We aspire to be the voice of a trusted friend, a friend who makes you feel more hopeful and connected.

By making a purchase from Guideposts, you join our community in touching millions of lives, inspiring them to believe that all things are possible through faith, hope, and prayer. Your continued support allows us to provide uplifting resources to those in need. Whether through our communities, websites, apps, or publications, we inspire our audiences, bring them together, and comfort, uplift, entertain, and guide them. Visit us at guideposts.org to learn more.

We would love to hear from you. Write us at Guideposts, P.O. Box 5815, Harlan, Iowa 51593 or call us at (800) 932-2145. Did you love *Treacherous Waters: Zahla's Story*? Leave a review for this product on guideposts.org/shop. Your feedback helps others in our community find relevant products.

*Find inspiration, find faith, find Guideposts.*

### Shop our best sellers and favorites at
# guideposts.org/shop

Or scan the QR code to go directly to our Shop

If you enjoyed Mysteries & Wonders of the Bible, check out our other Guideposts biblical fiction series! Visit https://www.shopguideposts.org/fiction-books/biblical-fiction.html for more information.

# EXTRAORDINARY WOMEN OF THE BIBLE

There are many women in Scripture who do extraordinary things. Women whose lives and actions were pivotal in shaping their world as well as the world we know today. In each volume of Guideposts' Extraordinary Women of the Bible series, you'll meet these well-known women and learn their deepest thoughts, fears, joys, and secrets. Read their stories and discover the unexplored truths in their journeys of faith as they follow the paths God laid out for them.

*Highly Favored: Mary's Story*
*Sins as Scarlet: Rahab's Story*
*A Harvest of Grace: Ruth and Naomi's Story*
*At His Feet: Mary Magdalene's Story*
*Tender Mercies: Elizabeth's Story*
*Woman of Redemption: Bathsheba's Story*
*Jewel of Persia: Esther's Story*
*A Heart Restored: Michal's Story*

*Beauty's Surrender: Sarah's Story*
*The Woman Warrior: Deborah's Story*
*The God Who Sees: Hagar's Story*
*The First Daughter: Eve's Story*
*The Ones Jesus Loved: Mary and Martha's Story*
*The Beginning of Wisdom: Bilqis's Story*
*The Shadow's Song: Mahlah and No'ah's Story*
*Days of Awe: Euodia and Syntyche's Story*
*Beloved Bride: Rachel's Story*
*A Promise Fulfilled: Hannah's Story*

# ORDINARY WOMEN OF THE BIBLE

From generation to generation and every walk of life, God seeks out women to do His will. Scripture offers us but fleeting, tantalizing glimpses into the lives of a number of everyday women in Bible times—many of whom are not even named in its pages. In each volume of Guideposts' Ordinary Women of the Bible series, you'll meet one of these unsung, ordinary women face-to-face, and see how God used her to change the course of history.

*A Mother's Sacrifice: Jochebed's Story*
*The Healer's Touch: Tikva's Story*
*The Ark Builder's Wife: Zarah's Story*
*An Unlikely Witness: Joanna's Story*
*The Last Drop of Oil: Adaliah's Story*
*A Perilous Journey: Phoebe's Story*
*Pursued by a King: Abigail's Story*
*An Eternal Love: Tabitha's Story*
*Rich Beyond Measure: Zlata's Story*
*The Life Giver: Shiphrah's Story*
*No Stone Cast: Eliyanah's Story*
*Her Source of Strength: Raya's Story*
*Missionary of Hope: Priscilla's Story*

*Befitting Royalty: Lydia's Story*
*The Prophet's Songbird: Atarah's Story*
*Daughter of Light: Charilene's Story*
*The Reluctant Rival: Leah's Story*
*The Elder Sister: Miriam's Story*
*Where He Leads Me: Zipporah's Story*
*The Dream Weaver's Bride: Asenath's Story*
*Alone at the Well: Photine's Story*
*Raised for a Purpose: Talia's Story*
*Mother of Kings: Zemirah's Story*
*The Dearly Beloved: Apphia's Story*

Interested in other series by Guideposts?
Check out one of our mystery series!
Visit https://www.shopguideposts.org/fiction-books/mystery-fiction.html for more information.

# SECRETS FROM GRANDMA'S ATTIC

Life is recorded not only in decades or years, but in events and memories that form the fabric of our being. Follow Tracy Doyle, Amy Allen, and Robin Davisson, the granddaughters of the recently deceased centenarian, Pearl Allen, as they explore the treasures found in the attic of Grandma Pearl's Victorian home, nestled near the banks of the Mississippi in Canton, Missouri. Not only do Pearl's descendants uncover a long-buried mystery at every attic exploration, they also discover their grandmother's legacy of deep, abiding faith, which has shaped and guided their family through the years. These uncovered Secrets from Grandma's Attic reveal stories of faith, redemption, and second chances that capture your heart long after you turn the last page.

*History Lost and Found*
*The Art of Deception*
*Testament to a Patriot*
*Buttoned Up*

*Pearl of Great Price*
*Hidden Riches*
*Movers and Shakers*
*The Eye of the Cat*
*Refined by Fire*
*The Prince and the Popper*
*Something Shady*
*Duel Threat*
*A Royal Tea*
*The Heart of a Hero*
*Fractured Beauty*
*A Shadowy Past*
*In Its Time*
*Nothing Gold Can Stay*
*The Cameo Clue*
*Veiled Intentions*
*Turn Back the Dial*
*A Marathon of Kindness*
*A Thief in the Night*
*Coming Home*

# SAVANNAH SECRETS

Welcome to Savannah, Georgia, a picture-perfect Southern city known for its manicured parks, moss-covered oaks, and antebellum architecture. Walk down one of the cobblestone streets, and you'll come upon Magnolia Investigations. It is here where two friends have joined forces to unravel some of Savannah's deepest secrets. Tag along as clues are exposed, red herrings discarded, and thrilling surprises revealed. Find inspiration in the special bond between Meredith Bellefontaine and Julia Foley. Cheer the friends on as they listen to their hearts and rely on their faith to solve each new case that comes their way.

*The Hidden Gate*
*A Fallen Petal*
*Double Trouble*
*Whispering Bells*
*Where Time Stood Still*
*The Weight of Years*
*Willful Transgressions*
*Season's Meetings*
*Southern Fried Secrets*
*The Greatest of These*

*Patterns of Deception*
*The Waving Girl*
*Beneath a Dragon Moon*
*Garden Variety Crimes*
*Meant for Good*
*A Bone to Pick*
*Honeybees & Legacies*
*True Grits*
*Sapphire Secret*
*Jingle Bell Heist*
*Buried Secrets*
*A Puzzle of Pearls*
*Facing the Facts*
*Resurrecting Trouble*
*Forever and a Day*

# More Great Mysteries Are Waiting for Readers Like *You*!

### Whistle Stop Café

*"Memories of a lifetime...I loved reading this story. Could not put the book down...."* —ROSE H.

Mystery and WWII historical fiction fans will love these intriguing novels where two close friends piece together clues to solve mysteries past and present. Set in the real town of Dennison, Ohio, at a historic train depot where many soldiers set off for war, these stories are filled with faithful, relatable characters you'll love spending time with.

### Extraordinary Women of the Bible

*"This entire series is a wonderful read.... Gives you a better understanding of the Bible."* —SHARON A.

Now, in these riveting stories, you can get to know the most extraordinary women of the Bible, from Rahab and Esther to Bathsheba, Ruth, and more. Each book perfectly combines biblical facts with imaginative storylines to bring these women to vivid life and lets you witness their roles in God's great plan. These stories reveal how we can find the courage and faith needed today to face life's trials and put our trust in God just as they did.

### Secrets of Grandma's Attic

*"I'm hooked from beginning to end. I love how faith, hope, and prayer are included...[and] the scripture references... in the book at the appropriate time each character needs help.*" —JACQUELINE

Take a refreshing step back in time to the real-life town of Canton, Missouri, to the late Pearl Allen's home. Hours of page-turning intrigue unfold as her granddaughters uncover family secrets and treasures in their grandma's attic. You'll love seeing how faith has helped shape Pearl's family for generations.

---

Learn More & Shop These Exciting Mysteries, Biblical Stories & Other Uplifting Fiction at **guideposts.org/fiction**

Printed in the United States
by Baker & Taylor Publisher Services